# HATCHET HILL

DAVID J. GATWARD

DG CREATIVE LTD

Hatchet Hill
by
David J. Gatward

Copyright © 2024 by David J. Gatward
All rights reserved.

Author photography by
@chrisbaileyheadshots, Facebook/chrisbaileyphotography

No part of this book may be reproduced in any form or by any electronic or mechanical means, including information storage and retrieval systems, without written permission from the author, except for the use of brief quotations in a book review.

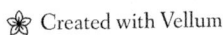

❀ Created with Vellum

*To Donna*

"For where God built a church,
there the Devil would also build a chapel."

— Martin Luther —

# ONE

Paul Edwards had always loved being a Police Community Support Officer, and what he was doing right now, and where he was doing it, only served to make that love deepen. To his mind, the role of a PCSO was akin to that of being a 'bobby,' a figure in a police uniform who knew everyone in the community, was trusted, respected.

It involved walking around local villages, meeting people, being offered mugs of tea with biscuits and cake, helping businesses with security, having serious chats with people who'd had a few too many in the local pub, visiting schools to do talks on safety and not talking to strangers offering puppies out the back of vans. Well, maybe not that last one, because it wasn't the 1970s anymore, but everything else, very much so.

He believed his role was to take people seriously, to listen to them, and to give them enough reassurance to know that if they needed help, then he and the wider team were there to provide it.

Paul understood that his view was perhaps a little rose-tinted, but he'd never had a problem with that. Always better a glass half full, than half empty, as his Granddad had always said. At least he thought it was something his Granddad had said. It might not have been, and Paul had been only six years old when the old man had died in a tragic, if not somewhat amusing, allotment accident involving a squirrel, a badly placed rake, an unfortunately positioned stack of clay plant pots, and a very well-rotted compost heap.

Which was why, at close to midnight, he was more than happy to have been asked to check out some strange lights reported by a man called Mr Rowe, who had been keen to point out that he was a member of a local running club, and who had called in and asked to speak with him specifically.

The conversation had been short and intriguing, and Paul had been genuinely excited to investigate.

'So, can you describe the lights for me, Mr Rowe?' Paul had asked, once he had taken down Mr Rowe's details.

'Well, they were lights, weren't they? You need to come and look for yourself, don't you? Yes, that's what you need to do. Not go asking me daft questions about how to describe a light. Bright and flashy? How's that?'

Mr Rowe's answer didn't give Paul much to go on.

'Where did you see them?'

'Can't remember the name of it, the lane, I mean. New to the area, you see? There's a telephone box, isn't there? Yes, there is, I saw it.'

'That's not much to go on.'

'It's the old railway line,' Mr Rowe went on. 'That's it, yes, that's where I was. There's a road that crosses over it. And a telephone box.'

The description made Paul's heart stop.

'You mean the one that runs out from near Great Elm and onto Radstock? That old railway line?'

'Yes, that's it.'

'The lane called Hatchet Hill?'

'Is it?'

'I'm asking you that.'

There was a pause, and in it, Paul heard whispers of his past, and other things, too, because Hatchet Hill seemed to be calling him. He'd not been there himself in years, though, and with good reason, but perhaps it was time to put his own history there to bed at last. And the other things he knew about the place—what he'd been looking into, which was little more than personal interest, research useful for his writing, albeit on the darker side of what he liked to dive into.

Or that was what he'd told himself. There had always been a part of him that had wondered, though, if the things he'd discovered had been somehow responsible for what had happened; if the black secrets held within the soil and the trees, that whispered on the wind and danced in the rain when the moon was high, had changed an old friend into someone he couldn't recognise.

'What? Oh, yes, that's it. Yes, must be, but you know where I'm talking about, don't you?'

For a moment Paul was caught by the tone of those last few words, like they'd been phrased not so much as a question, but more as a statement. He shook his head. He was probably reading too much into it, what with it being late and all.

Mr Rowe didn't sound too sure, but then, running at night was probably a little disorientating, thought Paul. And the description was enough for him to be absolutely certain of where Mr Rowe meant, and he felt sure it was Hatchet Hill.

He asked, 'Can you tell me why these lights struck you as suspicious?'

'They just were,' Mr Rowe replied, sounding a little agitated. 'Shouldn't be lights out that way, should there? All flashing around like they're dancing. Oh, and I heard voices, too,

I think. Singing, maybe? Or was it chanting? Yes, maybe it was that. But you'll be wanting to check up on it all, won't you? That's why I called in, to speak to you specifically. Talk to PCSO Edwards, they said. So here I am, Paul, speaking to you. I was told you'd take it seriously, not like the others.'

That made Paul smile; he'd worked hard to make sure he had a reputation for listening to people's problems, and not just dismissing them out of hand.

'Could they have been headlights perhaps, maybe a tractor doing some late-night work in a field?'

'No, because it was silent, wasn't it? Except for the chanting or singing or whatever it was, though I couldn't be sure. Only other thing I heard was an owl. Bloody close it was, too, hooting right next to me; nearly gave me a heart attack!'

'And there's nothing else you can tell me? Do you know if there's livestock in the fields?'

'Honestly, I don't know. It's foggy now, and that's made everything really quiet. Not much to go on, I know, and you probably think I'm daft for reporting it in the first place, but it just struck me as all a bit odd, which is why I called.'

Paul had thanked Mr Rowe for calling in, and after checking in with Detective Sergeant, Patti Matondo, who was back at the station in Frome, had been more than happy to jump into the incident response vehicle he'd commandeered for the evening, and head off into the night.

Having parked where the old railway line was leapfrogged by a narrow lane, Paul took a few moments to just sit and observe the dark of the night, and to think about what Craig Rowe had told him. Outside his vehicle, the night was oily and thick, the darkness swilling around him like the contents of a giant cauldron poured out onto the Earth, eerie fingers of fog caressing the silhouettes of trees.

Inside the vehicle, Paul was rather cosy, and he was a little tempted to just stay where he was, and see if he could catch sight of whatever Craig's weird lights were without having to leave his seat. Making the most of the warmth, he had a swig of the hot chocolate he always carried with him in the car when he as on night duty, the battered old flask was one he'd had for years, maybe even since he'd first joined the police.

With the steaming mug in hand, and the sweet taste of the hot chocolate on his tongue, Paul observed the night beyond his cocoon. Being alone, the silence of the moment grew exponentially, and he quickly became acutely aware of the sound of his own breathing, his heartbeat, the smell, not just of what he was drinking, but the thin silvery quiver of air slipping into the vehicle through the air vents, even the way his eyelids seemed to stick a little every time he blinked. It was as though the isolation in the gloopy Somerset darkness was forcing his senses to up their game, and they were now competing to overload him with things he'd not usually notice.

Beyond this, Paul became aware of sounds beyond his vehicle, the eerie orchestra of a thick night resting on fields, lapping at the feet of hedgerows. He heard the wind attacking the branches of trees, like a wrestler trying to force an opponent into submission; the yap-yap-yap of a fox calling for its cubs, and other, hidden things, rustling and scurrying through the gloom.

Finishing his hot chocolate, and stowing the cup and flask away, Paul pushed open his door and yawned, tasting the night on his tongue. The air was colder out here in the wilds, and ghosts of it snatched at his clothes, sank their thin tendrils down his neck to make him shiver.

He made a quick call on his radio to the station. Patti, who was on call as well, answered.

'All good?'

'Well, it's dark,' Paul replied. 'So, there's that.'

'You should be a detective.'

'I don't like the uniform.'

'We don't wear one.'

'Exactly.'

'Any sign of these mysterious lights?'

'So far, no; and it's a bit foggy, now, too, so I'll just have to see how I do.'

'You do realise it's probably nothing?'

'Of course I do,' Paul replied. 'But that's not how this works, is it? Mr Rowe was genuinely concerned. Could be someone out here trying to break into a barn, maybe even steal livestock; can't ignore that, can we?'

'Not really, no.'

'Anyway, I'm here, you have my location. If there's anything to report, I'll let you know.'

'You coming back to the station after?'

'I'll see.'

'Well, keep me posted.'

'Will do.'

Conversation with Patti over, Paul hunched up his collar, and with a torch in hand and on full beam, locked the car. He then made his way down from where he was parked and towards the old railway line.

The route, closed decades ago like so many others up and down the country, was now a popular walking, running, and biking route through the countryside, and he had wandered along it many times. But at night, the trail wore a different mask, the serene, sun-dappled peace of the daytime was now replaced with a sullen, depressive air, and the sense that something deep inside the dark was watching.

Laughing, and chiding himself for letting his imagination run away with itself, Paul took a walk up the path first, then back, dipping under the lane he had just parked on, not entirely sure what he was looking for. Craig Rowe hadn't given him anything else beyond the lights being strange, but that was what had interested Paul from the off; their strangeness.

He liked that, always had, his interest in things beyond the norm, not just a hobby, but something that had seeped into his working life as well. But how could it not? Somerset was a place built on myth and legend, and the soil was wet with whispered tales and strange goings on.

Having turned around to head back to his vehicle, and close to giving up on his search for the strange lights, something caught Paul's eye; the flash of a light from up above, right where he had parked.

Probably nothing, he thought, but it sent a shiver down his spine nonetheless. He upped his pace to get back and check on things, worried that some little bugger with mischief on their mind had seen the vehicle and been unable to resist the urge to let down a tyre or two.

Arriving back at the vehicle, Paul was relieved to find that all was well, and as he did a second sweep around the car, another light caught his eye, this one over a fence and a little way down a bridleway.

Paul walked to the fence and shone the beam of his torch along the rutted trail, which was lined with trees, their bows drooping over it like the bowed heads of mourners.

When was the last time he'd actually been down this way? he wondered. Twenty years? Longer? He'd been avoiding it, he knew that. Well, now he couldn't.

'This is PCSO Paul Edwards,' he called out. 'We had a call earlier about some lights, so I'm just here having a look around. Is everything okay?'

Paul's voice seemed to die short in the foggy darkness.

He called again, saw the light, got no response, and knew he had no choice but to push through the gate and see what was going on, if anything.

Marching along the bridleway, Paul was very aware of how soft the ground beneath him was, his footsteps barely audible as he pushed on into the emptiness ahead.

'Hello?'

The light came again, dancing almost from tree to tree.

Briefly, Paul remembered when he'd last been down here, who he'd followed, what he'd found, and why he'd ultimately done something that had broken a friendship for good. But that friendship had been a sham, hadn't it? There were secrets, and there was what he'd uncovered; funny how little you know about the people you think you're closest to, he thought.

Guessing that the lights were most likely teenagers playing silly buggers, Paul mentally prepared himself to be having a word with kids who should've been home in bed, who were no doubt out here with booze, or something stronger.

'There's nothing to be worried about. I'd just like to have a chat with you, if that's o—'

The night disappeared in an instant as Paul's world was filled with bright stars and an agonising pain in the back of his head.

He staggered, dropped his torch, tried to make sense of what had happened. He wondered if a hefty branch from a tree had fallen on him. Then the pain came again, another blow to his head, sending him crashing to his knees, forcing him to fall onto his hands.

Two branches? The odds of that were impossible, he thought, so what the hell was going on?

He tried to move, to force himself back up onto his feet, his focus now on getting back to his vehicle to call for help, when he heard something that made his breath catch in his throat. A laugh, light and bright, and filled with menace.

Paul had no words. He simply knew that he had to get the

hell out of there, get back to the station, get help. But as he tried to move, pain raked his body, forcing out a scream.

The laugh came again, then more pain, only this time it wasn't only to his back, but his legs, his arms, and he fell forward, his face slamming into the dirt.

'Please ...'

The last sound Paul heard, wasn't the laugh, but the sound of something hacking away at his legs, like a woodsman taking down a tree.

Then the night reached out and embraced him, and as his dying breath took its final dance in the gentle hands of the fog, the strangest of thoughts crossed his mind. The caller, Mr Rowe, had used his first name, but he was sure he'd never given it.

# TWO

*The previous day ...*

IT TOOK two seconds too long for Detective Inspector Gordanian Haig to realise that the scream, which had ripped her from her sleep, was her own.

Sitting up, the echo of the scream making her wince, she saw her duvet on the floor, as though her bed had shed its skin, and it now lay rotting in the moonlight spilling in through her window.

She shivered, leaned over to grab it, and noticed that her skin was slick with sweat, her bed sheet clinging to her as she moved.

Pulling the duvet over herself, the damp sheet beneath her caused her to flinch as she lay back.

She closed her eyes, breathed deep, sucking in the cold air slipping into her room from an open window, and imagined it coating her lungs with ice.

*It was just a dream, that's all, just a dream ...*

But it wasn't just a dream, not by a long shot, and though she didn't want to, she sobbed, her faint, soft whimpers hanging in the darkness as her tears fell, slipping down her cheeks to stain her pillow.

Moments passed like eons and seconds all at once, as her mind forced her to relive things she had tried so hard to run from. After all, wasn't that really the reason she had gone ahead with the move to Somerset? To get away from what had happened, the place it had happened in, the memories that choked every bend on every road, every turn on every path?

*Anna ...*

The name, and the bright face it belonged to, came to her then, separate from the memories. She saw her smile, the crinkle at the corner of her eyes, caught the sob in her throat before it had a chance to escape, and, with all the strength she could muster, forced herself out of bed.

The flat, now furnished, and with not a single unpacked box in sight, welcomed her with a quick shiver of cold, as she grabbed a dressing gown off the back of her bedroom door, then padded down the corridor to the kitchen. The room was small, a simple worksurface along one wall, with cupboards above and beneath, and a window staring out across the shared grounds below. There was no washing machine, but Gordy had come to enjoy her regular trips into the small town of Shepton Mallet, to drop off her washing, before going for a wander, or just sitting in a café, having a bite to eat, and reading.

Reading was something she had come back to of late, having drifted from it for a while not only due to the pressures of work before the move, but also because of the death of her love, her Anna. She had been unable to focus, to get beyond the first few sentences without her mind drifting, but now the pages of so many books had provided her with a much-needed escape into lives and worlds far removed from her own.

A couple of weeks ago, and to cheer herself up, Gordy had decided to treat herself to something she didn't really need, but absolutely wanted, and that was a decent coffee machine. In part, she blamed Vivek, the station's receptionist, for such a rash and expensive purchase, because if he hadn't been so insistent on always providing such exceptional coffee, then she wouldn't have found herself wanting to have it at home as well.

A couple of minutes later, and having enjoyed the sound of the coffee grinder filling the portafilter before tamping it down, and clamping it into the group head, she sat at her dining table in the lounge, window open, staring out into the night through the fronds of plants now populating one of the two window boxes she had inherited with the rental.

The coffee was rich and chocolatey, and it burned just a little as she sipped it. Whether the caffeine hit immediately or not she didn't care. It was the ritual more than anything that mattered; using the machine, the noises, and the smells, and then the moment of quiet to savour what had been made.

Coffee drunk, and with no urge to head back to bed for the remaining hours of the night, Gordy lay herself down on her sofa and reached for a book resting on the rustic coffee table she had purchased from a flea market. It wasn't really all that practical as tables went, its surface following the natural contours of the wood it was made of, rather than having been planed flat, and weighing about the same as a wet Alsatian should it ever need to be moved.

Opening the book, she started to read, and soon the words on the page pulled her away from where she was, her new life and the old memories, and took her somewhere else. And there she stayed just long enough for her eyes to close and sleep, again, to take her.

When morning came around fully, announced by sunlight cutting into the room from the windows of the lounge, Gordy picked her book up from where it had tumbled to the floor when she'd drifted off, and took herself through to the shower. The bathroom, which was barely large enough to house the sink, bath, and toilet, was soon thick with steam, which she allowed to escape into the hallway, chased by her own sorry attempt at singing with a playlist she had on her phone.

Back in her bedroom, and with her work clothes on, it was only when she went to grab her keys and head out into the day that she realised she'd made a mistake born of a tired mind, and a night spent half in bed, half on the sofa; it was Sunday morning, and she wasn't on duty.

With a mix of frustration at her own forgetfulness, and joy at being gifted the surprise of empty time, Gordy tore off her clothes and slipped into something more comfortable and considerably more colourful. Then, with little thought of what she was going to do or where she was even going, she left her flat and leapt into the day.

Strolling over to her car, the clear sound of bells caught her attention. She paused, listened, closed her eyes, and for the briefest of moments, was back in the Dales. She was with Anna, walking to church, ready to listen to the love of her life lead a service, give a sermon, talk to the people of her parish. The memory was so real she felt sure she could smell the cool, stony aroma of the church, cut through by wisps of smoke from lit candles.

Gordy paused, her hand hovering over the handle of her car door. She was ready to go, to drive off, to go exploring, but the sound of the bell came again, and with it, the soft coo of pigeons, and she was suddenly very aware of the beauty of where she now was. Not that Evercreech was the most attractive of villages, but what it was, was welcoming, alive, a place that had a stronger heartbeat than she had.

Turning from her car, Gordy found herself following the

sound of the bells. With each footstep, part of her wanted to stop, to go no further, but something else, something deeper, pulled her on.

A few minutes later, the church stood before her. She had passed the building enough times since moving into the village, standing as it did just a short distance from The Bell Inn. The pub hadn't quite become a second home as yet, but it, and the warmth of the people inside, had given her a place she could go and relax. She knew a few faces well enough now to give a nod and a passing comment about the day, the weather. Never work, though, or her past, because Gordy was private, and liked to keep it that way.

Following her first visit to the place with Jameson, a retired DCI, and old friend of Harry Grimm, she had adopted the pub's snack, the mousetrap, and a pint of cider as something of a ritual. There was just something she couldn't help but love about a packet of crisps, into which was dropped a huge chunk of mature cheddar and a large, pickled onion. It just worked, and every time she had it, washing it down with the cider, she found herself relaxing a little more into her new life.

Staring up at the church, Gordy hesitated. The doors were open, worship would begin soon enough. Who would be leading it she had no idea, only that it should've been Anna had she not ...

A voice called out, interrupting Gordy's thoughts. She looked over to the church door to see a man waving at her and, instinctively, she waved back.

'You coming in, then?'

'In a moment,' Gordy replied, not entirely sure that she wanted to.

'Best you make that moment now, if you don't want to miss the start,' the man said. 'Though I wouldn't blame you if you did, if you know what I mean.'

No, Gordy did not know what he meant at all, but she was intrigued enough to take a deep breath and walk over.

She held out a hand to introduce herself to the small man in a slightly dishevelled tweed suit. He was thinning on top and wore the scrappiest beard she'd ever seen.

'I'm—'

'Oh, I know who you are,' the man said. 'Ms Haig, yes? We've all been wondering how you're doing. I've even been around to your flat a number of times, but every time I turn up, you're not in. I've left a few notes as well, a few of us have, actually, but I suppose you've been too busy with settling in, yes? Fair enough, totally understandable.'

Gordy thought back to the handful of notes she had found over the weeks since she'd arrived, all of them shoved under her door, with names, telephone numbers, and various little messages to hopefully meet her soon. She'd ignored them all, terrified, she knew, of doing exactly what she was doing now; entering what should have been Anna's church. The kindness of the notes hadn't escaped her, though, and she wondered who else she would bump into inside the building, whose messages of goodwill and invites round for dinner, she had ignored.

'So, you'll be Mr Barker or Mr Gatcombe, then, yes?'

'Enough of the Mr! I'm Clive, Clive Gatcombe. You'll meet John and his wife inside, no doubt. My wife's around somewhere, too. Probably asleep in the vestry or something; only warm place in the church really.'

'Pleased to meet you.'

Clive stood back and ushered Gordy inside, just as a truly terrible sound hit Gordy square in the face.

'Good grief ...'

Clive gave a shrug.

'That's the organist, Mary Sykes.'

'What? Is she okay? Has she no' fallen on the organ or something?'

'There's a tune in there somewhere,' said Clive. 'Just don't try too hard to go looking for it.' He handed Gordy a hymn book and a service sheet. 'In you go. Sit where you want.'

Stepping inside the church, Gordy was hit so hard by a wave of memories that she stumbled back a little, but she forced herself on, and sat down in a pew at the back.

A few pews in front of her, two people turned around, saw her, smiled, glanced at each other, then stood up. Gordy watched as they made their way over to the pew directly in front of her and sat down. They were in their early seventies, she thought, and well dressed.

'You're Gordanian Haig,' said the woman, and she reached out a hand and rested it on Gordy's arm. 'So pleased to meet you at last.'

'I'm John Barker,' the man said. 'This is my wife, Doreen.'

'Awful name, isn't it?' said Doreen. 'I did think about changing it once to something exciting, like Chantelle, but I just never got around to it.'

The organist was still playing, and to Gordy, it sounded as though all she was doing was flapping her arms up and down the keyboard as though trying to swat a fly.

'It's no' an awful name at all,' said Gordy. 'Wear it with pride.'

Doreen smiled.

'You have a kind heart and a good soul,' she said. 'You've seen our messages, yes?'

'I've had a few,' said Gordy. 'Everyone here seems very kind. I've just not been, well, in the right frame of mind, I suppose.'

Doreen squeezed Gordy's arm.

'Well, we are rather busy this week, aren't we, Love?'

Doreen's question was obviously aimed at her husband, but she kept her eyes focused on Gordy instead.

'Free Tuesday evening though, if you are? Would you like to come round for dinner? Nothing too fancy, I'm sure. Just nice to get together, isn't it?'

'Would do us the world of good to have you over. Really cheer us up,' added Doreen.

Gordy was rather shocked by the sudden invite.

'I'm sorry to hear you need someone like me to do that,' she said.

'Just been a bit of a tough time, that's all,' said John. 'Anyway, you'll come round! How does seven-thirty suit?'

Gordy cast her mind through the week ahead, knew she was free that night, wasn't on duty, could think of no reason to turn down the offer, and just nodded and whispered, 'Thank you.'

Her social diary wasn't exactly full, after all. In fact, Tuesday evening would be a very lonely affair if she actually bothered jotting it down in her diary, surrounded on either side by days devoid of any social engagements at all.

With a glance at his wife, John, then Doreen, turned back around to face the front of the church.

Gordy still wasn't sure if she wanted to be there or not, but then the service started, with the choir being led in from the back, down the centre aisle. The vicar was a man, short and round, and he waddled rather like a penguin. As the choir settled into their stalls, he climbed up into the pulpit, where for a moment he disappeared from view. Then his hands appeared over the edge, and his head popped up behind the lectern.

The smile the man beamed out at the congregation, which Gordy noticed then was actually considerably larger than she would have expected for a village the size of Evercreech, warmed her immediately. And before she knew it, she was smiling back.

The next hour raced by, as the vicar, a Mr Alan Parker, peppered not just his sermon, but the whole service, with amusing anecdotes and stories. Laughter filled the church, mixing in cheerfully with the hymns, all of which somehow managed to ignore whatever it was the organist was trying to do.

When the service came to an end, and Gordy exited the church, she did so to smiles and handshakes, not just from the vicar and from Clive, and John and Doreen, but from so many others of the congregation. John and Doreen exchanged telephone numbers with her, and confirmed that she knew exactly where they lived.

By the time she was allowed to leave, she had at least half a dozen invites for coffee and cake, and for dinner, and when she arrived back at her car, she took a moment to think over what had just happened. Such a welcome had been so unexpected, that really, for the first time since moving to Somerset, she felt a sense that perhaps she could call the place home. Not yet, and perhaps not for a good while, but it was suddenly no longer an alien thought. Then, with a smile on her face so surprisingly genuine, she climbed into her car and headed off into the rest of the day, truly happy for the first time in a long, long time. And deep down, she could sense Anna smiling, too.

## THREE

A while later, Gordy found herself in Glastonbury. She'd visited twice since arriving in Somerset, the first time when she had been out exploring before starting work, and the second, a week or two into it. And now, here she was again, wandering its streets, and enjoying its ethereal charms, which in many shop windows had become real and took the form of crystals and dream catchers, wands and dragons.

A late breakfast was taken in a small vegetarian café, and was a celebration of everything you can do with eggs. Not that Gordy was complaining, because the vast omelette had been truly delicious. But, having finished it, she sensed that she would not be eating eggs for at least a month or two, perhaps longer.

Her appetite sated, Gordy attempted to go for a stroll, to browse the shops that lined Glastonbury's ancient streets, but shopping had never really been her idea of a good time, and she soon tired of it. And really, there were only so many scents of incense sticks and coloured healing crystals she could cope with.

Soon, early afternoon had faded into the later hours. So far, she had purchased a book on finding your spirit guide, from a small shop tucked away down a side street, an incense burner, and something called a smudge stick, whatever that was. With all that done, and with no urge, despite her best intentions, to go for a stroll up Glastonbury Tor, Gordy found herself back in front of a woman she had already visited twice before.

'You just can't keep away, can you?' the woman said, fanning out a large deck of cards in her hands. 'How's life as a detective in Frome?'

'You remember?'

'No, I don't, but the cards do, for sure,' the woman smiled back, then she winked at Gordy.

Gordy managed a smile in return and, remembering what to do, pulled out seven cards from the offered deck.

The woman took the cards in a hand that was more gold rings and jewels than visible flesh, and placed them face down on the table in the shape of a cross, five cards down the middle, and a single card on either side of the one in the centre.

'What brings you back to me this time, then? Same as usual?'

'That makes me sound very desperate and very lost.'

'Not at all; trauma like you've experienced is no small thing, so don't go treating it as such.'

Gordy's answer was a shrug because she had no answer.

'Well?'

'Well, what?'

The woman tapped a finger on the cards and the sound of her long nails made Gordy flinch.

'Why is it you're here? What do you want to know?'

Gordy really wasn't sure. There was Anna, obviously, because there was always Anna. There was the fact that she was living in a new place, and still didn't know anyone, and wasn't sure she wanted to. And then there was work, which was actually proving to be really enjoyable, with a great team. At least for now, because if—

'Is it love life, personal life, or work life?' the woman asked, butting into Gordy's thoughts. 'What is it that's bothering you right now, because I can see it written in the worry lines on your face clearer than if I'd scribbled it on in Biro myself.'

'Ha, ha.'

'You look very serious.'

'This is literally my most relaxed face.'

'Needs work.'

'I'll be bearing that in mind.'

With Gordy offering no answer to the question posed, the woman gave a sigh and proceeded to run through the cards, much as she had done the previous two visits.

After a while, Gordy realised two things: one, that she wasn't really listening, and two, that the woman had stopped talking.

'Uh ...'

'You're distracted.'

'That would be an understatement.'

'By what?'

'Everything.'

'So, that was your answer then, wasn't it? To what I asked before?'

'And what was that?'

To Gordy's surprise, the woman reached out and took the cards from the table, slipping them back into the pack.

'I could tell, as soon as you arrived.'

'Tell what?'

'That this is not where you need to be.'

'You can say that again,' Gordy replied, rolling her eyes. 'I've felt that since I've moved here. But what the hell am I supposed to do? And anyway, it's not all bad is it? It's just—'

The woman held up a hand, stopping Gordy from talking.

'No,' she said, shaking her head slowly. 'That's not what I meant. I wasn't saying that Somerset isn't where you need to be. I was talking about you being here, sitting in front of me.'

'Really?'

The woman rose to her feet and stood in front of Gordy, her hands held out to her.

'Take them,' she said.

Gordy hesitated.

'Take them! Come on, I've not got all day!'

Gordy lifted her own hands to the woman's, and was suddenly pulled to her feet.

'What are you doing?' Gordy asked. 'No, actually, what are we doing?'

The woman smiled so warmly that Gordy was fairly sure she felt the heat of it on her skin.

'I think it's about time that you started to take back a bit of control.'

'But I am in control,' Gordy replied. 'That's why I moved to Somerset, isn't it? I didn't stay up North in Yorkshire with what happened, with the memories. I made the decision, I moved, I started my new job. I even went to church this morning, the one Anna was supposed to be vicar of!'

'You're still not in control, though, are you? And don't answer, because I've not finished. What I mean is, you're letting everything that's happened to you this year define who you are. You're carrying it around with you like a huge sack, and it's weighing you down. No, scratch that, not a sack, more like a gorilla.'

'What?'

Gordy was starting to lose the sense of what the woman was trying to say.

'Yes, a gorilla. That's it. A huge thing on your back, that you can't carry, because it's so heavy, but for some reason, you're not just keeping it there, you're feeding it, giving it water, making sure it's comfortable, and all the time it's weighing you down. Yes, a gorilla. Definitely.'

Gordy tried to pull her hands free, but the woman's grip had them fast.

'I should go.'

'No, that's not enough, to just go. I need to hear something more positive.'

'Like what?'

'You tell me,' the woman said. 'You're the one who, once again, has turned up on my doorstep looking for direction. And you know what? I think you know what you need to do, don't you? I think you're here because you're afraid of that. And I don't blame you for it, but neither will I stand by and let you just continue as you are.'

The woman laughed.

'What's so funny?'

'I should charge more, that's what. You came here to have your cards done, and here I am providing valuable advice.'

'I still don't understand.'

The woman finally let go of Gordy's hands.

'Yes, you do,' she said. 'Stop running from the pain, from what happened, from your loss. You need to turn around and face it, embrace it, accept it, grieve, and instead of being defined by it, be defined by how you respond to it. Make sense?'

'No.'

'It will.'

The woman reached into her pocket and pulled out the money Gordy had given her for reading the cards.

'You'll be taking this back,' she said.

Gordy tried to refuse, but the woman shook her head.

'This one's on me,' she said. 'But on one condition.'

'Which is?'

'One day, and it could be in a month's time, a year's time, but one day, you'll wake up, and something will have changed. It won't be that you've moved on, because that's not what this is really about, is it? It's about growing with the grief and responding to it, and somehow using it to grow, to change. And a day will come, when you'll realise you have, that you've changed, and that you're not just okay anymore, but you're something more beautiful, more colourful because of it. You've work to do to get there, but my guess is, you know what that is, don't you?'

'Not sure that I do.'

'"Not sure," is very different to "no, I don't."'

And with that said, the woman led Gordy back outside into what was left of the day.

'Get yourself home,' she said. 'It's time to start living, you hear me? Don't let the dead, and the grief we all carry for them, stop you doing that. Understood?'

Gordy went to answer, but the woman had already gone back inside.

Later that day, with evening now reaching out to welcome what was left of it, Gordy pulled up into a parking space at her new home. She sat for a moment in the quiet, the engine popping and ticking as it cooled, and thought about what the woman had said, and about the welcome she had received at the church earlier in the day.

Then she climbed out of her car and, instead of being sensible and making her way to her flat and an early night, walked in the opposite direction. The Bell Inn was only a five-minute walk away, and right now she could think of no better way to spend her time than to get there as quickly as possible, and to treat herself to dinner and a bloody good pint of Stan's Trad cider.

## FOUR

For the second night in a row, Gordy was woken early by a sound that ripped through her sleep like a chainsaw. Only this time, instead of her own scream, it was the sound of her phone.

She reached out for it in the soft, grey light of the early morning, and answered the call.

'DI Haig ...' She yawned.

'Boss? Sorry, I mean, oh God, I ...'

'Patti?'

Gordy heard panic in the detective constable's voice, but there was something else there, too; absolute terror, ripping through her words like the screech of a violin breaking the dawn.

'PCSO Edwards, I mean Paul ... There's been an anonymous call, and I've called him, tried to contact him, and he's not answering. There's nothing. And I've tried the number of the person who called, and it's dead, it doesn't exist.'

'First, take a wee breath there,' Gordy instructed, now wide awake, like she'd just taken a shot of adrenaline to the heart.

'Now, start at the beginning, and tell me exactly what's going on.'

Gordy heard Patti take a deep breath, then exhale, in an attempt to calm herself.

'Paul attended a call out at around midnight. A runner had spotted lights down on the old railway line, and Paul decided to go and investigate.'

'Nothing about that sounds strange, other than the fact that I'd usually expect it to be more than just lights, Patti. What made Paul go? Did he no' speak to the runner?'

'He did,' Patti replied. 'Paul was sure that it was worth checking out, but then he likes to check out weird stuff. But he's not responding to my calls, and whoever it was that rang in, the number they gave doesn't exist.'

Weird stuff? thought Gordy. How are lights at night weird stuff? But that was odd about the number the caller had given.

'Weird how?' she asked. 'They could be anything, couldn't they? Farmers in the fields, another runner, someone just playing silly buggers, maybe even a wild camper; those buggers get everywhere!'

'I know, I know,' Patti replied. 'But the bloke who reported it, Craig Rowe, he was adamant that it wasn't a tractor or anything like that, because apparently, it was silent when he saw the lights. He was pretty spooked by it.'

'And it's this Mr Rowe you can't call back because the number's wrong?'

'Yes.'

'That doesn't make sense though. It'll be on the system, won't it?'

'That's the number I tried. It's dead. No tone. Nothing.'

Gordy shook her head, fought back a yawn and failed.

'Well, there's no denying that's suspicious.'

Patti said nothing for a moment, but when she did, her voice was a little calmer.

'Look, what you're saying makes sense, I know that, but Paul, he takes his role very seriously. He's very focused on being the person the community knows they can turn to, so, off he went. It's what makes him who he is. And like I said, he's always happy to check out weird stuff.'

'You've said that twice now. What do you mean, exactly?'

There was a slight pause.

'If I said he was a member of a local paranormal group, would that explain it?'

A shot of frustration sent Gordy's eyes wide.

'If you're calling to tell me that Paul's got lost looking for ghosts, I'm no' going to be very happy at all. In fact, I'd go so far as to say I may even be a little bit upset. And I trust you understand that's a marked understatement.'

Gordy heard herself using that exact phrase the day before in Glastonbury and wondered if 'understatement' in itself was how she responded to many things, and if it was all that healthy. A little bit of self-protection, she guessed, nothing more.

'I'm not saying that at all,' Patti replied. 'I'm just saying he's the one on the team who's always happy to take the slightly odder queries or stories seriously than the rest of us. And with this, there's actually a chance it might be something else, right? This is a rural area, could be livestock or farm machinery theft.'

Another yawn threatened, but Gordy forced it back down, only to have it come back even stronger, and make her eyes water. She knew Patti had a point; in the Dales, the theft of stock and machinery was a major issue for farmers.

'So, we've got Paul racing off to check out some mysterious lights,' she said, wiping tears of tiredness from her eyes. 'Not the best use of police resources, but that's for another day. And we've got no way of contacting whoever it was that called it in.

Like we've just said, it could be something serious, but why the panic? Why are you phoning me at—' Gordy checked her phone '—one AM? Really, Patti? I know I don't really need my beauty sleep, but some would be nice every now and again.'

'I know, and I'm sorry,' Patti said.

Gordy remembered what Patti had said at the start of the call.

'You also mentioned an anonymous call; what's that got to do with Paul? What was it about?'

Patti was quiet again.

'Patti?'

'The location Paul was sent to by the runner is a lane called Hatchet Hill,' Patti said.

'Sounds lovely.'

'The call mentioned the same lane.'

'In what context?'

'That Hatchet Hill is just the beginning.'

'What were the actual words? I know we'll have a recording, but was that it? Was there anything else?'

'Yes, but it was some crazy, occult kind of nonsense about being afraid of the one who can kill your body and your soul. Not exactly something I'm about to take seriously.'

Gordy said nothing in reply to that, deciding it was best to just get shifting and find out where Paul was, first, before thinking about whatever else was going on. She stood up and started to pull her clothes from her wardrobe with one hand, while the other kept the phone glued to her face.

'And you've no' heard anything from Paul at all?'

'Spoke to him when he arrived. That was it. He said if there was anything to report, that he would. But I didn't hear anything, so I didn't think anything of it. Then the call came in, so obviously I called him, but there was no answer, nothing at all, and that's not like Paul, it really isn't.'

'Maybe he's been delayed,' Gordy suggested, hearing the panic in Patti's voice again. 'Perhaps something else has come up while he was checking out the weird lights. He's not legally bound to keep you up-to-date with his every movement, is he?'

'Again, what you're saying makes sense, but this is Paul we're talking about, and he's different.'

'How?'

'He'd have been in touch to let me know what he was doing, where he was going, because that's what he does. He thinks nothing to report is as important as having something to tell me, and will usually take even longer to tell me what he's not found, than what he has! The fact that he hasn't called back has me worried, especially with the anonymous call. And I know I shouldn't have called you, that it's the middle of the night, that you're officially not on duty, but ... oh, God, I'm sorry ...'

Gordy gave Patti a moment to gather herself, taking the opportunity to put her phone on speaker, so that she could finish getting dressed.

'Can you send me Paul's exact location? I need something more than the name of a lane.'

'I will,' Patti replied. 'But it's a short lane, you'll see his car.'

'Send it to me anyway, and I'll meet you there.'

'No,' Patti began, 'you're right, I'm overthinking, worrying. I can sort this. I'll head out there myself.'

'This isn't a discussion,' said Gordy. 'Anyway, I'm awake now, aren't I? And there's zero chance of me getting back to sleep. So, do as I've just said; send me the location, and I'll meet you there. Is that understood?'

'Yes, ma'am.'

'Patti—'

But the line was dead, so Gordy wasn't given the chance to remind the detective constable once again that she really, really didn't like to be called ma'am.

# FIVE

Heading out into the blackest of mornings, Gordy narrowed her eyes to focus on the road ahead. It was mostly clear to begin with, but she soon found sections hidden by the spindly fingers of fog stretching across through gaps in hedges, or pools of the stuff hidden in dips, like cotton wool in a bowl.

Having barely left Evercreech, however, and taking a left up a steep hill, she rounded a bend to see a sign ooze its way out of the fog, to reveal that the road ahead was closed. Swinging around in the gated entrance to a field, and swearing a little under her breath, Gordy found herself diverted along a lane she sometimes used to head to Frome.

The night was still, the roads empty, and where trees lined them, they stood like mythical soldiers pausing during their advance to allow her past, their weathered branches barely moving, as though time for them had slowed to a crawl.

Eventually hitting the main road, Gordy's satnav had her slipping through the village of Nunney, a place she remembered well, not just for the history cast down upon it by the shadow the castle nestled in its lap, but the body that had been found there not long after she had arrived in Somerset. That case had been shocking on so many levels, not least because her new boss, DCI Allercott, had been responsible.

That brought to mind how she and the rest of the team were now waiting for a replacement Detective Chief Inspector to arrive, though there had, as yet, been no word who it would be or when they were expected. Gordy had applied for the role herself after a chat with Jameson.

The interview hadn't gone well, and thinking on it, she was hardly surprised. She'd taken on enough as it was, moving South under such difficult circumstances, so to take on anything else would have been foolish. She hadn't realised at the time that was what she had felt deep down, and her failure at getting the role had hit hard. But with a bit of time between her and it, Gordy saw that it had been for the best, for now, anyway.

The next village was Mells, not that Gordy saw much of it, the fog thicker than ever the closer she got to her destination. She was aware of narrow streets and old buildings, which slid past like images in a silent movie. Then she was back out again onto a lane where the fog rested so thick she was forced to slow to a near crawl, her headlights casting an eerie glow around her.

BY THE ENTRANCE TO A QUARRY, Hatchet Lane welcomed her, and she drifted into it, as a gap in the fog opened wide to swallow her whole.

The lane was dark and snaked its way up a steep, twisting incline. As they climbed, swirling fog kept their final destination a mystery, only ever allowing them to see just around the next bend, but never further. The lane's borders were given over to woodland that seemed to have become one with the walls that held it back. Gordy saw roots reaching over at through old stonework, branches resting on the walls frozen in the act of trying to topple them, thick carpets of moss rolling out from beneath the trees to suffocate what it touched.

Around another bend, two vehicles loomed out of the fog, and Gordy slowed down, seeing Patti standing beside one, waiting for her.

She parked up just beyond the two cars, and climbed out.

'Here we are, then,' she said. 'Any sign of Paul?'

'I've only just arrived myself,' said Patti. 'I've checked his car, though; it's locked, doesn't seem like anything's out of place.'

Gordy dropped her eyes to what Paul's car, then asked, 'Any particular reason this place carries the name it does?'

'Haven't a clue,' said Patti. 'To be honest, Paul would be the one to ask. There's lots of odd names around, though; Murder Combe is a favourite, and there's a Witches Walk, I think, over in Bridgewater.'

'Lovely.'

'Aren't they?'

Gordy looked around where they now stood, the lane slipping down into the fog behind her, and disappearing up into it ahead. The Woodland the lane snuck through, choked as it was by the fog, had the feel of a theatre backdrop, all shadows and strange angles and atmosphere. She could easily imagine Shakespeare's famous, prophetic witches cackling over their cauldron somewhere beyond where she could see, waiting for the arrival of Macbeth.

'It's an eerie place, isn't it?'

'Somerset can have that feel about it sometimes,' said Patti. 'But then most places do, when the weather's like this.'

Gordy wasn't so sure.

'The Dales never gave me the same feeling,' she said. 'You'd have thick fog on the moors, it would roll down the fellside to swallow villages, but it never struck me as anything other than comforting and cosy. That sounds weird, I know, but it's very different here.'

Gordy saw a faint smile chance its luck on Patti's otherwise stressed face.

'Watch yourself,' she said. 'Before you know where you are, you'll be racing off to Glastonbury Tor and trying to find the Holy Grail.'

That made Gordy laugh.

'So, that's where it is, then? I always wondered. Might give me something to do come the weekend.'

'Not only the Holy Grail, either; there's even a hidden cave that will give you safe passage into the land of the fairies. If you can find it, that is.'

'Which sort of implies there's another cave that's considerably more dangerous, doesn't it?'

'I'd not thought about it like that. Probably best to not go looking for that one.'

'My thoughts exactly. And if it's all the same with you, I'll be keeping myself well away from any land of the fairies as well.'

Gordy pulled a torch from a jacket pocket.

'So, where do you want to start?'

Patti clicked on her own torch, and shone it around.

'There's an old railway line beneath us,' she said. 'One of us could take a look there, while the other has a look in the woods?'

'I'd rather we stuck together.'

'So would I.'

'Then you lead the way.'

Gordy waited for Patti to stroll past her, then followed on, down a small path that took them to a thin line of tarmac running perpendicular to the lane above.

They both shone their torches left and right.

'Toss a coin?' Gordy asked.

'I don't carry cash.'

'Very regal of you.'

Patti gave a shrug and decided to go right, walking under the road above, and into a section where the fog was not so thick.

'This is the route the runner told Paul he was on,' Patti explained. 'It's a nice walk or a bike ride if you're ever looking for something to do.'

'I'll bear it in mind, but I wouldn't be so keen to be running down here on my own in the middle of the night, would you?'

They walked on in silence, the beams of their torches scanning the thick greenery around them.

'Needle in a haystack,' said Gordy, tempted to shout out for Paul, but something held her back. She wasn't sure what, but there was an atmosphere to the place, and something about it was putting her on edge.

'Paul's a big needle, but you're right. Shall we double back?'

Gordy's answer was to do a one-eighty and together they explored the other direction. The unease she felt only grew, and that annoyed her, because Gordy was not one for allowing odd feelings and hairs rising on the back of her neck to be her compass, not by a long shot.

'Did this runner say where he'd seen the lights?' she asked, coming to a stop.

'As far as I know, he saw them running along here. Not much to go on.'

Gordy stopped, shone her torch around.

'Not much to see, either, is there? Just open fields either side of us beyond the trees, and they've thinned out a lot here. Where the hell is he?'

She did her level best to remove any panic from her voice, but with the fog deadening the sound of the night all around, it was hard not to sense that something wasn't right. On the way over, she'd wondered if the anonymous call had been a prank, but then the coincidence with Paul's location and him not being around made her uneasy. And anyway, there was no such thing as coincidence, was there?

'Where we are doesn't strike me as the kind of place anyone would see strange lights,' she said. 'If this runner had seen the lights in the fields, then the natural conclusion would be farmers working, that kind of thing, right? Maybe someone out lamping for rabbits or foxes.'

Gordy saw Patti's eyes widen at this.

'What?'

'You know about lamping?'

'Knew a gamekeeper or two in the Dales. Plus, there's a bit of family history way back in the Highlands. I've some old black and white photos somewhere of my distant relatives; they were gamekeepers on an estate in Glen Etive.'

'Ah.'

'So, if there's nothing to see on this path, and nothing in the fields, and if Paul found the same, what would he have done next?'

'Headed back to his car.'

'My thoughts exactly, Patti; come on.'

A few minutes later, and back at the car, Gordy swung her torch around once again, narrowing her eyes against the darkness.

'There's a gate just up there,' she said, pointing up the road. 'And a little wooden signpost.'

She said no more, and marched up to the sign.

'Bridleway.'

Patti directed the beam of her torch over the fence and down the bridleway.

'Now, lights from down there? They'd be mysterious,' she said.

Gordy opened the gate, allowed Patti through, then closed it behind them, making sure that when they set off, she was in front.

She cast the beam of her torch to her left, saw brief slivers below of the path following the route of the old railway line, then thought to hell with it and called out for the missing PCSO.

'Paul? It's Gordy and Patti. Where are you? If you can hear us, make a sound, please.'

No sound came.

Gordy tried again, but the night still refused to reward her.

'I don't like this,' Patti said.

'Don't overthink it,' Gordy advised. 'Doesn't help at all. Worry never does. Clouds the mind. For all we know, Paul's tripped up, fallen, banged his head. Maybe even lost himself down a fox hole.'

That statement made Patti stop and Gordy glanced back to see confusion in her eyes.

'Down a fox hole?'

'Happened to a farmer up in the Dales,' Gordy said. 'A constable on the team only found him because his dog knew where he was, and even then, only because the poor bloke's feet were stuck out of the ground.'

'You're pulling my leg.'

'Remind me to tell you about it sometime.'

Gordy continued walking. In the light of the torch, she caught two bright circles ahead, staring back at her.

'Fox,' she whispered.

'That's not good,' Patti whispered back. 'It wouldn't be hanging around so comfortably if Paul was close by.'

The fox stared for a moment longer, then disappeared.

Gordy directed her torch beam to where it had been standing.

'Looks like we disturbed it after a kill,' she said, seeing something lying in the grass ahead.

'Probably a rabbit or something,' said Patti.

As Patti's words came to her, some dark part of the night reached into her gut and gave it a hard twist.

'Patti? Stay here.'

Gordy gave the detective sergeant no chance to respond, and pushed on down the bridleway, her pace picking up as she went.

'Gordy? What's wrong? What have you seen? Is it Paul? Is he okay?'

The beam of Gordy's torch fell on where the fox had just been, and what it been bothering itself with. She looked back, saw Patti drawing closer, held up a hand.

'Stay back,' she said, her voice commanding now. 'And that's an order.'

Patti froze.

'Why? What's wrong? What have you found? What is it?'

Well, thought Gordy, staring at the fleshy, fox-gnawed thing lying on the ground in front of her, there was one thing it very much wasn't; a rabbit.

## SIX

Gordy was not surprised in the slightest when Patti, after initially doing as she was ordered, and staying where she was, ran over to join her, and regretted it immediately.

'Oh, God ...'

'Patti ...'

'That's not Paul, is it? It can't be!'

Gordy, who was crouching on the ground, glanced up, over her shoulder, at Patti.

'We don't know who it is. There's not enough of whoever this is to be able to tell, is there?'

Patti didn't respond, just stared.

Gordy stood up, turned her back on what she had found in the grass, and forced Patti to look at her with nothing more than sheer force of will.

'Patti, I need you to call this in,' she said, her voice gentle and calm, but no less commanding for being so. 'Cordon the area off. Pull in extra officers. Contact Scene of Crime. You know what to do, Patti, so I'm leaving all of that to you.'

Patti didn't respond right away.

'Patti?'

Gordy watched the detective sergeant seem to shake herself and finally look at her.

'Of course, yes,' she replied. 'I'll get on with that now. But what about you? What are you going to do?'

'I'm going to see what else I can find,' Gordy replied, and turning from Patti, trained the beam of her torch on the ground in front of her.

'You sure you don't want me to come with you?'

'I've told you what I need you to do,' Gordy replied, following the doorway of bright, white light that her torch was calling her to step through. 'The sooner we both get on with what we need to do, the sooner we find out exactly what's happened to Paul.'

Gordy didn't give Patti a chance to respond, and pushed on.

Leaving the hand where it lay in the grass, and hoping that there wasn't another fox nearby that fancied padding on over to take it away for a nibble, she made her way slowly along the bridleway. Sweeping the torch left and right, the wide beam draped the trees and bushes in sudden sheets of light, causing darker shadows to dance behind them. The brightness of the light, Gordy noticed, seemed to turn what was beyond it darker still, as though beyond its reach nothing else existed. Or perhaps it was that the light itself brought the world around her into existence in the first place, and once the beam had moved on, the things it revealed faded.

Admonishing herself for allowing her imagination to run so wild, though in turn also rather impressed with the images and descriptions she had come up with, Gordy saw that bridleway turned a little to the left up ahead. When she reached it, the corner was deeply rutted by the passage of numerous travellers on foot and tyre and hoof. The ground was damp beneath her feet, and Gordy could just make out the faintest sound of trickling water, feeding puddles hidden beneath thick grass, turning the mud slick.

Watching her footsteps, careful to make sure she neither slipped nor placed a foot in a hidden well of muck, Gordy turned with the bridleway, the beam of her torch firmly on the tricky terrain. Then, when she was past it, and the ground was firm again, she brought the light back up in front of her, and stopped.

Dear God ...

Seconds passed, each one feeling like a year, as the hellish vista before Gordy held her attention with all the grim, ghoulish fascination of a car crash. She wanted to turn her head away, no, not just her head, but her whole body, and get the hell away from this sudden nightmare, this impossible scene before her that she knew could never be unseen. But that just wasn't an option, and fighting every instinct inside her, to turn tail and face back the way she had come, Gordy forced herself to take in everything she was now witness to, as though afraid that even the sound of her soft breathing could wake yet more horror.

Staying where she was, afraid for the moment to step any closer, Gordy moved her torch beam with deliberate slowness. It was the same beam as before, the same artificial light which had innocently caressed the sleeping branches of the night-cloaked world, yet now it was tainted by everything it touched.

Where many hues of green should have been, blood spatter painted the vista like graffiti. It shone bright red and black, switching between the two in moments, like the rich paint of an artist suddenly turned to oil. And it would flip between the two as she stared at it, sometimes cherry red droplets glinting in the light, and other times black marbles falling from branches to the ground. And it was those black marbles which Gordy found the most horrifying, their dark nature somehow suggesting what had happened in this peaceful dell, reflecting the violence of it in their silent journey to the ground.

There was, Gordy realised, no body. Not in the normal sense of the word. She had not stumbled upon a crime scene where the act of death was frozen in time by the position of legs and arms and torso. Oftentimes, she had thought how the body of a victim was like that of a dancer frozen in one final movement, but here, there was nothing, not in the normal sense, anyway.

Meat. That's what Gordy thought of now. A butcher's shop, but so much bloodier, and without any of the care shown in presenting the flesh in such a way as to distance the purchaser from the animal of origin.

No such care had been taken here. Unless, of course, the care was of an entirely different kind, focused only on displaying where each joint was from with both shocking clarity and absolute disregard for the stomach of the witness.

A leg was propped up against an old wooden fence post, as though left there by accident by a passing walker, who had somehow managed to continue on their way without it. A handless arm was draped over a low branch, like washing left to dry. The other leg was in front of her, lying on the bridleway like a limb ripped from one of the trees lining the path. As for the other arm, Gordy could see sections of it around and about, cast on the ground like joints of meat spilled from a trolley. She hadn't found the torso yet, but at the far edge of her carefully moving circle of light she did see a mess of blood and flesh.

Then, of course, there was the head.

Resting in a tuft of soft grass, a pale face stared passively up at her. There was no emotion in it, no sense that she could draw from the look it was giving her as to what had gone on here or why.

Perhaps it didn't really need to, thought Gordy, because enough had already been said by the way the whole scene had been painted. But there was something else as well, and its very existence rendered words hopeless in its presence.

Buried in the scalp of the severed head of PCSO Paul Edwards was a small axe.

## SEVEN

With the crime scene cordoned off with what she thought was enough tape to stretch to the moon and back, Gordy was standing at the roadside and leaning against the gate to the lane where Paul had been brutally butchered and displayed. The whys and wherefores of what had taken place were, right now, ghosts to her, much like Paul himself.

She turned around, forced herself to stare back down the lane into the oily darkness swilling between the trees. She thought about Paul, the most relaxed, easy-going PCSO she had ever had the pleasure of working with. That he was gone seemed utterly impossible. He just couldn't be, because she could remember so clearly how she had chided him for referring to himself as 'only a PCSO,' because to her mind, there was no such thing.

In the short time she had known him, Paul had never been *only* anything. He had been an exceptional PCSO, and a truly lovely human being. But he was gone. He was no more. His life had been hacked away from him so terribly, so violently, that what she had seen down that lane blasted into her mind as if from a water cannon, and she reached out to grip the gate just to hold on against the onslaught. When it finally eased, she was left with memories so real she felt she could reach out and grab them; her last conversation with him, his smile, how they had talked about the days ahead, the job, life in Somerset, his family.

Oh, God, his family ...

'Boss?'

The voice of Detective Constable Patti Matondo was firm, calm, and peppered with just enough concern for Gordy to know that she wasn't just trying to get her attention.

Gordy turned around.

'I'm okay, honestly, I'm fine.'

'No, you're not,' Patti said. 'I know I'm not, so I don't see how you can be.'

Gordy noticed how red Patti's eyes were, was about to ask how she was doing herself, when vehicle lights broke the moment with clinical brightness.

'Can't be Cowboy, not yet,' said Patti.

'Rest of the team, then?'

Two vehicles pulled up at the side of the road, doors opened, spilling figures into the night.

Detective Constable Peter Knight was first up, swiftly followed by Jack Hill, the PCSO Supervisor, then PCSOs Helen Kendrick and Travis Waring.

Helen's ginger hair shone bright in the glare of the headlights, whereas Travis's thick beard seemed to just swallow it like a black hole.

'Where is he?' Jack asked, and Gordy saw not just shock and grief in the man's face, but an anger burning hot enough to set the trees around them alight.

She understood the emotion, expected it in fact, but she would have to keep a check on it; the awfulness of the situation, the brutality of it, that was what they needed to focus on, and finding the person or persons responsible was only going to be possible with clear minds. As soon as thoughts became snared in anger, justice could flip to its darker side and become revenge, and she had no place for that, not anymore, anyway, not since ...

Pushing away a sudden memory, one so old and filled with menace it caught her breath, Gordy gathered everyone in close. She needed the team to focus on what they were there to do, and what the days ahead would involve. She also needed them to know that she understood what they were going through, and that she wasn't just their DI, there to order them about, to lead, but also someone they could confide in. That they were still down a DCI wasn't much help, but that was the way of things sometimes, and you just had to work with what you had.

Taking a slow breath in and then out, Gordy cast her eyes around the team.

'I'm not going to mess around with this, or soften the blow,' she said, though her voice itself rested in the air like duck feathers spilled from a burst cushion. 'PCSO Paul Edwards is dead.'

She gave those words just a few seconds to settle, watching the reaction of each member of the team.

'As hard as this is, and I think I can confidently say this will be one of, if not the hardest case any of us will ever work on, the best we can do for Paul now is our jobs. Understood?'

Nods all around, no words muttered.

'This is personal, unavoidably so, and arguably, we should probably all be taken off the case due to being too close to it. But we are a DCI down, and I can't think of people better placed to investigate what has happened than the people I have in front of me.'

Out of the corner of her eye, Gordy saw Travis fold his thick arms across his wide chest.

'I'll call Firbank first thing to discuss, but believe me when I say I can be very, very persuasive. Paul was our colleague, our friend, and our place is here, finding out who did this.'

'What did they actually do?' Jack asked. 'How did they ...?'

Gordy turned kind eyes on the PCSO supervisor.

'Paul's dead,' Gordy said. 'And for now, that's enough for any of you to be thinking on. Cowboy and the SOC team are en route. I will be heading back to the scene myself, but that I will do alone.'

There were mutters of objection, but Gordy ignored them.

'Pete? You're Scene Guard. No one gets in or out of here without giving you their details. Jack? Helen, I need you and Travis to not be here.' Gordy held up a hand to stop any complaints before they had a chance to be voiced. 'I called you over because I needed to tell you about Paul face-to-face. Now, however, I need you to focus on not only being PCSOs, but to think about everything you know about Paul. Yes, we all worked with him, and obviously all of you for considerably longer than I. However, you three have detailed knowledge of his life, who he knew, where he hung out. I'm not suggesting that he did anything to lead to him ending up here, but his background, his life, his world, may hold some clue, some link to it all.'

'Paul wasn't involved in anything dodgy, if that's what you're suggesting,' said Jack. 'I'm sure of it. He was about as criminally minded as Jesus.'

'I'm not suggesting that he was,' Gordy clarified. 'My point, however, is this; if what happened here turns out to be utterly random, I'll hand my badge in. That's not me jumping to conclusions either; I'm listening to my gut. Maybe Paul was simply unlucky to be here, maybe he wasn't. Only way to find out is to unpick everything.'

Gordy widened the focus to include Patti and Peter. 'What we know is that lights were apparently seen by a runner who called them in as suspicious. Paul came out to investigate, and was murdered. We have no way of contacting the runner, as his phone is dead, but we do have a name and a possible connection to a local running group.

'As far as what happened to Paul, we need to consider this: could it have been any of us taking that call and ending up here, or was what happened somehow designed to get Paul here specifically? Who is this runner who called in and why isn't their phone being picked up? And then, of course, there's the anonymous message.'

Gordy saw eyes widen.

'Anonymous message?' said Peter. 'What are you talking about?'

Patti said, 'Came in a good while after Paul had headed off to investigate the lights.'

'And what was the message?'

Patti went quiet for a moment, clearly trying to remember, then said, 'It was something about killing the body or the soul, I think ... Wait, yes, that was it, *Do not fear those who kill the body but cannot kill the soul; fear the one who can destroy both.*'

'What the hell's that supposed to mean?' asked Travis.

'No idea at all,' said Gordy. 'But it's worrying on every possible level.'

'Sounds biblical,' said Helen.

'Sounds like nonsense, more like,' said Travis.

Gordy looked at Patti. 'Paul's family; once I'm back from having another look at the crime scene, I'll need to visit them, talk to them. And I'll want uniform keeping an eye on them for a while as well, just to make sure they're safe.'

'I'll come with you,' Patti said. 'I know them. His daughter is at university. It will be better if there's two of us.'

'It will,' Gordy agreed.

The rumble of diesel engines tumbled into the small gathering, then lights swept down the road as two large, white vans came to a stop in front of them. The driver's window of the first van sunk into the door and Gordy saw the head of the Scene of Crime team, Keith 'Cowboy' Brown, staring back. Gordy noticed immediately that the expected blast of Country and Western music hadn't materialised, and that Cowboy wasn't wearing his white Stetson.

'Came as quickly as we could,' Cowboy said. 'You okay?'

The question took Gordy by surprise, not only because it had been asked, but also due to the genuine concern in the man's voice.

'No,' she said.

'I'll send the photographer in now. If you can show him the way, give us time to get our gear together. Ambulance on its way?'

'It is,' Patti said.

Gordy heard a van door open and shut, and watched as the photographer, dressed in an ill-fitting paper suit, walked around the front of Cowboy's van and approach her. She gave him a nod, then turned back towards the lane. Patti stepped in beside her.

'No,' Gordy said. 'You stay.'

'Ain't happening,' Patti replied, and to Gordy's surprise, she felt the detective sergeant's hand squeeze her arm. 'Shall we go?'

Gordy's answer was to lead Patti and the photographer back along the lane to see Paul.

# EIGHT

Seeing Paul for a second time somehow managed to shock Gordy even more than when she had first discovered his body. She had prepared herself for what she was going to see, verbally, too, with a quick pep-talk with Patti and the photographer, but somehow, knowing what was coming made it even worse. It reminded her of why, over the years, she'd realised that she wasn't much of a fan of horror films, because the scares the first time around were enough, but watching the same thing again, and knowing what was coming? That was the worst.

As they walked quietly into the space where Paul's final moments had been turned into an orchestra of pain and violence, heard only by the night and the creatures that wandered around in it, Gordy was impressed to see that Patti held herself together well.

The photographer, on the other hand, did not. Despite Gordy's warning of what awaited them, and the photographer's reassurance that he would be fine, he had, within moments of casting his eyes around the shattered remains of the PCSO, bolted back down the bridleway to empty his stomach. The sound of it had been violent, dramatic, and when he had returned, full of apology, he had carried out his job with a quiet efficiency, which seemed to be both hurried and deliberately slow all at once. Impossible, of course, Gordy knew, but it was the way the man floated around the crime scene that seemed almost otherworldly, bouncing between each vignette of horror like the metal sphere in a pinball machine, throwing blasts of light into the night like the erratically cast spells of a mad wizard.

His job finished, the photographer had simply slipped away, back down the bridleway, with not a wave or nod of farewell, leaving Gordy and Patti alone with Paul.

'How you holding up?' Gordy asked, as Patti stood beside her.

'I'm pretending I'm not really here,' Patti said. 'Seems to be working so far.'

'You don't have to stay.'

'It's not about whether I do or don't,' Patti replied. 'It's that I will, regardless.'

No, it isn't, is it, Gordy thought, and said, 'I appreciate you coming along, Patti. Thank you.'

Gordy sent the beam of her torch in a wide, slow arc, allowing the sharp-edged circle of light to flow across the ground and from tree to tree, like a sheet of silk spilled from a loom. She swung it back, this time trying to imagine what had happened, how Paul had ended up so scattered, and allowed the beam to come to a stop on the leg leaning against the fence post.

Walking over for a closer look, Gordy heard Patti following, and came to a stop just far enough away to be able to take it all in without being overwhelmed by it.

'Why is it displayed like that?' Patti asked.

'Wish I knew,' said Gordy, staring at the leg, before guiding her torch beam around to the other remains of Paul, the light flowing through the dark like water spilling from the mouth of a quiet cave. 'Walk with me.'

Gordy guided Patti from leg to arm to leg to torso, and finally, to Paul's head, on the way, stepping over fallen branches and large tufts of grass, which snatched at her heels and tried to pull at her legs as they explored. Something about what they were seeing struck her as planned, ordered almost, but for the life of her, she couldn't work out why.

'It's like everything is in a circle, isn't it?' Patti suggested, interrupting Gordy's thoughts. 'With ... well, with Paul at the centre. I mean, I know it's all Paul, but ... well, you know what I mean.'

Gordy knew exactly what Patti meant.

'Why, though?' she asked. 'What's the reasoning behind it, assuming there is any, of course. And no, I'm not expecting you to be able to give me an answer.'

'Good, because I don't have one.'

'It's worrying though. Suggests there's method here, as well as madness, doesn't it?'

'Method? How?'

Gordy's eyes fell on Paul's head, then followed thick lines of blood on the grass that seemed to reach out from where it rested like the legs of a vast, hideous spider. That was an image Gordy wished her mind hadn't created; something told her that when she next fell asleep, her dreams would be ripped apart by an arachnid with Paul's head as its body.

'Murder is one thing,' she said. 'But murder this brutal? It's something else entirely. To kill Paul in this way, then make the conscious decision to show him off? There has to be a reason for it, doesn't there?'

'You mean this was all planned?'

'I mean,' said Gordy, 'that you don't kill someone on Hatchet Hill with an honest-to-God hatchet, then take the time to lay out the pieces like this without reason. Even if that reason is glee at the kill, a celebration at what's been done, or just wild, untethered rage. There's still a good reason for it.'

'Good reason? How can there be a good reason for any of this?'

'To us, it isn't good at all, I know that,' Gordy tried to explain, 'but to the killer or killers? Well, perhaps the reason, whatever it is, is the reason Paul was killed in the first place.'

'What terrifies me most,' said Patti, a thin sliver of terror skewering her words and twisting her voice, 'is that this could just have easily been me, couldn't it? The call came in. I was there. It's just bad luck that put Paul here, that's all. But then does that make me lucky? Because I don't feel it.'

'Don't think like that,' said Gordy, turning to face Patti. 'It won't help us work outwhat the hell this is, why it happened, anything. Understood?'

'But—'

'No buts, not one,' Gordy said, voice firm. 'Life is fragile. Most of us are damned lucky to just get through the day without being hit by a car, tripping over and being stabbed through the eye by a stick, or contracting some hideous disease.'

Patti's mouth fell open again, but shut it when Gordy raised a finger.

'You go down that route, you'll end up blaming yourself for this, for what happened to Paul. Do not allow that to happen.'

Approaching lights caught Gordy's attention, and she turned to see Cowboy and his entourage slipping through the inky blackness of the night.

'I'm impressed,' Patti said. 'No music, no nonsense; seems he can behave when he wants to.'

Gordy led Patti over to greet the head of the SOC team.

'Had a quick chat with the photographer,' Cowboy said. 'I know what we're dealing with. How are you both doing?'

'Better than your photographer, so that's something,' said Gordy.

A hint of a smile hung itself briefly on Cowboy's lips, before disappearing again, like clothing snatched from a washing line.

'Well, best you leave us to it, now,' he said. 'We'll do the usual thorough job, might even throw a drone up as well, once we've got the crime scene floodlit, see if that picks up anything unusual; you never know, right? Anyway, my guess is that you've another journey to do, yes?'

'He's not been formally identified,' Gordy said, 'but frankly, right now, procedure and protocol be damned; that's Paul back there, and his family needs to know.'

'They do,' Cowboy agreed. 'And I can't think of anyone better to break the news to them.'

With that, he continued on his way, and his team snaked after him.

'At some point,' said Patti, 'you need to tell me exactly what it is you've done to have Cowboy talk to you with such deference and respect.'

'If I knew, I'd tell you,' said Gordy, then sighed. 'Time to visit Paul's wife, then ...'

Patti said nothing as they walked back along the bridleway, lost in their own thoughts. Gordy would've happily put money on Patti's being little different to her own—wondering just what the hell they were going to say when they arrived at Paul's house to wake his nearest and dearest with the news no one wants to hear.

# NINE

Having made it clear that the team were to be in the office late morning, to give them all a chance to rest after the harrowing and late night they had endured, Gordy herself had turned up just before nine. Having arrived in Evercreech at just gone six, she had at least attempted to rest. But sleep had not come easily, and after nearly two hours of staring at the back of her eyelids, she'd given up, took a quick shower, dressed, and driven to the station.

'Whether you want some or not, I'm making you coffee,' Vivek said, as she walked towards him, the main doors swinging shut behind her, just not quick enough to leave everything she was now dealing with on the other side. 'And I won't insult you by asking how you are, either,' he added. 'Paul was a good man. I'm not ashamed to say I cried when I heard, and have cried again here, at my desk.'

Gordy gave Vivek what she was sure was the saddest of smiles, because though her face moved, her eyes were still small windows to the trauma of it all, and she was struggling to open them.

'I'm assuming no one else is in.'

'Just you and I, for now,' Vivek said. 'You head up, and I'll sort you that coffee. My guess is you've not had breakfast either.'

'Wasn't really hungry.'

'Hungry or not, you need to eat.'

'I don't.'

The stare Vivek returned was enough to tell Gordy that he wasn't listening, and even if he was, he was taking no notice.

'Oh, yes,' he said, 'you're that special kind of human, aren't you? The kind that doesn't need food to convert to energy to actually live? Let me guess, you don't drink water either, do you?'

'Water? Of course I drink water.'

Vivek's stare was unchanged.

Heading upstairs and into the incident room, she shuffled wearily over to her little office at the far end, kicked open the door, and slumped behind her desk. She didn't even bother to put the light on, the darkness, for the moment forming a blanket of comfort.

Gordy wished tears would come, that she could feel something beyond the numbness, but her eyes remained dry. Closing them didn't help either, which was probably why she hadn't been able to sleep; such intimate darkness took her to one place only; Hatchet Hill.

'Here you go.'

Vivek was padding across to Gordy from the door to her office. He was carrying a mug of steaming coffee and a small plate.

'I'm not hungry.'

'You've not seen what it is yet.'

'And what is it?'

Vivek placed the mug and plate down in front of Gordy.

'Little invention of my own, a breakfast muffin.'

Gordy stared at the thing on the plate. It was huge, the size of a heavyweight boxer's fist.

'And how is a muffin something that's got anything at all to do with breakfast?' she asked. 'Muffins are for midmorning with coffee at a push.'

'By adding chorizo, tomatoes, cottage cheese, and onion, that's how.' Vivek smiled back. Somewhat proudly, too, Gordy noticed.

'You just so happened to have this with you?'

Vivek gave a shrug.

'I bake when I'm sad,' he said. 'I also bake when I'm happy, or when I'm upset, or when I'm bored. Sometimes I even bake when I can't sleep.'

'You're not leaving much room for doing anything other than baking, are you? And what was the reason that made you make these, then?'

Vivek answered with the saddest shrug and shake of his head.

Gordy understood.

'Paul's death, it's going to be hard for everyone,' she said. 'I'll be honest, I'm impressed that you've worked out a way to channel your grief. That's very impressive and admirable. Wish I could do the same.'

'I could teach you to bake?'

That suggestion made Gordy smile.

'Baking requires too much finesse,' she said. 'I'm good with savoury stuff, stews and roasts, anything like that, but doing something that requires measuring the ingredients with a huge amount of accuracy, and following instructions to the letter? That's just not me.'

'Well, begin with bread,' Vivek suggested. 'It's very forgiving, and there's nothing like the smell of a freshly baked loaf, that's for sure. As for the muffins, I've made enough to make sure the whole team has something decent inside them. I figured you'd all be hungry after last night, even if some of you manage some breakfast or whatever; there's just no way any of you can be trying to find out what happened to Paul if you've empty stomachs, can you?'

Gordy reached for the muffin. It was soft, and it was warm.

Vivek made his way back to the door, paused, turned back around.

'His family ... how did it ...?'

Gordy said nothing, just held Vivek's eyes long enough to let him know, then he continued on his way, leaving her alone with her thoughts and the savoury treat he had provided.

A few minutes later, Gordy still hadn't made much progress with the muffin. It was still in her hand, and the warmth of it, the smell, were still very much apparent, but she was almost unaware of either. Instead, she was just staring at it, lost for a while to the grief and the shock. She'd managed a few nibbles, and there was no denying just how delicious it was, but her body seemed to reject the idea of taking anything in, the muffin turning to ash on her tongue.

The phone rang.

Gordy answered.

'I've heard.'

The voice was direct but no less concerned because of that. Detective Superintendent Firbank had been Gordy's old DCI's senior officer, back when he had worked in Bristol, and was now hers.

'I was going to call you.'

'No need. What do you need?'

'Gin.'

A laugh.

'Too depressive. A fine single malt would serve you better, surely. Especially with you being a Scot.'

'Can't stand the stuff.'

An audible gasp.

'I'm serious,' said Gordy.

'Bad experience?'

'When I was a teenager, yes,' Gordy replied, but kept the details of what that experience had been to herself, as she had done for all the years since.

'Then we need to do something about that.'

'No, we don't.'

A moment's quiet, then ...

'Other than your request for mother's ruin, what else?'

Gordy put the muffin down on the plate, rubbed her eyes, yawned.

'Sleep would be good,' she said. 'But in all seriousness, for now, nothing. I know you'll want to put someone else on this, because the whole team is too close, but—'

'Ignoring the fact that I can't actually spare anyone right now anyway, I can't think of anyone better for the job,' Firbank said. 'You've not been in Frome that long, have you? Three, maybe four months, isn't it? I can't quite remember.'

Gordy wasn't so sure herself, and kept quiet.

'My view,' continued Firbank, 'is that the team has the best local knowledge around and therefore the best chance to actually find out what happened, why it happened, and who the bloody hell is responsible. Wouldn't you agree?'

'Yes, I would, and I'm relieved to hear you say that,' Gordy said.

There was a noticeable pause then, and Gordy felt sure she could hear Firbank thinking about what she was going to say next.

'And how are you, yourself?' Firbank eventually asked. 'And don't go replying like I'm talking to you as your senior officer now, understood? I know we don't really know each other, but there's enough between us, and with our shared relationship with Harry, that means we go beyond just work, is that clear?'

Gordy wasn't sure how to answer. Anna was with her every moment of every day, and she wondered sometimes if there would ever be a day that she wasn't. But then, would that be a bad thing? And now, all of that grief was getting mixed up with what had happened to Paul, the grief she felt about that now, too, the need to track down those responsible, to bring them to justice. And then there was the rage, because really, that was the only word that came anywhere close to describing what she felt about what had happened.

'I finally decided to get some counselling,' she said, knowing full well that by finally she actually meant she'd only just booked a session a few days ago, and it was later that week. 'Good days and bad. Just have to lean into them, as a certain retired DCI has told me on more than one occasion.'

'Jameson?'

'He reminds me a little of Harry,' Gordy said. 'He's rough, and there's a darkness there, isn't there? His edges are smoother, though.'

'That's not exactly difficult. And it's age that's done that more than anything else, trust me.'

Gordy found that to be an interesting comment and wanted to know more about the man who had been so instrumental in the life direction of Harry Grimm.

'He smiles more, too,' she said. 'I sometimes wonder, when I'm with him, if I'm seeing Harry in years to come.'

'That would be no bad thing.'

'True. But anyway, yes, I'm no' doing so bad. Thank you for asking.'

Another pause, then, 'Well, keep me posted on the investigation, and before you ask, no, I still don't have a DCI to fill Allercott's vacancy. That bother you at all?'

'Not in the slightest.'

'Good. I hoped you'd say that. We'll talk soon, I'm sure.'

And with that, the phone call came to an abrupt end.

Gordy placed the phone down.

'You going to eat that, or can I have it as seconds?'

Spinning around in her chair, the sound of someone else being in the room taking her by surprise, Gordy found herself staring up into an old face wearing a kindly, concerned smile, albeit one now sporting a few crumbs.

'Jameson.'

'Gordy.'

'I was just talking about you. Here for the food, then?'

Jameson, a retired DCI who had come to her rescue in some ways, by calling her weekly for a chat, on the pretence of seeing how she was settling in, but more often than not to ask if she fancied a pint at the Bell Inn. It was he who had introduced her to the Mousetrap.

Jameson sat on the only other chair in the room, and did so rather gingerly, eyeing it warily as though half expecting it to collapse as soon as he sat down. It hadn't escaped Gordy's notice how most of the furniture in the office was in a similar state, and she wondered if the station in Frome was where knackered furniture was sent to die.

'I heard about Paul.'

'I guessed as much. How though?'

'That kind of news, there won't be a police officer in the country who doesn't know by now, retired or not.'

There was a lot of truth in that, Gordy thought.

'I'm okay, if that's the reason you've popped in,' she said. 'Well, that and the food.'

'I know you are,' Jameson said. 'And my presence here doesn't suggest otherwise, I assure you.'

'Then what does it suggest?'

Jameson eased a crumb from the corner of his mouth between his lips, then lifted his hands and wiggled his fingers.

'That an extra pair of these might be useful.'

'No' if that's all you can do with them; you look like someone doing a bad impression of a deeply unconvincing magician.'

'It's not an impression either,' said Jameson. 'I'm awful at magic tricks.'

'Please don't do one.'

'I'll save that as a treat for later, then. Much, much later.'

'That's a relief.' Gordy sighed. 'Firbank just offered the same, you know; that was her on the phone. Well, not exactly that word-for-word; she didn't offer her actual hands in the same weakly flamboyant manner, or to do magic tricks, but she did ask if I needed anything.'

'And you said no.'

'I'd rather keep things small for now. She agreed. Big teams mean—'

'Big problems, oh, I know,' said Jameson. 'But I'm just one person, and I'm local. I know the area.'

Gordy leaned her elbows on her desk.

'Are you offering your services as a consultant?'

'That makes me sound very professional, doesn't it?'

'Are you?'

'What, professional?'

'Yes.'

'Of course not.'

Despite herself, Gordy smiled at that.

'The team isn't in till later. I wanted them all to try and get some rest before we got down to things.'

'Rest you didn't take yourself, I assume?'

'I'll sleep next year.'

'Lies.'

'Little white ones.'

'Well then,' Jameson said, pushing himself to his feet. 'Why don't I go score us some more of that amazing coffee, grab some muffins, and you can tell me everything? How does that sound?'

'Like I'm about to have a counselling session?'

'I'll fetch the couch, too.'

# TEN

By the time the rest of the team had slouched into the office, eyes filled with both sadness and tiredness, their bodies weighed down with grief, Gordy had discussed everything from the night before with Jameson. Despite this, however, nothing was any clearer.

'Main thing to remember right now,' Jameson said, 'is A, B, C.'

Despite her own exhaustion, her shock, her worry about what she was going to say to the team, how she was going to lead the investigation, Gordy laughed, and loudly, and received a confused look from Jameson.

'What's so funny?'

'A, B, C; assume nothing, believe no one, check everything? Did Harry get that from you, or was it the other way around?'

'I'll have you know I taught that lad everything he knows,' Jameson said confidently. then added, 'Though, arguably, that probably wasn't that much.'

Gordy couldn't help herself.

'What do you want, a coconut?'

Her laughter was eclipsed by Jameson's own roar.

'What, a prize? Now that one really is mine!'

'No idea where that bubbled up from,' said Gordy. 'Honestly, I don't think Harry's said it since those first few months when he arrived in the Dales, like it was an echo of his life in Bristol, but I always liked it. Had the ability to defuse a situation like nothing I'd ever heard.' She leaned out a little to see past Jameson and into the room beyond. 'Everyone's here. And it looks like Vivek's just provided coffee and muffins. You ready?'

'For my grand entrance and the applause your no doubt eloquent and gushing introduction will garner? Of course.'

Gordy stood up and led Jameson out of her office.

The team was all drinking coffee and munching on the treats Vivek had provided, and her approach had them all turn and stare, not just at her, but at the man with her, clearly a stranger, their conversation dying as she drew close.

The whiteboard, with its wobbly wheel taped in place to stop the damned thing from toppling over, or just taking it upon itself to start drifting off in some random direction like it was possessed, was pushed up against a desk. As Gordy came to stand in front of it, the team instinctively gathered round, leaning against other desks, grabbing chairs.

'First things first,' Gordy said. 'The Action Book.' She looked straight at Patti. 'Right now, I have zero interest in it. Nothing on any list of the no doubt numerous jobs we need to do, floating around this office, is as important as our task right now. Are we all in agreement?'

Silence roared back at her, confirming what she thought.

'Good. Second, you'll have noticed we've someone new with us today ...'

Everyone glanced at Jameson, who was leaning against a desk to Gordy's side, obviously trying to keep out of their direct line of sight, so as to not intrude on what was happening.

'This is retired Detective Chief Inspector Jameson,' she said. 'He's an old friend, he's local, and for reasons known only to himself, and against all sense and good reason, he's decided to set himself up as a freelance consultant.'

'An old friend? But you're not from round here, are you, Boss?' asked Peter, and Gordy heard confusion in the detective's voice. 'How did you meet?'

'Is it the kilt I'm wearing? Is that what gives it away?' Gordy asked. 'No, it'll be my pet haggis, the one I keep under my desk, is that it?'

Gordy saw from the look on Peter's face that perhaps her sarcasm hadn't come out as gently or as good-humoured as she had intended. She went to explain how she knew Jameson, when to her relief he came to her rescue and said, 'We share a mutual friend; DCI Harry Grimm.'

To Gordy's surprise, the mention of Harry's name garnered wide eyes and gasps in response. Then, from all eyes being on Jameson, they all turned back to her.

'You worked with Grimm?' said Patti. 'Really?'

'He was my DCI in Yorkshire,' Gordy said. 'Arrived a few years ago, never left. Didn't really cross my mind to mention it.'

Jack said, 'And he's a friend?'

'Very much so,' said Gordy, noticing a tone in Jack's voice she couldn't quite place. She wouldn't have said it was fear as such, but there was caution there, wariness, and a lot of respect. Grimm's reputation was clearly a fearsome thing; she would bear that in mind, she thought; it could come in useful.

'You've heard of him, then?' Jameson asked, a glance at Gordy as he sent the question to the rest of the room.

'Everyone's heard of him,' said Patti. 'I'd say I was surprised you've never mentioned him until now, but then again, maybe I'm not.'

'Why do you say that?' Gordy asked.

'You worked with him, so you must know his reputation,' Patti replied.

'If you ask me, his bark is worse than his bite,' Gordy said. 'But I know a little. Not that he shared much about his past, really.' Keen to move away from discussing Harry, and onto the job in hand, she then said, 'Jameson will be working alongside us. He has good local knowledge, stretching back decades, huge experience, and, I think, will prove to be an invaluable resource.'

Jameson added, 'I also know a handful of unconvincing magic tricks, and tell some of the best jokes known to humanity, usually at really inappropriate times, or when I get nervous.'

'Like what?' asked Travis, and Gordy heard a challenge in the way the PCSO asked the question.

Without hesitation, Jameson said, 'Why did the thief wear blue gloves?'

The room was silent.

'Because he didn't want to be caught red-handed!'

Jameson's laugh at his own joke rattled around the room like it was desperately trying to find an open window to escape through. Gordy was inclined to do the very same herself.

'Tough crowd,' Jameson said, but Gordy heard the smile in his voice.

Then she took a deep breath, exhaled slowly, allowing it to iron out the creases of stress she was feeling, and to calm her down a little. Best to get straight to the point ...

'The body of Police Community Support Officer Paul Edwards was discovered on Hatchet Hill at approximately one-thirty this morning. He was investigating strange lights reported by a runner, someone who we are now unable to contact due to the phone number being disconnected. So, that's obviously got my spider senses tingling. Though the actual cause of death has yet to be established, we do know that at some point, his body was dismembered, either by the person or persons responsible for his death, or their associates. A weapon was found at the scene, a small hand axe, or hatchet, so obviously everyone is thinking there is at least a connection between what happened and the location itself, Hatchet Hill. That is the brutal truth of it, and I've stated it as clearly as I have because it needs to be said. What happened to Paul was horrific and shying away from it, ignoring it, not talking about it, or seeing it for what it is, just isn't healthy. Now, it is our job to find those responsible. Any questions?'

The silence that had followed Jameson's joke grew thicker, and Gordy sensed so much hiding inside it—disbelief, shock, grief, and the heat of rage.

She reached for a pen to start jotting things down on the board, but Patti was already on her feet and had grabbed one before she had the chance.

'First things first, then,' Gordy said, 'and I say this because I care and I don't want anyone to think that their feelings haven't been considered: this case is horrific, disturbing, and deeply personal. You are going to see things and hear things that will upset you and shake you to your core, indeed you already have. That's not to say you've not experienced similar before, or that you're not capable of dealing with such, but this is someone you know; a friend, a colleague, so it's very, very different. My point is this: if any of you, at any point, feel it's too much, talk to me immediately. I'm a DI, but I'm also just me, Gordanian Haig. You all knew Paul considerably better than I, and this has shocked me to the core, so I can only imagine how you are all feeling. We can do this if we all work together, but that only comes from open communication and honesty. Are we clear?'

'We are,' said Patti, clearly deciding to be the voice of the team.

'Obviously we're waiting on the crime scene photographs, the postmortem, and a report from the SOC team. That kind of information can take days, but something tells me that Cowboy will be pushing to have it all to us sharpish. Regardless, we can't sit around here and wait on it. So, over to you; ideas?'

Every member of the team raised a hand.

'Jack?'

'Out of everyone here, I think I knew his wife and daughter the best. You spoke to them last night, I know, not just because you had to, but because I've already been in touch with Gill, and she told me.'

The way Jack said those last few words had Gordy narrowing her eyes. There was an edge there, for sure, but she couldn't tell if it was one that was there because of something Paul's wife had said, perhaps, or simply because of the situation they were all now facing.

'That's good to hear, and also what I would expect.'

'She also mentioned that she's seen uniformed officers outside, keeping watch,' Jack continued. 'And if it's okay with you, I'd like to go around and visit them this afternoon, see how they're doing.'

'Kelly's on her way home from uni today,' said Gordy, remembering the name of Paul's daughter. 'I was aiming to head over myself once we are done here.'

'We could go together.'

Jack's reply was more direct than he had intended as he flushed a little under Gordy's glare.

Gordy saw Jack's attention flip to Patti, as though looking for approval, and possibly some support, worried he'd upset their DI.

'Makes sense,' said Patti. 'Jack's right, and perhaps you might be able to find something useful together?'

'That's us sorted, then,' said Gordy, and turned to the team member sitting next to Jack, PCSO Helen Kendrick, whose red hair was pulled back in a tight plait.

'Travis and I will head straight out after this and get knocking on doors,' she said, which received a firm nod from Travis, who was sitting on her other side. 'There's not much out that way in terms of houses, but there's a few farms, some cottages, and someone might have seen or heard something, you never know. Even the smallest change or detail can mean something.'

'That reminds me of something Harry used to say,' Gordy said, and took a second or two to make sure she could remember what it was exactly, before directing it at the whole team. 'What any investigation boils down to is this: it's all about looking for something that should be there, but isn't, or the opposite of that; something that is, but shouldn't be. Bit of a mouthful, I know, but it always made sense. And like I said, it always struck me as the best summation of what we do when we're investigating something.'

'That one's mine, too,' Jameson said, with a wink, just quietly enough for only Gordy to hear.

'Running club is worth contacting,' added Travis. 'It was a runner who saw the lights, right? Well, I'm not a member now, but I was a good while back before my knees gave up. I'll chat to whoever it was that called in with the report, and see if anyone else has ever seen anything strange out that way. Might be that it was a regular gathering, though of what or why, I've no idea. But if Paul stumbled into something he wasn't supposed to ...'

'Great,' said Gordy, and moved her eyes over to Peter Knight, the detective constable.

'And you?'

'I'm going to see if I can find anything out about Hatchet Hill,' he said. 'Can't be a coincidence, can it, the name of the place, and what was done to Paul?'

'If there's one thing I don't believe in, it's exactly that,' said Gordy. She turned then to Patti. 'Two things,' she said. 'First, I want you to come along with Jack and me, to visit Paul's wife and daughter. That way, if necessary, you can look after Kelly, while Jack and I chat with Gill. Then, once we're done there, I'd like you to chase up Cowboy. See if we can get the photographs over today; that shouldn't be too difficult. I'm not expecting much yet from the SOC team, but they might have something. And get in touch with the pathologist, Doctor Charming, as well. If he asks you to go over, I'm happy for you to do so, but if you need someone to go with you, let me know.'

'I'll be fine,' Patti said.

'Thought you might say that.'

With nothing else to add, she looked at Jameson.

'Where do you think you can best help, then?'

Jameson looked from Gordy to the team.

'Think I might do a little stroll through Paul's free time,' he said. 'You knew him, but if you go snooping around, it'll possibly be more suspicious than some random old bloke who can't tell a joke to save his life. So, what clubs was he involved with, interests, favourite pub?'

Gordy remembered something Patti had mentioned.

'Wasn't there something about a paranormal group?'

'Paul was well into all of that stuff,' Patti replied, her eyes flicking from Gordy to Jameson. 'I can give you the contact details. And there's a Facebook page.'

'Anything else?' Jameson asked.

'The Lamb and Fountain, and the Griffin,' said Jack. 'I think they were the main pubs he went to.'

'I know them both,' Jameson said.

'There's a writers' group as well,' added Travis.

'He was a writer?' Gordy asked.

'Horror, mainly,' Travis replied. 'Good stuff, too; right up my street.'

'Published?'

'Small press, that kind of thing. I don't know much about it.'

'Gill will know, for sure,' said Jack. 'We can ask.'

'That's plenty to be going on with,' Jameson said.

Gordy gave the team another moment or two, to see if anyone had anything else to raise. With nothing forthcoming, she decided it was time to send them out to do their jobs.

'Keep in touch,' she said. 'Communication is vital. Talk to each other, to me. We work together, we can do right by Paul. And above all ...' Gordy gave Jameson a look before she spoke again. 'Assume nothing, believe no one, check everything. Now, go!'

And with that, the team disbanded.

# ELEVEN

With the rest of the team on with their various tasks, Gordy was in her vehicle with Patti and Jack. Instead of heading right at the roundabout on the main road to head through town, she had instead gone left, to take the bypass. It was six and two threes, she knew that, but she knew that the bypass would be an easier drive, with fewer frustrations over badly parked vehicles. And that meant she would be able to think.

'You must have some stories about DCI Grimm, then,' Jack asked from the rear seat, as Gordy took them down a long, straight hill, that she'd heard locals refer to as the ski slope.

'I do,' Gordy replied. 'Though if I'm honest, what I remember most is how soppy he was with his dog.'

Patti gasped.

'We're clearly not talking about the same Harry Grimm, then,' she said. 'The one we've heard about wasn't the kind of person who would have a pet. An attack dog, perhaps, but that's about it.'

'It took him as much by surprise as the rest of us, I think.'

Gordy smiled, remembering when her old DCI had turned up at the office with a black labrador puppy that he'd rescued from an illegal puppy farm. 'Like I said, his bark is worse than his bite.'

'That's not what those who've worked with him or been on his wrong side say,' muttered Jack.

'Well, don't you go believing everything you hear,' said Gordy. 'He was a hard man, I'll give him that, and he looked terrifying enough to make most people run like hell just from a narrowing of his eyes and a growl, but he wasn't—'

'Boss?'

Gordy was slowing down to approach another roundabout when Patti's question interrupted her.

'What is it?'

'You mind taking a right?'

'But that's not the right direction.'

'Doesn't matter,' Patti said. 'I know plenty of little routes around here. We both do, don't we, Jack?'

Gordy saw Jack nod in the rearview mirror.

'Why, though? What's up?'

Patti pointed a thumb over her shoulder.

'I think I recognise the driver in the vehicle behind us.'

Gordy stole a quick look in her wing mirror, saw Jack look over his shoulder.

'You do? And I should be worried why?'

'Humour me.'

Gordy slowed down, turned right, and watched as the car behind them followed suit.

The car was quiet for a moment or two, then Patti said, 'Just ahead, take the next left. It's a singletrack lane. We can follow it round back to where we need to be, I promise.'

Gordy took the left, and behind them, she saw the car once

again turn to follow, slowing down a little, she noticed, in a very poor attempt at trying to not seem suspicious.

Rolling along the lane, Gordy asked, 'So, are you going to tell me who it is, or is the mystery to remain until the shooting starts? Which reminds me, I didn't bring a single gun, sorry about that.'

'T-junction ahead,' said Patti, glossing over what Gordy had just said. 'Take a left. Jack? Have another look round, see what you think, but I'm right, aren't I? It's her ...'

Jack turned in his seat as Gordy headed left at the junction. The car behind followed.

'Not seen her around in a while,' said Jack.

'You can't even bring yourself to say her name?' Gordy asked. 'Who on Earth is she?'

The road took them over the railway, and then, as the way ahead was blocked by huge, concrete blocks, round to the right and onto another lane.

'I'd prefer it if I wasn't kept in the dark as to who's trailing us,' said Gordy.

'It's Alison Read,' Patti said. 'Journalist.'

Jack laughed.

'Hack, more like.'

'And why would this journalist be following us?' Gordy asked.

'That's exactly what I want to find out,' Patti said, and turned in her seat to look at Gordy. 'There's another junction coming up. I need you to speed up enough to lose her so that I can jump out and hide in the bushes. Then, at the junction, stop and wait. When she comes round and sees you, get out and give her one of those hard stares you're so good at. She'll try and reverse, but she'll have me glaring at her in her mirror. Then we can have a little word, can't we? Find out what she's up to, though I can guess ...'

'You think that'll work? And what's that about my hard stares?'

Patti's answer was a big smile and a firm nod.

Gordy sped up, as Patti had requested, and the junction ahead came up fast, the car behind disappearing from view. Gordy stopped and, with no warning given, Patti was out of the door, disappearing from view.

A moment or two later, the car that had been following them appeared around the corner, skidding a little as it came to a halt. Gordy opened her door and climbed out. The driver of the car stared back at her, then started to reverse. Only Patti was now standing behind her in the middle of the road.

The car stopped. Gordy waved. The driver did not wave back. Instead, she reversed, faster this time, directly at Patti. Just in time, Patti threw herself into the bushes, her howls of anger, shock, and pain at all the prickles, suddenly drowned out by the sound of the vehicle careening into the bushes a little further along.

Gordy ran over to Patti, quickly followed by Jack.

'I'm going to guess that wasn't part of the plan.'

'Not really, no.'

'Bloody lunatic, reversing like that!'

Patti, with a helping hand from Gordy, pulled herself out of the bush.

Jack ran over to the vehicle, and called back, 'She's managed to get stuck. Not sure she can get out without a shove.'

'She'll be getting more than a shove,' Gordy said, looking at Patti. 'She'll be getting a boot up the arse! Come on.'

Along the lane, and with Patti's barely disguised laughter at what she had just said chasing them along, Gordy and Patti joined Jack as they jogged over to the stranded car. At seeing them approach, the driver kicked open her door, but she was too slow, finding a very unhappy-looking detective inspector waiting for her on the other side.

'In a rush?' Gordy asked, blocking the woman's escape.

The journalist was a few years younger than Gordy. Thin like a rake, medium height, with dark hair in a neat ponytail. She was dressed in jeans and a fleece top.

The woman hesitated just long enough for Gordy to know she was trying to work out a way to explain herself out of what had happened. Good luck with that, she thought.

'What are you doing stopping like that on the road?' the woman asked. 'And why was that police officer standing behind me? I was terrified! It's no wonder I crashed; it's your fault, all three of you!'

'Is that why you tried to run her over? Because you were terrified? I mean, Officer Matondo is one of the most terrifying people I've ever known. Isn't that right, Detective?'

Patti bared her teeth and made a growling sound, which Gordy was rather impressed by.

The woman did not look impressed.

'I did nothing of the sort!' she said. 'I didn't know what was going on. I panicked, that's all. You panicked me! And now you've made me crash my car. Just look at it! How am I supposed to get out of there? I'll be putting in a complaint, that's for sure.'

Gordy folded her arms.

'Oh, I don't think you will,' she said.

'I've done it before.'

'She has,' said Patti, leaning in closer to Gordy. 'Something about wrongful arrest, I think.'

'You mean she's tried to run someone else over?'

'I did not try and run Patti over!' the woman said, and that got Gordy's attention.

'First-name terms, is it?' she said. 'Friends, are you?'

'Not a chance of it,' said the woman. 'Detective Sergeant Matondo has never been what I would call helpful. And is certainly no friend.'

'And who can blame her, if you're trying to run her over every time you see her?' Gordy said. 'Would certainly put me off forming any kind of relationship with someone.'

'I was not—'

Gordy held up a hand, and the woman fell quiet.

'Name,' she said, though she didn't bring out her notebook to jot it down. She knew it anyway, and also guessed that she was well known enough for her details to be on file.

'Alison Read.'

'Occupation?'

'Journalist.'

Gordy ignored the stifled laughs from Jack and Patti.

'And can I ask where you are heading?'

'No, you can't,' Alison replied.

'So, it's just a very odd coincidence that you've been following us all the way down this random little lane, is that it?'

'I don't need to tell you,' said Alison, sounding to Gordy's surprise, somewhat emboldened, though by what, she hadn't the faintest idea. 'I'm not under arrest, am I? The only thing you should be worrying about is how to get my car out of that hedge, and how to explain it when I report you.'

'I'll no' be doing any of that,' Gordy said, her soft, Highland accent becoming rich and clear. 'And I think we all know that, don't we, Alison?'

Alison's mouth snapped shut.

'Now, answer my first question; where are you heading? Actually, no, don't. Answer this one instead, because it's a wee bit clearer, I think, and that might help you: why were you following us?'

'I wasn't fo—'

Gordy's hand went up fast, and was firm enough to stop a truck in its tracks, never mind to stop a journalist from talking.

'Alison, please don't take me for the fool you're clearly trying to pretend you are, and doing very well at it, might I add.'

That reply, Gordy was happy to see, had Alison screw up her face as she tried to work it out.

'I know something happened at Hatchet Hill,' Alison said. 'There, that's it. That's why I was following you. But I wasn't following you, I just happened to see you, and thought I'd—'

'Follow us,' said Patti.

Gordy stepped in close, and stared at the woman.

'Who?'

'Who what?'

'Who told you something happened at Hatchet Hill?'

'I'm not at liberty to divulge my contacts.'

Gordy raised one eyebrow just enough.

'You're no' at liberty? Well, that's me told, isn't it? You see, the thing is, Alison, I am also at liberty, by which I mean I can throw the book at you if I want, and it's a hefty thing, for sure. There are whole chapters in it on endangering a police officer's life, obstruction—'

Gordy watched Alison's eyes grow wide.

'I don't know.'

'How convenient,' Jack tutted.

'And what have you been told about Hatchet Hill?' Gordy asked. 'What is it that you know, assuming that there is anything to know, of course?'

Alison's mouth opened, but no words came out.

Gordy sighed.

'Look, Alison,' she said, easing back on the tough cop tone, because she'd never really found that it suited her all that well. She was always better at the softly-softly approach. 'I've worked with journalists so often over the years that they've all become blended into one huge, annoying memory of too many questions asked under the pretence of *the public has a right to know* when, in fact, it was all about the story and their own over-inflated ego. Is there any chance, Alison, that this can be different? And understand, right now, we both know what I want you to say, don't we? So how you answer me could be quite important, and influence exactly where you and I move on from here, understood?'

Gordy saw stunned stares aimed at her from both Patti and Jack.

'Different how?'

'We could work together.'

Alison's eyes went wide. Patti and Jack audibly gasped.

'What? How? I don't understand.'

'Right now, I'm not sure, but what I do know is that if I've got you sneaking around, following me, following my team, poking your nose in where it might get chewed off. And before any of us know where we are, that's going to be making things difficult, having the public think one thing when, in fact, the opposite is true—all kinds of nonsense I could well do without. That's going to put me on edge a little. And believe you me, you won't like me on edge, not one little bit.'

'That sounds like a threat.'

Deep down, Gordy wondered if it was. Something about what she'd been through with Anna, with the move, had stirred something in her, something from long, long ago. She wasn't sure she liked it, knew she would have to control it, but another part of her knew it could come in useful.

'What do you say?' she asked, ignoring the journalist's words.

Alison was quiet for a moment, then said, 'Look, I really don't know who tells me stuff, and neither do I know why they do it; they just do, and it's useful sometimes, isn't it?'

'What were you told about Hatchet Hill?'

Alison hesitated just long enough for Gordy to use that hard stare Patti had mentioned earlier.

'Just that a body was found, that's all, so I thought I'd see what I could find out, didn't I? That's all.'

'And you thought you'd do that by following us?'

'Yes.'

Gordy leaned back against the bonnet of Alison's car. The suspension complained, though she decided not to take that too personally.

'This is a very sensitive investigation,' she said, dropping her voice just enough to add to the gravity of what she was telling Alison. 'The last thing anyone needs, especially the family and friends of the person who was found on Hatchet Hill, is everyone knowing about it. Does that make sense?'

'Yes, but—'

'This is very, very sensitive,' Gordy continued, ignoring whatever Alison had been about to say. 'We need to do our job, and those closest to the deceased need to be given the time and space and respect to try and come to terms with what has happened.'

'I know that,' said Alison. 'I really do.'

Gordy was a little taken aback for a moment, because it actually sounded like Alison did know.

'Then I'm asking you to hold off, okay? If you can work with me on this, and trust me going forward, then I'll make sure that you can also be the first port of call regarding any press involvement.'

Gordy let that sink in for a moment before continuing.

'I won't go to anyone without going to you first. In return, you step back, and wait, be sensitive. I'm not trying to stop you from doing your job, and neither am I going to stand here and say you can't widen your own investigation as a journalist, find out more about Hatchet Hill, and see if other things have happened in the area, ask around, see what people know. All I'm asking is that you don't take me for a fool; if you do, you'll only do it once, I promise.'

'That's another threat, isn't it?'

Gordy pushed herself away from the car, held Alison's eyes just long enough for her to understand that it was answer enough, then turned to the two officers.

'Jack? Patti? You reckon the three of us can give this enough of a push to help Alison on her way?'

'Don't see why not,' said Jack.

'Sure,' agreed Patti.

Gordy looked again at Alison, this time holding out a hand.

'Do we have a deal?'

Alison frowned, scratched her cheek, then took Gordy's hand.

'We do,' she said.

'Good,' said Gordy, 'then get yourself back into your car, and let's have you on your way.'

A few minutes later, with Alison duly rescued, and Gordy driving the remaining couple of miles to Paul's home, Patti said, 'You do know she's going to do exactly what you said, don't you?'

'Like what?'

'Nose around, about Hatchet Hill, the area, see if anyone knows or has seen anything.'

'Of course I do,' said Gordy. 'In fact, I'm counting on it.'

'You are?' asked Jack, leaning forward a little, his head between the two front seats. 'Why?'

'Because I've now got control, haven't I? I've had her agree to hold off, but also given her something to get on with. And my guess is that Alison might prove to be more useful than any of us realise. If we're not directing her, there's no knowing what damage she might do. But because I've quietly suggested something, she's focused on what we need her focusing on.'

'Clever,' said Patti.

'Oh, I wouldn't say that,' said Gordy.

'Then what would you say?'

Gordy smiled.

'Cunning.'

## TWELVE

Jameson was outside the Lamb and Fountain. He wasn't hesitating about going in, but was just enjoying being there and taking it in. It was a pub he had visited plenty of times over the years, but not for a good while. Not since he'd lost his wife, anyway, mainly because half the fun of going had been to see the look on her face when he arrived home courtesy of a taxi and tried to tell her why he liked it.

She had never seen the charm of the place, never understood why anyone would want to drink somewhere that hadn't been redecorated since the fifties. She had zero interest in its supposed trapdoor that led to the mysterious tunnels under Frome, and had never really regarded pork scratchings and a pint of cider as a good way to pass the time.

But their differences had always been, in many ways, what had kept them together, and she'd had her own funny ways, too, hadn't she? The basket-weaving, for a start. That thought made him laugh, the memory of her first stabs at the hobby, which had been distorted beyond all use, to her creations later on, and the sheer quantity of them. There was, after all, only so many baskets anyone needed, though now, with her gone, he had kept enough of them to remind him of her, the log basket being his favourite.

The day was clear, and the pub, with its unassuming exterior more befitting a farm building than a public house, and its weathered black and white sign on the wall, beckoned him in.

Stepping under the stone lintel, Jameson was standing in a short corridor. He knew that if he continued, he would be in the back room, with its superb views over the town of Frome itself, staring down on the higgledy-piggledy world of roofs all vying for a little bit of space, and the jumble of lanes they twisted themselves along. The building also had a spiralling stone staircase, which was more reminiscent of a castle than a pub, leading down to the toilets and the cellars beyond.

Instead, he pushed through the first door on his left and found himself in a small room with the bar to his right. A small, square pub table sat in the centre of the room, with a number of chairs around it. To his left, a window looked out across the street, beneath which a wooden bench was attached to the wall. The room was decorated haphazardly, with the odd shelf here and there, weighed down by a strange and eclectic collection of ornaments.

Jameson spotted porcelain ducks of various sizes, a porcelain sheep, and even something that looked terrifyingly like a small clown's head. Three flying ducks were attached to the wall above the window. A small noticeboard was pinned with flyers promoting local interest groups, as well as events at the pub itself, including everything from live mic nights and local musicians to a drum therapy workshop, ghost-walks, and to his bemusement, dog massage, whatever that was. Pictures were also hung on the wall, all of them faded, some comprising photographs of classic cars, others of what Jameson assumed were local patrons of the place.

As he glanced around, he remembered his wife's love-filled look of confusion whenever he tried to tell her why the pub was so perfect. Shaking his head at the memory, he headed over to the bar and the woman standing on the other side.

'Quiet, isn't it?' Jameson said, as he perched himself on a stool.

'Early afternoon's never anything else. It'll perk up later, though, after work. What are you having?'

Jameson cast his eyes around the bar, allowed them to dally a while on the scant selection of snacks, noticed that the pump clip for the beer was turned around to face the other way, and said, 'Cider it is, then.'

'Good choice. Not that you had one, really, did you?'

'Too early for something short and strong, that's for sure.'

'Exactly what I tell my husband if he starts getting frisky in the morning.'

They both laughed.

The pint of cider was placed in front of Jameson, and he requested some pork scratchings and a couple bags of crisps.

'You're hungry, then?'

'Always.'

'I can do you a cheese toasty.'

That was music to Jameson's ears. The muffins back at the station had been good, but the day he turned down a cheese toasty would be a bad one indeed, and he wasn't about to make it today.

'Sold; cancel the crisps.'

The woman left Jameson alone for a moment as she headed off to to produce what she had offered.

No one else entered the pub while Jameson waited. Daylight took swipes at the dust motes in the room, its golden blades cutting through them with the ease of a cutlass in the hands of a cavalryman. A quietness sat in the room like another patron, and Jameson wondered, if he listened hard enough, would he be able to hear the memories of all the conversations that had happened in that room, somehow still floating around beneath the beams holding up the ceiling.

The woman returned, and presented Jameson with two golden slices of bread oozing thick, glistening cheese from between them.

'Here you go,' she said, proudly. 'And this, too, if you want some.'

A jar of Branston Pickle was placed next to the plate.

Jameson paid for the drink, scratchings, and toasty, took a deep gulp of the cider, then spread some pickle on the toasty and took a bite.

'Now that's a pub snack,' he said, holding the crispy sandwich up in celebration and wonder.

'It's all down to the cheese,' the woman said with a wink. 'Cave-aged, properly strong. Can't beat it.'

Jameson continued to eat and sipped on the cider, allowing his gaze to waltz gently around the pub, taking it all in.

'Love this place,' he said.

'You do? Can't say as I recognise you.'

'Been a while, too long, really. A friend of a friend reminded me about it, so here I am, taking a little walk down memory lane, I suppose.'

'You're not local, then?'

'Used to be, a good while ago. Moved away a few years back, after I lost my wife. Not too far, but just far enough, if that makes sense?'

'I'm sorry to hear that, and yes, it does.'

'Yeah, it was rough. Still is, actually.' Jameson broke his sudden grief with a much-needed laugh. 'She was never a fan of this place, though, you know? Almost made it more fun to visit!'

The woman smiled.

'What's not to like? I've always thought coming in here was like travelling back in time. Back to when the days were simpler.'

'Not sure they ever really were, though,' said Jameson. 'I think we all just hear about it more, don't we? The news, bad stuff going on. It's not healthy. I don't even bother with it anymore; never buy a newspaper, and I certainly never go looking for doom and gloom on the Internet, mainly because that seems to be about the only thing on there now.'

Jameson finished off the toasty, wiped away the crumbs, and washed it all down with more cider.

'Where are you now, then?' the woman asked.

Jameson ignored the question and said, 'I guess the good thing about this place is that the bloke who reminded me of it, and who clearly loves it enough to share it with others, shows just how good it is. He's a bobby ... well, near enough; PCSO.'

'Really?'

Jameson gave a nod.

'And if the police like you, you must be doing something right, right? Plus, it hasn't got a flat roof, and if there's one rule I live by when it comes to pubs, it's that. Never trust a place that has a flat roof.'

'Not letting the wrong sort in, that's what it's about.' The woman smiled. 'Anyway, we attract a certain type, don't we? People who like old pubs, quirky pubs, pubs that aren't all about ...' She waved her hands in the air as though trying to conjure something out of thin air. 'You know, all that fancy stuff, where everything's just so, and the food has words like artisan in front of everything.'

'No, you're not fancy, I'll give you that. You do have flying ducks, though.'

'No desire to be, either. It's not what Mother wanted, and it's not what this place will ever be about.'

Jameson clocked the mention of the pub's original owner, and gave a nod of respect.

'Like I said, if the police think it's alright, then there's a good chance that it is.'

'If it's a PCSO you're talking about, then my guess is you mean Paul, right?'

A bite, thought Jameson, but gave nothing away in his response.

'That'll be him.'

'Lovely chap. Bloody good at his job, too. He was in here just a few days ago. Off duty. Did his usual of just sitting in the corner with a pint, writing in that notebook of his.'

Jameson's interest was immediately piqued, but he made sure to not respond too obviously, and went with a causal, 'In with a couple of mates, then?'

The woman shook her head.

'You know, he's always in here on his own. Been like that for years, now.'

There was more behind that statement, Jameson thought, but what?

'Things change when you grow older,' he said. 'You grow to like a bit of alone time in a pub, rather than sinking the jars at pace with a group of mates.'

'I guess, but it wasn't like that with Paul, you know? He was never someone who'd have a skinful. No, it was always just him and his mate, until that thing happened ...'

Jameson had come to the pub on the off chance that a little bit of chatter with someone who knew the place, perhaps knew Paul, would maybe lead to something. He wondered if he had, against the odds, struck gold.

'That sounds a bit ominous.'

'Awful, really,' said the woman. 'And to think they were old school friends.'

Jameson sunk what was left of his pint, ordered another, thinking it would make sense to stay a bit longer. A taxi home would be on the cards for sure, or at the very least, a long walk around town or a kip back at the station, assuming no one would mind. There was always the off chance as well that he'd be able to grab a lift off Gordy or from one of the team.

'So, what happened, then?' he asked, as he lifted the fresh pint to his lips. 'You can't just leave that mystery hanging there! Was there an accident or something? Losing a friend, it's always awful. Not sure you ever get over it, if you even can.'

Jameson forced his mind not to immediately think about his wife, but her smile flashed up in his mind, regardless.

'Well, I don't know the ins and outs of it,' the woman said, her voice quietening, 'but I do know it was his mate that was involved. Didn't die, so far as I'm aware, though there's been a lot of water under the bridge, hasn't there, and you never know what can happen, do you?'

'Involved? How do you mean?'

'Some drug thing, I think, or so I heard, anyway. It was before Paul became a PCSO, actually. Some think it might have even been the reason he became one; felt like he'd do more good helping people that way.'

'What was he before that, then?'

'Shop manager, nothing special. He probably told me what shop once as well, but I've forgotten.'

Jameson took a gulp of cider.

'So, his friend was into drugs, then? That's never good.'

The woman pointed behind Jameson, over to the bench beneath the window.

'Used to sit there, the pair of them. Thick as thieves, they were. Would get up to all sorts, loved exploring, and there's those tunnels of Frome, you know? So, they were always pestering me about heading down into the cellar here and seeing what they could find. Loved a bit of spooky stuff, too; ghost-hunting, or whatever it was. No idea how you hunt something that doesn't exist, but what do I know? Kept them amused, anyway. Well, the next thing we know, it's just Paul on his own, isn't it? Never really spoke much about it, but you know what things are like in places like this; soon everyone knows, even though no one will admit to talking about it, or who they heard it from.'

'Are you saying his friend was put away, then?'

The woman gave the most nonchalant of shrugs.

'All I know is that something made Paul shop his best mate. I don't know what it was, but it was enough to turn him against someone he'd been friends with for years, since they started coming to the pub, I reckon, back when they were faking their ID and lowering their voices to sound older.'

Jameson laughed at that.

'Takes all sorts to make a world,' he said.

'And the world needs more people like Paul,' the woman replied. 'Salt of the Earth, he is, and no mistake.' She glanced at Jameson's glass, which was already empty. 'You got a thirst on? Need another?'

'Need? Yes. Want? Also yes, but I'm going to be sensible and head off, or I'll be asleep in the corner before I know it. And I snore terribly, which you really don't want, especially when it gets busy later.'

Jameson made to head back to the door.

'Wait,' the woman said, and Jameson paused.

'I've not left my wallet, I know that for sure,' he said, patting his pockets just to make sure.

'No, it's this,' the woman said, and held something out in front of her.

Jameson took it, and found it to be a small book with a worn, black cover.

'Remember I said about how Paul would come in and jot things down in his notebook? Well, that's his notebook. One of them, anyway. I think he has a few of them. Left it here a few weeks ago. Every time he was in, we'd both say we needed to remember to for him to take it, and every time we both forgot.'

'I'll pass it on,' Jameson said. 'Thank you.'

Outside, the afternoon air hit Jameson hard, and the impact of the very strong cider doubled in a heartbeat.

He looked at the notebook the woman had given him, flicked through its pages, saw lots of scribbled notes, diagrams, drawings, even little maps, and then he stuffed it in a pocket.

'So, Paul's friend was put away for drugs,' he muttered to himself. 'Now that's interesting, isn't it?'

A few minutes later, Jameson stepped through the doors of the second pub on his list to check out, The Griffin, and wondered if he would get as lucky again. He doubted it, but what the hell, he thought. With a quick prayer sent Heavenward, asking for a helping hand, and a text sent to Gordy's phone about what he'd found out, he walked up to the bar and ordered a pint.

## THIRTEEN

Gordy was sitting in the lounge of a typical 1960s semi-detached house with Patti, Jack, and Paul's wife Gill and their daughter, Kelly.

On arrival, and having given a nod of acknowledgement to the uniformed officers in the car outside the house on her way in, it had been patently clear to Gordy that Gill hadn't slept or even rested since she had seen her earlier that morning. Her eyes were sunken, and beyond them lay nothing but the bleakest landscape, a place that had once been beautiful and lush, now blasted to burned rock and ash by the events of the previous night.

A fresh pot of coffee sat on a small table in the middle of the room, and had so far been ignored by everyone. There were biscuits, too, but Gordy wasn't about to reach for one of those and start munching.

The conversation so far had been somewhat lacking, and Gordy expected nothing else. This was a house ripped in two, and there was nothing anyone could say or do to soften the impact of it. Not now, not ever. This was seismic. The loss of

Paul the husband, Paul the dad, had slammed into Gill and Kelly with all the tact of an intercontinental ballistic missile. The damage it had caused would never truly heal, and the scars would remain forever. That much was clear, if only from the look in their eyes.

Having allowed everyone sufficient time to just relax into being in each other's presence, Gordy knew that it was down to her to get things moving.

'Gill, Kelly,' she said, 'first, can I ask about the support you have locally? Obviously, you've been put in touch with a police family liaison team, and that's all well and good. However, I think that in situations like this, family and friends are where the most valuable support come from. And I'm speaking from experience here. Recent, too, I might add.'

'I don't think people really know what to say,' said Gill. 'How can they?'

'You've spoken to someone, then?'

Gill gave a nod. Kelly, Gordy noticed, was statue still, her face pale behind thin strands of long, black hair, which hung like railings around a churchyard.

'Not many, not yet. I don't think I'm ready. I'm still processing it all. Doesn't seem real. It can't be, but it is, I know that. I'm not making sense.'

'You're making absolute sense. You're in shock. Losing someone close is difficult, but like this? No one can truly understand what you're going through.'

Patti asked, 'Are you able to make sure you have company when we're not here? Not the whole time, because you'll need your own space, but to have someone, or a number of people, able to pop by, to just be with you can be helpful.'

'Maybe to provide some simple supplies as well,' Jack offered. 'In fact, if there's anything you need, I'm happy to do that now.'

The faintest, most fragile of smiles dared to flicker on Gill's face.

'I can't think about food or anything like that, not right now,' she said.

Jack stood up.

'Well, you'll need to eat, Gill. You both will.' He looked then at Gordy. 'What about if I just have a quick look through what's in the fridge, come up with a quick list, then pop out while you're here? There's a Spar just a short walk away, so I wouldn't be long. How would that sound?'

'Just like the kind of "beyond the call of duty" I'd expect,' said Gordy. 'Especially from someone who knew Paul so well. That okay with you, Gill?'

Gill gave a nod, but said nothing.

Jack left the lounge, and Gordy could hear him checking through the fridge and freezer, then heading out. She guessed the reason for his sudden spurt of action was born out of his need to do something helpful, and perhaps sitting in silence wasn't his idea of being useful.

'Jack and Paul were great friends,' Gill said.

'Everyone loved Paul,' said Patti. 'No one can believe ...'

As the detective constable's voice broke on her words like waves against a sea wall, Gordy took out her notebook and said, 'The reason we're here is that we really do need to ask you a few questions, if that's possible? And perhaps have a look around the house? Only with your permission, of course.'

Gill's brow furrowed deeply.

'Why would you need to do that? What questions? What could be here, what could I know, that has anything to do with what's happened to Paul?'

'I honestly don't know,' Gordy said. 'But I hope you can understand that we need to do everything we can to find who did this.'

'I know, but this is our home. There can't be anything here, can there? Paul was never really involved with anything, not as a PCSO, anyway. And all his interests outside work are innocent enough.'

That struck Gordy as a little odd. She would ask in a moment, however, because first was the most difficult question.

'Before we go on, Gill, can I ask where you were last night?'

Gill's response was the kind of silence cold enough to freeze blood.

'This is just procedure,' Gordy continued. 'In any case such as this, it's vital to establish the whereabouts of family, so that they can be—'

'I didn't do it!'

'It's just a question I have to ask,' Gordy said, her voice calm, as she made sure she didn't say anything to suggest Gill either was or wasn't involved; she'd been party to too many investigations where the closest family members who were responsible, and she knew that so many murders ended up being traced back to husbands and wives. Not the happiest of thoughts, warranted, but that was just the way of things.

'But I loved Paul! Why would I ... I mean ...'

Gordy gave Gill a moment or two.

'Gill,' she said eventually. 'It's just something I have to ask so that we know where you were, okay? That's all. It's as much for your own good as anything.'

Gill shook her head.

'I can't believe he's gone.'

That's not an answer, Gordy thought, so she waited.

'I was here,' Gill said eventually. 'On my own. Because Paul was at work, wasn't he? And Kelly was at uni. And before you ask, no, I don't have any witnesses to that. Why would I?'

Gordy gave a nod, jotted it down in her notebook.

'My next question is about something you said a few

minutes ago. You mentioned that Paul wasn't involved with anything as a PCSO; are you saying he was involved with something before he became one? It was just an odd way of saying it, that's all.'

'That was years ago,' Gill said, dismissing whatever it was with a weak wave of a hand. 'No way that has anything to do with this. It just can't, trust me.'

'No way what, exactly, has anything to do with this?' Patti asked. 'And we do know how hard all this is to talk about, okay? So if you need a break, just say.'

Gill sighed, rolled her eyes, went to speak, but Kelly stood up, interrupting her.

'I'm going upstairs,' she said. 'I have work to do. For uni.'

Gordy caught Patti's eye, and Patti stood up as well.

'Mind if I come with you?'

Kelly just gave a shrug, then headed over to a staircase on the far wall and started to climb. Patti followed, and soon Gordy was left alone with Gill.

'So,' she began, but Gill cut in.

'It was too long ago to mean anything now,' she said. 'A friend of Paul's, he was into some kind of drug thing. I don't know what. Like I said, it was years ago, before he became a PCSO.'

'What kind of drug thing? What happened?'

'It was before Kelly was even a glint in her father's eye,' said Gill. 'We'd just got married. Billy was around all the time. They'd known each other through school. He was even Paul's best man. But when Paul found out what he was into, he cut all contact. It broke him apart. They'd been friends since they were kids, got up to all kinds of mischief, apparently.'

'And nothing happened after that, after Paul cut contact? They just stopped hanging out together?'

'To be fair, it was more than cutting contact,' said Gill.

'How so?'

'Paul found a kid who was in a right mess because of something he'd taken. He called an ambulance, contacted the kid's parents. Kid only just survived; if Paul hadn't found him, that would've been it. Don't think he was ever able to forgive Billy after that.'

'What did he do, then?'

'Paul? Oh, he reported Billy in a heartbeat,' said Gill. 'Never seen him so angry, before or since. Half of me thinks the only reason he did that was to stop himself going round there and telling Billy exactly what he thought of him by way of his fists.'

'Certainly the more sensible action.'

'He gave up his best mate to the police. And with the evidence from the kid, they had him. Billy was put away for a fair while, I think. But like I said, that was years ago. Paul then became a PCSO, didn't he? And he's not heard anything from Billy since.'

'What was Billy's surname?'

'Parker, I think. Something like that. But there's no way it can be anything to do with him, can it? He was put away.'

'And people who are put away are later released,' said Gordy. 'But if this was all before Kelly was around, then it does seem a bit too long in the past.'

Gill leaned forwards and started to pour the coffee. As she did so, the pot slipped from her hand and sent black liquid spilling across the table and onto the floor.

Gordy rescued the pot from her hand as Gill broke down.

'It's okay, I'll grab something from the kitchen,' said Gordy, and quickly nipped through to see what she could find. As she was searching, Gill appeared behind her, positioning herself in front of a drawer almost deliberately, Gordy thought.

'Over there,' said Gill, pointing at another drawer. 'Tea

towels, a roll of kitchen towel as well, I think, that's where I keep all of that.'

Gordy checked the drawer, found what she needed, then headed back through to the lounge to clear up the coffee, Gill following on behind.

As she mopped up the spilled liquid, she asked, 'The drawer you stood in front of; is there something in it that you don't want me to see?'

Gill shook her head.

'What drawer? What do you mean?'

Spilled coffee dealt with, Gordy stood up.

'Gill,' she said. 'Please understand that we're only here to help. That's literally it. We've no other purpose. We're not prying, we're investigating; very different, I promise.'

'I know, but there's really nothing in there, I promise.'

Gordy said nothing, just waited.

'I'm telling the truth.'

'A little too forcefully,' said Gordy. 'Because if that is the truth, then you wouldn't mind me having a look, would you?'

Gill spent a moment or two mulling that statement over, but Gordy wanted to hurry things along, and said, 'So, please, Gill, what is it in that drawer you seemed so keen for me to not see?'

'It's nothing. It really isn't. It's just that ... well, it was Paul's thing, and I don't want you to think he was ... well, you know, a bit odd.'

'To be honest, all you're doing right now is making it odder by not telling me or showing me or whatever.'

'But it can't have anything to do with what happened, can it? I just want everyone to remember Paul as they knew him. Just without this other thing.'

'Still not helping with the oddness,' said Gordy. 'Wouldn't it be easier if you just told me and showed me?'

'I don't know.'

Gordy held out her hand.

'Look, let's both go and have a nosy together, shall we? I doubt very much that whatever is in that drawer is going to be damning enough to make everyone think they'd got Paul wrong.'

Gill reached up for Gordy's hand and used it to pull herself out of her chair. She didn't let go.

'You think so?'

'I know so,' said Gordy. 'Paul was a beautiful human being. His loss isn't just tragic, it's horrific. We all want to find out who did it, and why. And if there's even the tiniest thing in this mystery drawer that might help, then I need to see it.'

'It won't help though,' said Gill. 'It's just something he was into, that's all. I can't see how it's relevant.'

'Maybe you should let me be the judge of that?' Gordy suggested. 'What do you say?'

Gill hesitated for a moment, then with her hand still in Gordy's, walked them both back into the kitchen and to the drawer.

'You'd best open it,' she said. 'I was never into any of it at all. Creeped me out, if I'm honest.'

Gordy opened the drawer; Gill was still talking.

'People are weird, aren't they? The things they're into. I love a scary movie, but that's about it for me, really. Paul was fascinated, though. I think it started with him and Billy; they were into ghosts and legends and myths, and there's plenty of that round here, isn't there? Can't walk ten yards without bumping into some story or tale. Anyway, Paul saw it as research for his writing. But some of the stuff? I thought it was a bit more out there than a haunting or two. I've not really looked at much of it, but it's quite disturbing, to me, anyway. It's probably all gibberish and nonsense.'

Gill's voice faded as Gordy started to take out the things from the drawer; notebooks—lots and lots of notebooks—maps, drawstring bags with things in them she would look at later, evidence bags with bones.

'See?' said Gill. 'Weird, isn't it? It was just a hobby, really. It helped with his writing, helped him focus, gave him ideas.'

Gordy shuffled through the books, then the maps, saw that one had Frome on it, so she opened it, and traced a finger along the lanes that reached out from it like the searching arms of a squid.

The map was annotated by Paul, she guessed. Lots of red pen, lots of arrows, things circled in biro. And then she spotted it; a location she now knew well, also circled in red pen, Hatchet Hill. And next to it, the words, 'Notebook two, page thirty-four'.

It took her no time at all to realise that notebook two was missing.

## FOURTEEN

Travis was tired, but thanks to the two cans of energy drink he'd just necked, he was also rather wired. A part of his brain wanted him to sleep, but another part was refusing to listen.

Having spent the last three hours with Helen, driving around the lanes and knocking on doors, the only thing matching his tiredness was his frustration. Paul was dead, brutally murdered, and here they were, to his mind, wasting time.

'This is pointless,' he said, voicing his frustration. 'No one knows anything, because of course they don't. No one out here will have seen or heard anything. And why should they have done? It was the middle of the night, down a bridleway. Only witnesses were probably furry and live underground.'

'I've always fancied living underground,' said Helen. 'Reckon it would be proper cosy, don't you?'

'Do I look like a hobbit?'

'Not sure how to answer that.'

Travis fell silent, stared out of the window, and tried not to think about what had happened to Paul, which meant that was all he could think about.

'It doesn't make sense, any of it,' he said, as Helen slowed down for a sharp corner ahead. 'Why Paul? Why do that? What is wrong with this world?'

'A lot,' Helen answered, then gave a nod forward, and said, 'Maybe we'll learn something here, eh?'

Travis glanced at the house they were approaching, a small, detached bungalow surrounded by a garden that was mainly vegetables. Trees loomed over it from behind, like they were trying to take a sneaky peek over its roof at some hidden wonder by the front door. The bungalow was painted white, and as they pulled into the drive, Travis saw that the paint was peeling and patches of damp were creeping up the walls from the ground. The roof was almost completely hidden by the moss it wore, and from its chimney, grey-blue smoke curled skyward, stopping on the way to taunt the branches of trees with promises of freedom.

'It's both idyllic and depressing, isn't it?' he said, as Helen brought them to a stop.

'How do you mean?'

'Well, just look at it; on the one hand, it's a lovely little place in the country, with a vegetable garden, trees, that kind of thing.'

'And on the other?'

Travis leaned forward as though doing so would afford him a better look at it. It didn't.

'It's gloomy,' he said. 'The house looks like it's not so much a bungalow as a normal house that's slowly sinking into the ground due to depression or something. Those trees, they must make this place so dark all the time. And just look at the vegetables.'

'What? Why? They look amazing.'

'Exactly. Whoever has that much time on their hands clearly has issues.'

'They could be retired. Or maybe they just like gardening.'

'Or maybe they do it because if they didn't, they'd be out on the streets doing a nice little bit of murder.'

Helen gasped.

'Did you really just say that?'

'I'm just saying that it's odd, that's all.'

'Growing vegetables is not odd.'

'It is.'

'And it certainly doesn't mean you're suppressing an urge to go on a murder spree.'

Travis unclipped his seat belt and opened his door.

'All I'm saying, is that if you ever find me growing vegetables, get me professional help.'

'I never realised you had such a deep-seated mistrust of anyone who grows their own food.'

'Really? Well, don't get me started on those who show their produce at the local show ...'

Travis climbed out of the vehicle and met Helen as she climbed out from behind the steering wheel. He heard a door being opened and turned around to face a man in his mid- to late-fifties standing before them. He was wearing just about enough to be decent and had the shiniest bald head Travis had ever seen.

'I'm not imagining this, am I?' Travis asked.

'What? The fact that he's wearing a Speedo?'

'Not imagining it, then?'

'No.'

'That's disturbing.'

'Afternoon,' the man said, approaching them. 'Just going for a dip, so whatever it is, I hope you don't mind if I warm myself up.'

'A dip?' said Travis, glancing down at Helen, then back at the man. 'You have a swimming pool?'

The man laughed, then pointed at something sitting in the middle of the garden, a structure made from sheets of corrugated metal, atop which sat a wooden lid. It looked to Travis a little like a large cooking pot.

'And what's that, exactly?'

The man was now stretching his body into all kinds of strange shapes, while at the same time making very odd breathing noises.

'Ice bath.'

'Ice bath?'

'Yes, an ice bath. I use it at least twice a day, you see. Good for the heart, the mental health, that kind of thing.'

The man, who seemed to be more pretzel than human, started to slap his chest like a gorilla, before moving his hands down each arm, continuing the slaps as he went, all the way to his face.

Helen asked, 'Are you okay?'

The man's slaps, Travis noticed, had a resonance as his fingers bounced off his cheeks, and the sound echoed a little beneath the trees.

'What? Of course I am. Never better.'

Travis was working really hard not to stare at what the man was wearing, but it was proving to be almost impossible; not only were the Speedos so terrifyingly tight, they were also almost illegally worn, the material as close to transparent without actually being so.

'I'm PCSO Waring, and this is PCSO Kendrick,' he said. 'We were just wondering if—'

The man let out a huge huff of a breath, then turned on his heel, and marched across his garden towards the ice bath. Standing at its side, he lifted off the lid and rested it on the ground.

'Perfect!'

With no warning given, the man gripped the side of the tub, which rested just below his chest, and with the agility of someone at least forty years his junior, leapt up and over.

Water and ice burst out of the tub, chased by a roar of either pain or delight or both from the man.

With a little trepidation, Travis, with Helen beside him, made his way over to the tub. He leaned over the edge to see the man up to his chin in water, the surface of which was thick with ice cubes.

Travis gave his head a scratch.

'Where are the ice cubes from?'

'I have a freezer inside that I use just for ice,' the man said. 'It's not very efficient, I know, but I'm saving up.'

'Saving up?' Helen asked. 'For what?'

The man turned his head to look up at Travis and Helen.

'Some kind of chiller unit. Not sure how it'll work yet, but I've sketched it out. I'll just need to run power out here, get it all fixed up, and I should be able to have ice-cold water all year round. Won't that be fantastic?'

Travis reached a hand into the water and snatched it out again.

'That's absolutely bloody freezing!'

'Well, of course it is, otherwise what would be the point?'

'And you do this every day?'

'Twice.'

Travis dried his hand on his trouser leg.

'Will you be long?' Helen asked.

'I'm up to fifteen minutes now,' the man answered. 'Not sure I'll manage much longer, but I'm aiming for twenty. Can I ask why you're here?'

'Just need to ask you a few questions, that's all,' said Helen.

The man held up his hands, palms to the sky.

'Well, I'm not going anywhere, am I? So, ask away.' He

frowned thoughtfully, and added, 'Unless you'd both like to get in as well? There's plenty of room, and it really is very good for you, I promise.'

'I'll take your word for it,' said Travis.

'Can we take a name?' Helen asked.

'Roger,' the man said, dropping his hands back into the water. 'Roger Mason.'

While Helen made note of that and a contact number, Travis said, 'Were you home last night?'

'I was,' said Roger. 'It was a foggy one, wasn't it? I was hoping for something a little brighter, what with the promise of a full moon, you see? Because you can't beat a dip in the moonlight, I promise you.'

'Did you notice anything strange or out of the ordinary?'

'Like what?'

'Lights,' Helen said. 'Or maybe you heard something?'

'Again, like what?'

Travis wasn't sure how to answer that, because all he could think of was Paul's last moments, his imagination doing a good job of running away with itself.

'Hard to say,' he said. 'We believe there was something going on over on Hatchet Hill, had a call about it last night, so we're just out and about seeing if anyone noticed anything.'

Roger gave a shrug.

'Didn't notice a thing,' he said. 'It was just me in the tub, here, praying for the fog to clear just enough to see the moon, and that was it.'

'So, nothing, then?' Travis asked.

'Nothing strange or out of the ordinary,' said Roger. 'Just me, the quiet, the pool, the fog, a delivery driver turning up at the wrong address, and the hoot of owls; it was actually quite beautiful.'

'Delivery driver?' Helen asked, as Travis caught her eye.

'It's easy to get lost round here,' said Roger. 'Postcodes are no use at all, just gives you a general area and next thing you know, you've driven past where you need to be. Happens a lot, trust me.'

Roger gave a shiver, but didn't make any attempt to climb out of the tub.

'Do you know what company the driver worked for?'

'Not a clue. Just said he was lost, and if I could point him in the right direction.'

'Of where?' asked Helen.

Roger slapped the surface of the water, sending enough of it out to splash both PCSOs.

'Is there a problem?' Travis asked.

Roger stood up, the surface of the water tugging at his speedos just enough to have Travis turn his head in case more was put on display than he was prepared to witness.

'I'm a fool!' Roger said.

Travis resisted the urge to voice his agreement with that statement.

'Is something the matter?' Helen asked.

Roger stood in the tub, his head and shoulders poking out above the corrugated metal rim.

'He asked about Hatchet Hill. Not specifically, but said he had a delivery down that way, had been driving around and been unable to find it.'

'No satnav?'

'No signal,' said Roger. 'No surprise there; it's a dead spot for anything like that round here. Some nights, I'm fairly sure the wind is strong enough to blow the signal away.'

'And this delivery driver asked about Hatchet Hill?' said Travis. 'What time was this?'

'Oh, it was late, actually,' said Roger. 'Midnight easily. Thinking about it now, it was a little late for anyone to be out delivering, wasn't it? But I guess that's just the way of the world now, isn't it? We're all so impatient.'

'Did the driver give you a name?'

'He did not,' said Roger. 'Stand back!'

A second later, Roger was out of the tub and marching back towards his house, his flesh marshmallow pink.

'What about a description?'

Roger was already at his front door and before either Travis or Helen could do anything, he disappeared inside, reappearing a moment later in a long dressing gown clearly made of numerous, multicoloured donor garments.

'What do you think?' Roger asked, swishing the dressing gown around a little, a proud smile on his face. 'Made it myself. Not bad for a first attempt, I think.'

Travis repeated his question.

'A description?' Roger said. 'I can do better than that.'

'You can?'

Roger lifted a hand and pointed a finger at the side of the bungalow.

'You can never be too careful out here,' he said. 'Things go missing, you know.'

Travis and Helen both looked up and there, attached to the corner of Roger's home, was a small security camera.

'Missing?' Helen asked. 'How do you mean? Have you suffered a burglary? Did you report it?'

'I'm reporting it now,' said Roger, then pointed across the garden, this time towards the trees.

Travis and Helen both stared.

'I'll be honest, all I'm seeing is trees,' said Travis.

'Exactly,' said Roger.

'Can you be a little more specific?' Helen asked.

'The woods belong to someone who doesn't take too kindly to me nipping over the fence to help myself,' Roger said. 'It's only ever stuff that's fallen in a storm or whatever, but he still gets very upset about it.' He pointed then to the front of the house where a large, well-organised pile of wood had been stacked. 'So, I'm afraid I have to buy supplies when I need them. Had that lot delivered last week. Burns well, but some of it's a bit large and I need to chop it up so it's the right size for my stove. Except I've got a problem now, haven't I?'

'You have?'

Roger placed his hands together as though holding the handle of something. He then lifted them above his head and swung them downwards.

'My axe,' he said.

'What about it?' Travis asked.

'It was there last night, but this morning? Gone. And axes don't just disappear, do they?'

'No,' Travis said, his mind turning to the mysterious delivery driver. 'They very much don't.'

# FIFTEEN

After discovering a notebook was missing, and with no clue as to if or why it could be important, Gordy had called for Patti. The detective sergeant had returned from sitting upstairs with Gill and Kelly, with little to report other than a lot of crying.

Jack had returned shortly after, having gone somewhat overboard with provisions for Gill and Kelly, and the sight of him carrying the numerous bags of food had warmed Gordy's heart. What he had done had been a gesture of practical goodwill and care, perhaps in place of words he had been unable to find, and it could only be admired.

Together, they had helped Gill unpack, and then left her and Kelly to their evening. Gordy had made it clear that she would be in constant contact with them, not just to keep them up-to-date on the investigation, but also to make sure they were okay. Which, clearly, they weren't, and Gordy knew that, so keeping an eye on them was vital. She'd known people to go off the rails under such circumstances. It didn't take much for the seemingly strongest of people to lose it completely, and the last thing she wanted was to turn up at their door with more bad news about one of them.

The afternoon was getting on by the time they got back to the station. While Gordy drove, she'd had Patti call Cowboy and arrange for them to head over to have a chat, and to also go through the postmortem with the pathologist. Because of the nature of the case, and the victim, both Cowboy and Dr Charming had been happy to work a little later than usual, which was a relief.

With Jack dropped off to get in touch with the rest of the team to find out what they had uncovered, and to see what he could dig up about Billy Parker, and what he had been involved in and put away for, she had then swapped seats with Patti to let her drive, and together they had headed off to the city of Bath.

The ride from Frome had been uneventful, the road almost hypnotic as they'd followed it, the white lines and hedgerows zipping past at speed.

Gordy said little for much of the journey, instead allowing them both to think about what they were doing, and what they'd found out, which really wasn't much. A missing notebook could be anything, could be everything, could be nothing. At least, that's what she had thought until Jameson had called in and she'd told him about the missing notebook.

'And you're sure it's notebook two?' she asked.

'Says so on the spine,' said Jameson, his voice on speaker so Patti could hear, too, thus saving Gordy the pain of having to repeat everything. 'The cover is black, but Paul's put a little round sticker on it on the spine and there's a number two on it.'

'He left it in the pub?'

'Apparently so.'

'Any idea why?'

'None given, so no. Could be he just forgot it. Easy to do,

isn't it? I've lost count of the number of things I've left behind in pubs. Phones, wallets, keys, hats, even a dog once.'

Gordy was sure Jameson was pulling her leg.

'A dog?'

'Belonged to a friend. I was looking after it for a couple of days. Little Jack Russell. Fitted right in at the pub, I can tell you. I kept seeing it pop up at other tables and being made a fuss of. By the time I left, I'd completely forgotten I'd even taken it with me. Didn't realise till the next morning.'

'The poor thing!'

Jameson laughed.

'Oh, don't you believe it,' he said. 'That animal had the best time ever. The owner took it home, had seen it with me and figured I'd be back in the morning, but didn't have a contact number. Anyway, let's just say that it very quickly developed a taste for leftover steak. Refused to eat the food my mate had left for it. Can't say as I blamed it, either.'

'So, what's on page thirty-four?' Gordy asked.

At that, Gordy was met with silence.

'Jameson?'

'I'm here,' he said. 'I'm just not entirely sure how to describe what's in front of me.'

'Not sure I understand.'

'Neither do I, and neither would you, if you were looking at what I'm looking at.'

Gordy willed the retired detective to get to the point.

'You ever been to the witchcraft museum?'

The question caught Gordy off guard.

'The which museum?'

'Witch*craft* museum,' Jameson repeated, emphasising the second half of the word to make it clear what he was talking about. 'It's a museum of, well, I guess the clue's in the title, isn't it?'

'Witchcraft?' said Gordy. 'There's a whole museum about it? Really?'

'And magic, too,' added Jameson.

'I've been there,' said Patti, jumping in. 'It's down in Boscastle, isn't it? Beautiful little place. Lovely walks along the coast. Bit bleak at times, especially when a storm comes in, and it's been badly flooded a fair few times. But that museum is definitely worth a visit.'

'It is?' Gordy asked. 'Why?'

'Hard to say, really; it's an experience, I think. Certainly makes a change from going to one of those modern, hi-tech museums full of pull-this and flashing-that. It's pretty basic, lots of display cabinets showing all kinds of weird stuff, but then belief is weird, isn't it?'

'How so?'

Patti was quiet for a second or two, then said, 'I'm not saying there's anything wrong with it at all, just that I find it hard to get my head around sometimes. Not least because I also find it hard to not believe in something, if that makes sense.'

'We seem to be straying into philosophy here,' said Gordy.

'And if it's all the same with you, I'd prefer it if we didn't,' said Jameson.

'Then perhaps you could get to the point and just tell us what's on page thirty-four?'

'Symbols,' Jameson said. 'Pentagrams, that kind of thing. There's a sketch of some kind of horned goat-man thing—'

'That's the god, Pan,' said Patti.

'Is it? Well, he's there, anyway, and then next to him and the pentagram thing, there's a list of six words; procession, purification, hymns, sacrifice, prayers, feast.'

Gordy sighed, rubbed her eyes.

'What a load of old shite,' she said. 'Pentagrams? Pan? It's nothing but more of Paul's notes to help with his writing, isn't it?'

'It is odd, though,' said Patti. 'I didn't realise he was so into it.'

'Plus, there's the connection with Hatchet Hill, isn't there?' said Jameson. 'And we all know what we think about coincidences, don't we?'

'Even so, I'm not convinced,' said Gordy. 'Paul was murdered, and brutally. We now know that he may have played a key role in a close friend being put away, possibly for drugs. Hopefully, Jack will have something more on that for us by tomorrow.'

'But that was years ago, wasn't it?' said Patti.

'Look, I'm just not going to go down the witchcraft, Pan the god of who knows what, ritual sacrifice, people dancing naked under the moonlight, road, okay?'

Neither Patti nor Jameson said anything to contradict her statement. And Gordy was pleased, because she really, truly didn't want to have anything to do with that world, not again. Years may have passed, decades even, but some memories, they stayed with you. And though all of that was so long ago now, what she had witnessed, what she had seen, none of it could ever be unseen. Which was why, for so long now, she'd never returned to the Highlands for more than a brief visit. Perhaps she never would, no matter how much the place tugged at her heartstrings.

'Boss?'

Patti's voice cut into Gordy's thoughts like a razor.

'Yes?'

'You drifted off a bit there.'

'I did?'

Patti gave a nod, then said, 'We're just coming up to the hospital now.'

'I'll leave you to it, then,' said Jameson. 'I'll see you in the morning. Need to get a taxi now, don't I?'

'You do?'

'I think I got a little bit too into character as a pubgoer.'

'Ah.'

'Indeed.'

Jameson hung up, and Patti pulled the car around to the hospital entrance.

'Ready to get lost in a maze of corridors?' she asked.

'Every day's an adventure,' said Gordy, and as Patti found them somewhere to park, she did her best to forget something buried deep in her past that Jameson's description of what he had discovered in Paul's notebook had brought to the surface.

# SIXTEEN

Like all mortuaries, this too was a cold place, which seemed both utterly unreal and so completely real at the same time, that she sometimes wondered if such places existed between worlds. Which, she pondered, in many ways, they did. This was where the dead came before they were buried or cremated. It was a waiting room for corpses, a storeroom of fleshy shells that had once been filled with souls, and which now only the cold kept from rotting. There were no dreams here, no loves and broken hearts, no memories and thoughts of tomorrow; just a special kind of silence born of the nothingness that only the absence of consciousness could create.

With Patti by her side, Gordy stared across at two pairs of eyes. Keith 'Cowboy' Brown was directly in front of her, with Dr James Charming, the pathologist, standing opposite Patti. They were all dressed in the uniform of those who dealt with death; white overalls, white boots, white facemasks.

Why then, Gordy wondered, were funerals a place where black was worn? White seemed to be such a more hopeful colour, even though, like black, it wasn't a colour at all. But at least it held the promise of brightness, of light, whereas black did not.

'Shall we get on?'

The question was from Charming, a man Gordy had met once before, and as yet had only ever seen the man's eyes. They were bright, and held in place by laughter lines that gave her the impression of someone who smiled a lot, was perhaps even smiling now, and she wasn't sure if that was reassuring, disturbing, or both.

Gordy turned to Patti.

'You sure you're okay to do this? You don't have to. I can manage on my own.'

Patti met Gordy's eyes, and she saw there only stony resolve.

'I'm the eyes of the team,' she said. 'I need to see it for them, for his family, for Paul. I need to know, to see what was done with my own eyes, and not just hear about it secondhand.'

'I know, but ...'

'Gordy, I was at the crime scene. I know what's coming.'

Gordy noted not only the firmness of Patti's voice, but that she had used her first name.

Patti started at Gordy for a moment longer, then dropped her eyes to what lay between them all; the shape of a body currently hidden from view by a white sheet, and resting on a stainless-steel table.

'Anyway, this isn't Paul, is it? Not anymore. I choose to remember Paul as he was, and that's what I'll hold on to. We all will.'

Gordy understood, rested a hand briefly on Patti's shoulder, then gave a nod to the pathologist.

Reaching up to the end of the table, Charming took hold of the white sheet, and with considerable care and reverence, eased it downwards.

No one spoke, no one breathed, as Paul's body was revealed.

Charming had, as far as Gordy could tell, done as much sewing as cutting. Paul was now in one piece, but to her mind had more in common with Frankenstein's monster than the PCSO she had come to know and regard so well in such a short period of time.

Switching off the part of her brain that would regard what was now in front of them with horror and shock, Gordy simply observed.

Paul was a jigsaw again made whole, the pieces she had seen scattered around that small clearing on the bridleway brought together by the technical brilliance and careful, steady hands of a pathologist. His flesh was pale, close to grey, but not quite there yet. The stitched lines of the violent wounds that had hacked his life away and the careful cuts by Charming were dark, almost black in places.

'Shall we begin at the top?' Charming asked, but didn't wait for an answer. 'As you are aware, there is a catastrophic wound to the head, caused by a small axe or hatchet. There are also two further wounds round the back and closer to the base of the skull.'

'You say that like it's significant.'

'Not done by an axe, so yes, potentially,' said Charming. 'From the bruising, the fractures to the bone, I would suggest something blunt, a hammer, perhaps.'

'They hit him with a hammer first, then attacked him with an axe?' asked Patti. 'Why?'

Gordy said, 'Probably to stun him. A hammer is a very effective weapon. Devastating actually.'

'I am inclined to agree,' said Charming. 'Those two wounds show all the signs of being the first suffered by the victim. As to the rest of the trauma to the head, this was done after, well, after everything else, actually.'

'After? How do you know?' asked Patti.

'The wound contained a considerable amount of material from the clothes Paul was wearing. This would have been from when all the other wounds were caused, fibres and so on sticking to the axe head.' He pointed to Paul's head. 'These fibres were then transferred to here, so it had to have happened after. I'll come back to this in a moment, if that's okay?'

Gordy frowned.

'Come back to it? Why?'

Charming didn't reply, simply guided everyone to Paul's torso.

'As you can see, his limbs were removed. What you will also see is this ...' He pointed to the middle of Paul's chest where a jagged line sat. 'This wound is directly above the heart. The ribcage has been hacked apart, and the heart removed.'

At that, Patti gasped.

'Removed?'

Charming gave the smallest of nods.

'Again, this was done after the other wounds, with various fibres found inside the chest cavity. But yes, removed.'

Gordy looked at Cowboy, who shook his head.

'No, we didn't find it; the heart wasn't left at the crime scene.'

'Which brings me back here,' said Charming, pointing again to Paul's head. 'This wound, there's more to it than you may think.'

'How so?' asked Gordy.

'The top of Paul's skull wasn't simply cracked by the axe, it was hacked off, then replaced, but only after ...'

The pathologist paused, glanced at Gordy, Patti, and Cowboy, then continued.

'Paul's brain was removed, then replaced, but only after something had been taken.'

Gordy could feel her body temperature dropping with every new and wholly disturbing revelation.

'What was taken?'

'The section of the brain which contains both the pituitary and pineal glands. Both are tiny, maybe about the size of a pea, so finding them in the middle of the night when your only surgical tool is an axe, and perhaps a knife, is rather difficult. But there we are; the heart and that section of the brain, which contains those glands, are missing. The brain was then pushed back inside the skull, and not exactly neatly, either.'

Gordy hung her head for a moment, folded her arms, closed her eyes.

Just what the hell was this? At first, it had struck her as just a brutal murder of one of her team. But with what the pathologist had just told them, there had to be more to it, but what?

'Why the hell would anyone remove either the heart or these glands you're talking about?' she asked.

Charming said nothing, but Gordy spotted the briefest of glances between him and Cowboy. And that told her there was still more to come.

'What are these glands anyway?' asked Patti. 'What do they do? What are they for?'

'The pituitary gland is part of the endocrine system,' Charming explained. 'It makes various hormones, such as adrenocorticotropic hormone, or ACTH, which stimulates the adrenal glands to produce cortisol, growth hormone, and so on. The Pineal gland secretes melatonin.'

'But why take them? Why hack open Paul's head and remove them? What's the point?'

At this, Cowboy entered the conversation.

'Maybe at this point, it might be worth me telling, or showing you, something from the crime scene?'

'Is it going to make any of this any clearer?' asked Gordy.

Cowboy reached behind him to a small table and turned back around, holding a brown folder.

'Mainly, the crime scene was a case of collecting body parts. The team found various prints in and around the area, but with it being a bridleway, it's impossible to tell if any of them are from whoever did this or just from walkers or runners. We also found dog hair, dog excrement, a child's woolly hat, various sweet wrappers, cigarette stubs, a couple of used condoms, and a few empty vodka bottles.'

'But I'm guessing none of that is relevant?'

Cowboy shook his head.

'We have to record everything we find, as you well know, and that's only part of the list. But really, it's what's here that I think you need to see.'

Cowboy held the folder out for Gordy. She took it, opened it, and found herself once again in the presence of the awfulness of that night.

'The crime scene photos,' she said as she started to shuffle through them.

The photographs were crystal clear, each one showing an astonishing depth of detail. Gordy was struck by the simple beauty of blades of grass, the weary branches of trees, how leaves up close seemed more like maps to distant lands so criss-crossed were they with veins. In juxtaposition to all of this was the blood, the gore, and the bits and pieces of Paul seemingly scattered at random around the place where his life had been so cruelly taken from him.

'It's the ones at the back I think you'll find interesting,' said Cowboy. 'You remember we used a drone? Well, they picked something up that none of us spotted, mainly because I just don't think you could unless you were way up above it all.'

Despite what Cowboy had just said, Gordy didn't skip to the photographs at the back. She made a point of pausing at each still, taking it in, trying to see if something, anything, jumped out at her. Then, when she at last turned to the final photographs, she stopped, and lifted her eyes to Cowboy, holding one of the photos out in front of her.

'You can't be serious.'

'You're seeing the same thing, then, yes?'

Patti leaned over to look at the photograph.

'What is it? What are you seeing?'

'The next one is clearer,' said Cowboy. 'Mainly because I've annotated what I think it is that we're looking at.'

Gordy lifted the next photograph and saw that dotted yellow lines had been added.

Patti reached out and took the photograph.

'That's ... it's a ...'

'It's a pentagram,' said Gordy. 'A huge one drawn out on the ground with Paul's blood.'

'And resting at each of the five points, we found a body part,' said Cowboy. 'Something else, though; it's inverted. At least we think it might be.'

'What? How can you tell?'

'We can't exactly, sure, but if you look, that bottom point? It's pointing back down the bridleway.'

'You're clutching at straws.'

'Also, Paul's head, it was set in the centre of the pentagram facing the same way.'

'Why is any of that relevant?'

'There's a sheet attached to the back of that photograph.'

Patti flipped the photograph over and showed Gordy a print-out of a pentagram, which seemed to contain the face of a goat, the creature's nose and jaw in the bottom point, the face in the centre, and the four remaining points containing its ears and its horns.

'That's the sign of Baphomet,' said Cowboy. 'The official insignia of the Church of Satan.'

Gordy said nothing, took the photograph back from Patti, placed it with the others, and closed the file. As she did that, Charming covered Paul's body with the white sheet.

'Paul's head was dead centre, wasn't it?' she said. 'But before we all start jumping up and down about rituals and Satanism or any other such nonsense, perhaps you can explain to me why I saw you both look at each other when we were talking about the removal of those glands?'

'You sure you want to know?'

Gordy's eyes went wide.

'Of course I want to know!'

She clenched her jaws and released them.

'Sorry,' she said.

'No apology needed, okay?' Cowboy replied. 'According to Descartes, the pineal gland is the seat of the soul.'

'I thought the heart was?' said Patti.

'The pineal is also often called the third eye, and apparently, some even see it as a connection between the physical and spiritual worlds.'

'Let me see if I'm understanding what it is I think you're saying,' she said, and she cast her eyes over both Cowboy and Charming. 'Paul wasn't just murdered, was he? Someone hacked him to pieces, removed organs that, for whatever insane reason, some people think contain the soul, then laid him to rest in an inverted pentagram painted in his own blood.'

The silence from both Cowboy and Charming was all the confirmation she needed.

## SEVENTEEN

Tuesday morning welcomed Gordy with dark clouds and rain, mirroring how she felt, almost as if it knew.

She had slept, of that she was sure, but as she padded around her flat and got ready for work, she remembered enough snippets of her dreams to tell her that the night hadn't been restful. Another sign of her tossing and turning was that when she'd woken up, she had been the only thing still on the bed, her duvet and pillows scattered across the floor.

The drive from Evercreech to Frome was a wet one. The rain that had gently pitter-pattered against her windows as she had managed to force herself to eat some breakfast had decided to up the intensity. The whole way over, it was akin to driving through rods of glass, which shattered against her vehicle with such ferocity, she was forced to ease off on the speed and take her time. Some of the lanes wore huge puddles like enormous, proudly displayed gems, and though she managed to slow down for most of them, one particularly large one had hidden itself in a dip and it snatched at her front wheels as she slammed into it, yanking her steering wheel from her hands just long enough to send her heart into her mouth. The sight of a tractor coming the other way hadn't helped, especially as it took up most of the lane and forced her into the hedge.

Arriving at the office, Gordy was frazzled, but Vivek's coffee soon had her back online, especially as it came with a generous slice of lardy cake.

With a little bit of time to herself before the rest of the team arrived, Gordy shut herself away in her office. Tempted though she was to have a nap, she instead waited for the caffeine and sugar to hit, and thought through what the day in front of her held. The answer, though, was disconcerting; she really didn't know. Paul was gone. His family would be forever broken by what had happened. And what little she and the team had learned so far seemed to be either of little use, or so outlandish it was all she could do to not discount it all without a second thought.

Still, perhaps something will come of the team meeting, she thought. She hoped so, anyway, because right there and then, she had nothing.

Gordy was about to have another look through the crime scene photos, when a knock at the door yanked her from her thoughts. She looked up, and peeking around it was Jameson.

'Penny for your pondering?'

'Pondering?'

'I could've said thoughts, but I prefer the alliteration.'

'Well, regardless, I'll give you them for free,' said Gordy, and gestured to the other chair in the room.

Jameson walked in, grabbed the chair, dropped it in front of Gordy's desk, and sat down.

'Go on, then,' he said. 'I'm all ears.'

'Hard to know where to begin.'

'Something like this, there's no beginning anyway, is there? It's just this big pile of stuff you have to sort through, with no obvious place to start. Best thing to do in that kind of situation? Just dive straight in.'

'You sure?'

'Go for it.'

By the time Gordy had stopped speaking, having rattled through everything from the day before in as much detail as she could, she was feeling the need to grab another coffee from Vivek. She could also see through the glass wall of her office that the rest of the team were now milling about outside her office, clearly doing their best to look engaged in important jobs and tasks, but constantly flicking their eyes to her door.

'Feel better?' Jameson asked.

'Not in the slightest,' said Gordy. 'I think I need more coffee.'

Jameson stood up.

'Allow me,' he said, then exited the office, the door swinging shut behind him.

With a glance at a photo of Anna she kept on her desk, the sight of which seemed to calm her a little, Gordy stood up, grabbed the folder of crime scene photographs, and followed Jameson out to meet the team.

Patti was the first to greet her.

'Jameson said he was fetching you a coffee.'

'He is.'

'You look like you need it.'

Gordy glanced at the rest of the team.

'Looks like we all do.'

The board was already in position, so when Jameson came back and handed her a fresh mug, she called everyone around.

'We've all had a good night's rest, I hope,' she said, then raised her mug. 'And if you haven't, there's always jitter juice.'

That got a laugh, which was as unexpected as it was welcomed; the sound of it had the effect of visibly relaxing everyone in the room, so Gordy pushed on quickly to take advantage of the change in atmosphere.

'I'll start,' she said, taking a glug of coffee, imagining it fuelling her synapses, setting her brain alight with energy. 'Chip in when you want to, and we'll probably find we've covered everything soon enough.'

Patti stood up beside the board and grabbed a pen. Then, as Gordy was about to go into what had happened at Paul's house with Gill and Kelly, Vivek entered the office.

'There's someone in reception, wants to have a quick word,' he said.

'Who?'

'Alison Read. Says she's in a bit of a rush.'

An audible groan from the team matched Gordy's thoughts at the news.

'Well, if she wants to talk to me, she'll have to wait, regardless.'

'I don't think she will.'

'Well, if she doesn't, then just take a note of whatever it is she wants to talk to me about, and tell her I'll call her when I'm done.'

Vivek gave a nod of acknowledgement, then left the office.

'Now, where was I?' said Gordy.

Jameson was first to raise his hand.

# EIGHTEEN

'I won't bore you with my pub reviews,' Jameson began, 'but if you're interested at all, The Lamb and Fountain is still the gem that it's always been, and historically important. And The Griffin is a wonderful little place, serving fantastic beer from the Milk Street Brewery, which is based in Frome. Can't get more local than that, can you?'

'How is any of that relevant?' asked Helen.

'It isn't,' said Jameson. 'But what is relevant is that Jack was right, and that Paul was well known to both, especially so in The Lamb. Been going there for years, from before he became a PCSO. Used to go there with an old friend of his, Billy Parker.'

'Is this where I jump in?' asked Jack.

Gordy looked to Jameson.

'You want to mention the notebook?'

'You mean this one?' said Jameson, pulling an evidence bag out of his pocket with a slim, black book inside.

'Not sure you're supposed to just keep evidence on you,' Gordy said.

'I looked after it last night, had a read through, and I've now brought it to where it should be.' He handed it to Gordy, then said to the team, 'As you all know, Paul was a writer. That's one of his notebooks. But I'll leave why that's important for your boss to explain soon enough. Anyway, this Billy was a childhood friend of Paul's. Grew up together. Hung around together. Then all of that fell apart when Paul found out what his mate was doing when they weren't in the pub sinking pints of cider.'

'And what was he doing?' Travis asked.

'Class A,' answered Jameson. 'Supplying. Apparently, Paul only found out when he found a kid in a real mess because of what he'd got from Billy. And that was it for Paul. He found out all he could about what Billy was up to, then reported him to police. Might even be why he became a PCSO.'

Gordy glanced at Jack.

'You're up,' she said.

Jack stood up, but a look from Gordy had him back in his chair again.

'Billy Parker was given life for possession with the intent to supply a class A drug.'

'How long ago was that?' asked Jameson.

Gordy remembered something Gill had said about it all being before Kelly was around.

'Must be twenty years.'

'Exactly, actually,' said Jack.

'Which means—'

'That he's been released,' Jack finished, confirming what Gordy was thinking. 'Just under a year ago, actually.'

'On licence?'

'Yes, until he went missing.'

That statement got an audible gasp from everyone in the room.

'What? How?' Gordy asked. 'Where the hell is he?'

Jack's answer was a shrug.

'I've tried to find out, but there's nothing.'

'People don't disappear.'

'Billy seems to have done. There are records of him meeting up with his supervising officer, and it looks like he stuck to all the usual, you know, good behaviour, no re-offending, living at an approved address, but then he just goes missing. There was some attempt to try and find him, but I think it all just got lost in the system in the end.'

'Bigger fish to fry, you mean?' said Travis.

'Don't forget budget cuts, stretched resources, all the usual excuses,' added Helen.

'I guess.'

Jack looked again at Gordy.

'He was a violent man,' he said. 'Seems almost as though he was living two lives; the one Paul knew, where they were best mates, hung out together, went to the pub, then this other life, where he got more and more into supplying, and had a reputation for taking no prisoners.'

'What do you mean, exactly?' Helen asked.

'Basically, Billy was someone you just didn't cross. His favourite weapon was a hammer. He never killed anyone, or so far as can be proved, anyway, but there's plenty of evidence to support numerous violent attacks on those in the circles he mixed in.'

That last sentence faded into the distance as Gordy had got stuck on one particular word.

'A hammer?'

'Apparently.'

'My God!' said Patti, jumping in. 'That was Billy's—'

'Favourite weapon,' said Gordy, finishing off what she knew the detective sergeant was going to say.'

'So, Billy did this?' Travis said. 'Billy got released and

hunted down his old best mate to exact some kind of horrific revenge?'

'It's easy to jump to that conclusion, isn't it?' Gordy agreed. 'Use of a trademark weapon, the history between the two.'

'You don't sound convinced,' said Jameson.

And Gordy wasn't.

'I know that there's every reason to think that makes sense, that perhaps Billy is using his favourite weapon as a warning or a message perhaps, to let everyone know that even after twenty-odd years, he'll come after you if you cross him.'

'But?'

'I don't know,' said Gordy. 'Just seems off. A little too neat. And why go to all the trouble of doing all that other stuff to Paul? If it was a message, then why not just kill him with the hammer? Why go from that to such brutality?'

'Could've been he just went into a frenzy,' Travis suggested.

'And just so happened to have an axe with him? No, that doesn't sit right either.'

Gordy went quiet for a second or two, her thoughts caught on how difficult it must've been for Paul to deal with, finding out that his old friend was a violent, drug-supplying criminal. The sense of betrayal must've been immense. That he had turned against him, take an active role in bringing him down? That was brave. And it really did look like it had cost him his life.

She looked at Patti.

'That's one suspect, then, isn't it?' she said, as Patti jotted down the name. 'He must have family and friends in the area; Jack?'

Jack stayed silent, and Gordy didn't like the look on his face one bit.

'What's wrong?'

'His parents disowned him. Never turned up in court.

Never visited him in prison. Refused to have anything to do with him. Even changed their names.'

'To what?'

'Not a clue.'

'And how do you know this?'

'Files on the case include a letter from them to Billy.'

'One letter? That's it? Must be signed, then, with their real names, surely?'

'It isn't.'

Pete raised a hand.

'There's a link with Hatchet Hill,' he said. 'With Billy, I mean.'

'How so?' asked Gordy.

'It's where he was arrested. He used to stash some of his stuff down there when he started out, dealing with cannabis, mainly. Then he got into the class A stuff, like Jack said. Apparently, he kept his personal supply down there as well because it was nice and out of the way.'

'He wasn't worried about folk using the bridleway, then?' asked Helen.

'I guess not,' said Jack. 'And maybe his reputation was enough. Hard to say, really; it's a long time ago, isn't it?'

'In plain sight is often better than spending time and energy in trying to make sure something's really hidden,' suggested Gordy. 'It's a bridleway, so it's not exactly the centre of Frome, is it? It'd be easy to pop along at any time, day or night, really, and no one would be any the wiser.' She looked at Jack. 'Anything else?'

'I'll keep looking to see if I can find anything else about him,' Jack said. 'But I can't promise I'll find much.'

'Who's next, then?' Gordy asked.

Pete lifted an arm.

'I've found a few other things about Hatchet Hill,' he said.

'First, the name most likely comes from Hackett; it's a variant of that surname. At some point it became Hatchet.'

'I'm going to assume that's not all you found out?' said Gordy.

Pete shook his head.

'Mr Rowe, who called in about those funny lights?'

'And who we can't get back in touch with, which isn't suspicious at all, is it?'

'Yes, him; he's not alone in seeing weird stuff out that way.'

'Define weird stuff ...'

'After a fair bit of digging, I ended up on the Facebook page for a local paranormal group. Seems like there's loads of sightings at Hatchet Hill. Paul was a member of the group. They visit there regularly. They even do ghost walks down the bridleway on Halloween.'

'So, both Paul and Billy have a history with Hatchet Hill,' said Gordy. 'And it's haunted.'

'I managed to meet the head of the paranormal group,' continued Pete. 'She said Paul was fairly regular with their meetings, would attend ghost hunts when he could, but when it came to Hatchet Hill, he never went, not even once.'

'Well, that probably ties in with what we know about Billy and Paul, doesn't it? It must've been rough on Paul, what he learned about Billy, then turning him in. Sometimes it's best to leave the past where it is.'

'I've also been in touch with the local writers' groups,' continued Pete. 'Paul wasn't a regular as such, but he'd pop along to see them now and again. Sounds like he was well-liked by everyone, was only ever full of praise and support and advice for other writers.'

'So, we're still with just the one suspect,' said Gordy, 'and he's disappeared. What else do we have?'

'A missing axe,' said Travis.

Gordy snapped around at this.

'What?'

Travis ran through his and Helen's bizarre visit to Roger Mason's house.

'And he thinks the axe was taken by the driver of the delivery van?'

'He does,' said Travis. 'And judging by the huge pile of wood he'd just had delivered, he needs it.'

'Do we have any details of the delivery van?'

'Roger has a security camera. Decent one, too. Though the van driver is hard to make out, the numberplate was very clear.'

'We've traced it,' said Helen.

'And?'

'And it was reported stolen last week.'

'What?'

Gordy couldn't disguise the frustration in her voice.

'We've got the address of the owner. We'll go and have a chat once we're done here. But yes, stolen.'

'Which gives us another suspect who's about as much use as our first, doesn't it?'

Gordy watched as Patti did her best to keep jotting things down on the board in a way that made sense. Which wasn't easy, as nothing was making sense.

'Me next, then,' she said. 'First, the notebook Jameson mentioned. When myself, Patti, and Jack visited Paul's wife and daughter yesterday, there was a drawer full of Paul's notebooks and other bits and bobs. Gill seemed embarrassed about it all, but let's no' be worrying about that. One of the notebooks was missing; the one Jameson found by accident in the Lamb and Fountain. It's important because it ties in with Hatchet Hill as well.'

'How?' asked Helen.

'Paul had various maps of the area, all with notes on them,

locations of hauntings and legends, that kind of thing. One map had Hatchet Hill circled, alongside the words "notebook two, page thirty-four."'

Gordy held up the notebook open on page thirty-four for everyone to see. Looking at the pages herself for the first time, she saw the pentagrams, the sketch of the horned goat-man Jameson had described, and which Patti had suggested was the god Pan. Now, however, she knew it was someone else. She also saw the words that Jameson had read out to her: procession, purification, hymns, sacrifice, prayers, and feast. Various numbers had been jotted down as well; grid references, she thought, though one or two seemed too long for that. Regardless, there was no denying that whatever Paul had got himself involved in, was certainly bizarre.

Pete said, 'That doesn't make sense. On the one hand, we're hearing that Paul stays away from Hatchet Hill, probably because of what happened with Billy, right? And now we find out he's got maps and notes about the place, with loads of weird symbols and whatever the hell else that all is?'

'It's a puzzler for sure,' Gordy agreed. 'And there's more … First, not only was Paul hacked to death, organs were removed from his body, namely his heart, and the part of his brain where the pituitary and pineal gland are kept.' She noticed mouths open to utter shock, words of disgust and horror, but she kept talking regardless. 'Second, the crime scene photographer used a drone and spotted something no one would've seen from the ground.'

At this, Gordy opened the folder and, keeping the rest of the gruesome photographs out of sight, held up the one taken by the drone, which Cowboy had annotated in yellow.

'You'll recognise this as the same symbol that's in Paul's notebook,' she said. 'It's inverted. I'm also led to believe that the goat-man you see in Paul's notes isn't the god Pan as we first thought, but Baphomet.'

'Well, I don't know about anyone else,' said Travis, scratching his thick beard, 'but I've not a clue what's going on now. What is all this? What are you saying?'

Gordy returned the photograph to the darkness of the folder, and took a slow breath in and out.

'What I'm about to say is not something I wish to become public knowledge,' she said. 'It stays here, in this room, among this team. Understood?'

Everyone acknowledged Gordy with a sharp nod.

'As insane as it may sound, my working hypothesis—and believe me when I say that I've only just come up with this as we've been talking—is that Paul, for whatever reason, wasn't just murdered, he was sacrificed.'

That got a response, but Gordy kept talking.

'I've no idea what Billy has to do with any of this, if anything. I don't know what this delivery driver was doing at Roger's place. The axe is clearly significant, though, and we need to check if it's the same one. There are too many questions and no bloody answers, not yet, anyway. Hatchet Hill is a place with a history for Paul, and for Billy. If we are to believe that Paul kept away from the place—and it certainly sounds like he did, according to the paranormal groups—then, like Pete said, why have it marked on a map, and why have it in his notebook? Why is it relevant? Why is he drawing pentagrams only to end up being one himself? Who the hell was the runner who reported the lights? Why ask for Paul by name? Who did this? Who?'

Gordy realised that as she had been speaking, her voice had grown louder and louder. She paused, turned down the volume.

'We've a lot to do,' she said. 'So, listen up, and I'll tell you what you're on with next ...'

# NINETEEN

With the team dispersed to get on with the tasks she'd set for them, Gordy shuffled back into her office to give herself a moment before she headed down to Vivek to see what Alison Read had popped in for. She slumped down at her desk, her mind a jumble.

Patti and Jack were on their way to try and track down the mysterious Mr Rowe, whose call on Sunday night had led Paul to his death. Jack had been rather vocal about hoping that it wasn't going to involve actually having to go along to the local running club, and when pressed as to why, he'd muttered something about Park Run, then clammed up.

Pete was on with seeing what else he could find out about Billy, if anything, and also to look into the footage from Roger Mason's security camera to see if they could identify, or at least get some form of description, of the mysterious delivery driver, perhaps even link them to the missing axe.

As for the axe, that was something Helen and Travis were looking into on their way to follow up on the stolen vehicle.

There was a lot going on and Gordy felt rather like she was

trying to knit a scarf while invisible hands kept pulling at the wool to undo her work, or to tie it into knots.

'Clear as mud, then?'

Jameson was at the door.

'What?'

'Your thoughts.'

Gordy shook her head despairingly.

'None of it makes sense. I refuse to believe, despite everything we've seen so far, that what happened to Paul is some kind of satanic, cultish nonsense.'

'Why?'

Gordy screwed up her face as she tried to work out why she felt like that.

'It's just too full on,' she eventually managed. 'Know what I mean?'

'Explain.'

Gordy leaned forward, resting her elbows on her desk, head in her hands.

'I can't,' she said. 'Well, I can, I just don't want to.'

'A SOMEWHAT MYSTERIOUS ANSWER.' Jameson sat down in the only other chair in the small room. 'This is a safe space, you know that, right? If tsomething's bothering you ...'

Gordy's mind cast itself back decades, even though she tried to stop it. Though she was in that little office with Jameson, she was also somewhere else. She could smell wet peat and moorland, taste thick fog in the air. She could remember how the ground had refused to give up what she had clawed at it for, and for so long, the muck and mire between her fingers, coating her hands, her arms, the way the smell of it hung around on her skin for days after. She could hear the wind laughing at her as it blasted across a wilderness so terrifyingly bleak that, had she not known where to go that night, then ...

'Gordy?'

Jameson's voice snatched her out of her memories, and for that she was grateful.

'It was a long time ago,' she said. 'A case I was involved in, up in the Highlands, before I came to England.'

'And what we're dealing with here reminds you of it?'

'A little.'

Jameson said nothing for a moment. When he eventually spoke, there was a firmness to his voice that Gordy hadn't heard before.

'We're all haunted by old cases. But those ghosts, they can only scare us if we let them. Better to confront them, make use of them, don't you think? I mean, what's a ghost, other than a memory trapped or lost, maybe even looking for a way out, an echo of unfinished business?'

'Oh, that business was very much finished, I promise you that,' said Gordy, and as she spoke, the sharp screech of a hawk cracked her head in two as it called to her from the past.

'That may be so, but there's clearly still enough of it in you to bubble up to the surface because of what happened to Paul, what we've uncovered. Are there similarities?'

'That's exactly it,' said Gordy. 'I've dealt with a murderous cult before, I know all about Satanism, the Church of Satan, how those two things aren't actually the same thing, black magic, rituals, all of it! Damn it, I've put people away because they thought human sacrifice was the way to bring about some kind of rebirth of Creation, where Lucifer, the Morning Star, would rule! But it was nothing like this, not at all!'

'The Morning Star?'

'Yeah, I remember it in a lot of detail. Kind of hard to forget it, really.'

'So, how was that different to this? And do you think there's a connection?'

Gordy laughed at the suggestion, but the sound was cold, dark, and hollow.

'That's history, long dead history,' she said. 'Trust me. As for this being different? It's just too over the top, if that makes sense?'

'Ish.'

'What happened to Paul, it was brutal, more like a message, like something a gang would do as a warning to anyone thinking of crossing them, that kind of thing. What I dealt with before, I mean, three of the victims actually volunteered to be sacrificed! And those who didn't—yes, there were quite a few—were drugged up to their eyeballs. I doubt they had a clue what was going on. And it was all done with care, with this makeshift altar out in the middle of nowhere. There was a knife, they were killed quickly, cleanly, because the blood was so important. There was no hacking someone to pieces, no drawing a massive pentagram on the ground in blood, no body parts removed. As messed up as it all was, there was a reverence to it, and yes, it does make me shudder to describe something like that in such a way. But Paul's murder? That was frenzied, brutal. He was lured there, hacked to pieces, and I think the whole thing with the pentagram—it's just window dressing, that's all.'

'What about his heart? The pineal gland?'

Gordy threw her hands into the air.

'How the hell should I know? How the hell should any of us know? I'd never even heard about the bloody thing till this week, didn't know it existed!'

'Well, you've got the team trying to find out more, so, hopefully, we'll have more to go on soon. What do you think the journalist wants?'

'A story,' said Gordy. 'My guess is that she's uncovered

something she thinks is useful, but that she'll only give it up in exchange for something. She has a source, you know?' she added. 'Someone on the SOC team.'

'No surprise.' Jameson shrugged. 'You worried about it?'

'I meant to mention it to Cowboy yesterday, but my mind was more focused on the postmortem. God in Heaven, what a mess ...'

Jameson stood up.

'I'll leave you to it,' he said.

Gordy forced the old memories to the dark recesses of her mind and rose to her feet.

'I'll come with you,' she said.

Leaving the office and heading downstairs, she found Vivek alone in the reception area.

'She didn't stay, then?'

'No,' he said, and held out a sheet of notepaper, neatly folded in half.

Gordy took it.

'And what's on here was important enough for her to want to come and give it to me in person?'

'She seemed a little hurried,' said Vivek. 'Agitated, maybe? There was definitely something up. She was distracted.'

'Probably got a sniff of another story,' said Jameson.

Gordy opened the sheet of notepaper. She frowned.

'Something wrong?' Jameson asked.

Gordy showed him what was written on it.

'And what's that when it's at home?'

'It's the address for a Dropbox folder,' Gordy explained. 'At least, I think it is. And I assume what's written beneath it is her address and mobile number.'

'Norton St Philip? Nice.'

'Is it?'

'Amazing pub there; The George Inn.'

'Do you navigate your entire life by pubs?'

'Yes, yes I do,' said Jameson. 'The George is ancient; fifteenth or sixteenth century. Samuel Pepys stayed there.'

'Fascinating.'

'Isn't it? So, what do we do with whatever that Dropbox file is, then?'

'We head back up to my office and see what we shall see, won't we?'

And with that, Gordy headed back up the stairs, with Jameson trailing along behind her.

# TWENTY

Having endured a little bit of resistance to being switched on, her computer making the kind of noises reserved by a mythical, and undoubtedly irritated, beast woken from its slumber to deal with some travelling hero intent on its demise, Gordy typed in the Dropbox address.

'You're a bit of a whiz with computers, then?' Jameson stated.

'Very much so,' Gordy replied. Crossing her fingers, she added, 'Me and Bill Gates? We're like that.'

On the screen were various movie and photo files. Gordy clicked on the first one, which was a photograph of a bustling pedestrianised area in an old marketplace with a bandstand in the centre. Market stalls were set out, and it was clearly very popular.

'That's Shepton Mallet,' said Jameson. 'When was that taken?'

Gordy checked the date.

'Yesterday afternoon. So, she must've headed there after she'd tailed me.'

'Or maybe she had been heading there anyway, and you were a distraction? What do you think we're supposed to be looking at?'

Gordy leaned in. Jameson, who was standing behind her, did the same. She caught a faint note of mint on his breath, and wood smoke from his clothes.

'Can't say I rightly know.'

Jameson leaned back and Gordy watched his reflection on the computer screen as he gave his head a scratch.

'It's just a crowd, isn't it?'

'Looks that way.'

'So, you think there's someone important in it?'

Gordy didn't answer, just moved on to the next file, another photograph.

It was the same crowd, only it seemed as though whoever had taken the photograph—Gordy assumed it was Alison—was homing in on one section of the crowd, who were milling around a stall selling various baked goods. The croissants looked particularly good, she thought, as she zoomed in for a closer look.

The next photo was closer still, but the three after that were from the same position, and she realised then, from the way the focal point of the photographs changed, that the subject seemed to be a figure in a black jacket. They had their hood up and were facing away from the camera.

'It's videos next,' she said, seeing three further files.

'And here's me with no popcorn,' said Jameson.

The first video was from the same position as the previous four photographs, and Gordy could now tell that, like the photographs, it had been taken from around waist height. She guessed this because a number of people walked in front of the camera, and provided her with some delightful close-ups of various backsides, one of which had been dangerously close to being exposed due to how low his trousers and boxers were being worn.

The next video had Alison on the move, following the one in the jacket at a distance, as they mingled with the crowd, checking out what was at various stalls.

'One to go, then,' said Jameson.

Gordy clicked on the last file. This one opened with the figure in the black jacket being the primary subject. They were no longer at the market, and were walking along a narrow street, along which tall houses stared down. Alison was keeping her distance, but she was very clearly following whoever it was.

'It's not exactly Hitchcock, is it?' said Jameson.

Gordy continued to stare at the screen, and for some reason found herself growing a little anxious. She wasn't sure why, exactly, but something about what they were watching had an undeniably sinister air. The photos, the video footage from the market, had all felt quite relaxed, just normal people getting on with the day-to-day. But this? It wasn't that. This was Alison following one person, and Gordy guessed she had been alone. The whole situation chilled her.

The figure in the black jacket swept around a corner, and from the way the image grew shaky, Gordy guessed that Alison had picked up her speed, perhaps worried she was going to lose whoever she was following. Gordy assumed the journalist figured the person to be of interest to her, but photos and videos of the back of someone in a jacket weren't all that much help.

On the computer screen, Alison swept around the corner after the person she had been following, and the image became immediately gloomy.

'That's not an alleyway I'd want to venture down in the middle of the night,' observed Jameson.

Gordy became aware of the sound of Alison's rapid footsteps, her breathing, as she upped her pace to get to the end of the alleyway.

'Judging by how Alison's racing down it, I don't think it's one I'd like to go down, even on the brightest summer's day.'

The end of the alleyway was in sight, showcasing a particularly high wall. Gordy hoped the path didn't finish in a dead end.

A figure stepped out in front of Alison. She stopped sharply, and Gordy heard her gasp. It was the person in the black jacket, their hood still up. They ran at Alison, and, camera shaking, Alison turned on her heel, and ran.

Gordy sensed the panic the journalist was feeling, felt her stomach twist as Alison came to the mouth of the alleyway and retraced her steps, her breath sharper now, more desperate, her pace not slowing. And behind it, they could hear the thundering impact of larger feet getting closer.

'Bloody hell,' said Jameson.

Alison stumbled back into the marketplace, disappearing into the crowd. Trying to hide, Gordy guessed. But even as she did so, she lifted her phone to point back the way she had come, and there, standing far off in the shadows, was the figure in the black jacket.

Gordy paused the video, scrolled back, stopped it where the figure had appeared at the end of the alleyway. She zoomed in, to try and get a better look at whoever it was, but she couldn't make out any facial features at all. And that made no sense. The jacket hood was large, deep, and lined with fur. Some kind of parka, she thought. But why couldn't she make out the face?'

'Whoever that is, they're wearing a balaclava,' said Jameson.
'What?'
Gordy leaned in close to the computer screen once again.
'You know, the kind you'd wear under a motorbike helmet or

for skiing. Not that I've done either of those things or have any interest in starting.'

Jameson was right. Whoever this was, their face was hidden by a black balaclava that made it look as though they had no face at all, hidden as it was in the dark recesses of the jacket's hood.

Gordy skipped forward to the last image from where Alison had returned to the marketplace. The balaclava was clearly still being worn.

Shutting down the computer, Jameson went back around the other side of her desk and took a seat. Gordy lifted her office phone and punched in Alison's mobile number. While she waited, she stared at Jameson. She let it ring just long enough to have Jameson stare back at her, worry lighting his eyes.

'No answer?'

Gordy tried again. Still nothing.

'No,' she said, replacing the phone in its cradle. 'How long will it take us to get to Norton St Philip?'

'Twenty, twenty-five minutes.'

'I'll be aiming for twenty,' Gordy said, and was out of her office chair and half running across the office, Jameson puffing along behind.

Something about what Alison had sent them was very, very wrong. That she wasn't answering her mobile had Gordy's mind doing backflips through various horrors that only the mind of an experienced police officer could dream up. Because they weren't dreamt up at all; they were real experiences stored away, memories of man's inhumanity to man, and the only use they served was to work almost as a sixth sense that something bad either had, or was about to, happen.

Leaving the car park outside the station, Gordy's wheels spun.

## TWENTY-ONE

Arriving in Norton St Philip, Gordy spotted the George Inn on their right, but Jameson said nothing about it, didn't even pass comment on the quality of the pints pulled, and instead directed them around to the left, down a hill, then right, and along a thin, horsetail of a lane. That the satnav was giving her the same instructions clearly didn't matter to him, and she said nothing, as she guessed it was helping him to keep focus, instead of worrying about what they were going to find.

'It'll be along here, somewhere,' Jameson said.

Gordy checked the satnav, saw that it was pointing to a location a couple of hundred metres along from where they were. She decided there was no need for stealth, no advantage in parking away from the house, then walking quietly in. If something was wrong, and she hoped to God that it wasn't, then they needed to be on it immediately. She'd even had Jameson call in for backup on the way, and Patti and Jack were racing to catch them up. According to Jameson, they were only a few minutes behind them. She wasn't going to wait, though, not a chance of it.

At the address Alison had given, Gordy whipped her vehicle into a gravel driveway, sending a spray clattering against a garage door as she skidded to a stop.

'You don't hang around, do you?' said Jameson.

'Life's too short to dilly-dally,' Gordy replied.

Despite the worry they were both consumed by, Jameson laughed.

'Oh, I'm absolutely stealing that one,' he said. 'Dilly-dally? Brilliant!'

Jumping out of the car, Gordy didn't even bother to shut her door, as she raced over to the front door, noting little on the way about the house other than that it was a fairly recent build, and had an air about it of everything being in order, all neat and tidy. That much was obvious just from the quick view she got through the window into the diner kitchen, a place sparse and clean, with no wall cabinets. Aa huge worktop-slash-breakfast bar sat in the middle of the space, and a neat stack of logs sheltered by the adjoining garage door.

The small lawn beside the driveway was mown short, with neat edges, and was bordered by a collection of clearly well-curated ferns, bushes, and other plants. The way they sat so neatly put Gordy in mind of a primary school classroom, children all sat on the floor in front of their teacher, desperately waiting for the next chapter of the story they were being read.

At the front door, Gordy went to press the bell.

'It's open,' said Jameson, just as Gordy noticed that herself.

She stared at the small gap between the door and jamb, felt her gut twist, then pushed the door inwards.

It swung silently on well-oiled hinges to reveal a hallway of grey carpet, white walls, and a single painting on the wall. Gordy took no interest in it as she stepped into the house, first checking the room on the right, the lounge.

'Alison?' she called, as she took in the tan leather sofa, the flat screen television, the large, full bookshelf, the books arranged by colour. The impression given was that of a collection of tiny sections of a rainbow, all stacked neatly together and prevented from escaping by various book ends, some of which were solid squares of wood, others of which were creations of fired clay.

Back in the hall, Gordy led Jameson through to the kitchen diner. It was quite something, she thought, wondering just what kind of money Alison was earning to be able to afford such a place. Maybe she had a partner, or perhaps an inheritance? But affording a place like this on her own seemed quite the stretch.

With nothing going on in the kitchen, Gordy and Jameson walked back into the hallway to find Patti and Jack at the door.

'That was quite the drive,' Jack said, and his wide eyes were enough to tell Gordy that Patti hadn't held back on the accelerator.

'What's the point of blues and twos if we don't get to drive fast when using them?' said the detective sergeant. 'Is she here? Alison, I mean?'

'Downstairs is clear,' Gordy answered. 'And we've had no response to us calling out.'

Jack said, 'Have you checked outside?'

'Not yet; you two mind doing that? There's the garage, and the garden wraps round the side and to the back of the house.'

Jack and Patti ducked back outside, and Gordy took the stairs, two at a time.

The landing was bordered by four doors. The first led to a small room which had been converted into an office. It, like the garden, and the rest of the house, was organised, tidy. The desk was clear, nothing left out at all. A few shelves contained books, and to Gordy's surprise, a collection of snow globes. Two walls had a large noticeboard displayed on each of them. Both were covered in notes, all joined to other notes with lines of thread. It was the kind of thing she'd seen on television programmes and films about the police, how they work, how this crime scene connected with that person. The ones in real life were just never that neat or well-organised, and the threads always ended up in a tangle.

She had a quick check of what was on each board, saw Paul's face staring back at her, a section of map that had, surprise-surprise, Hatchet Hill dead centre. No pentagrams, though, so perhaps Alison hadn't uncovered everything.

Moving on, she found the next room to be a bathroom. The bath was a standalone thing that must've cost a small fortune, and looked deep enough to swim in.

'Two rooms left,' said Jameson.

'And no sign or sound of Alison,' said Gordy. 'This is all very odd, isn't it?'

'Maybe she's out and left the door open.'

'You are walking around the same house as me, aren't you? There's no way someone who lives in a place like this, keeps it like this, leaves the door open. It's just not in their nature.'

Moving on to the next room, Gordy was starting to feel like this was playing out like a scene from a thriller, where each room checked simply ratcheted up the tension until the final door opened to the big reveal.

She pushed open the next door, and what stared back at her was more than enough to persuade her that this was no thriller.

This was real life.

And real life, when it wanted to be, was horrifying.

# TWENTY-TWO

For the first few seconds, each of which seemed to stretch out into aeons, neither Gordy nor Jameson said a word. And it wasn't just the shock of seeing what was before them that held their tongues; it was that words could never, would never, be able to truly capture what had been done to Alison.

No, thought Gordy, done was not an adequate word. Done implied little thought behind it all. It didn't take into account of what she could really only describe as the creativity which had been spent in turning Alison from a living, breathing human being, into ...

'Shitting hell, Gordy,' said Jameson, his voice sticking in his throat, as though ashamed to even be a witness to what had happened in that room, even simply as an observer. 'I ... I mean ... God in Heaven ...'

Gordy sensed that Jameson was close to leaving the room. His legs were fidgeting as though they were keen to take control and whisk him as far away as possible from the horror of it, and soon.

But the man stayed, and she felt that there was a determination in him to not just stand there with her to take it all in. No, there was more to it than that. She saw his fists clench, saw his whole body tense, his jaw set itself firm; this was a man dedicating himself to the ruination of whoever did this.

'It's okay,' Gordy said. 'You can take a moment.'

She said it because she felt she needed to, because she was the ranking officer, but she knew what his response would be even before Jameson had taken a breath to express it.

'I'm good,' Jameson said, the darkness in his voice so thick, so impenetrable, that Gordy caught an echo, perhaps, of the officer he had been so many years ago, the determination, the fierce and relentless nature of how he'd gone about his work. And that reminded her of someone, because of course it did; there was more of Jameson in Harry than Harry would ever care to admit.

Gordy reached into her jacket pockets, pulled out protective covers for their shoes, disposable gloves, and face masks. She handed Jameson what he needed, and noticed him holding his own small tub of vapour rub. He held it out for her.

'I've my own,' said Gordy, and they both dabbed liberal amounts beneath their nostrils.

Stepping into the room, Gordy quickly took as many photographs with her phone as she could. She had to work especially hard to switch off the part of her brain that was horrified and burning with rage at what had happened. She knew she had such emotions in abundance, but she had worked on her self-control for years. And what use were those emotions at a time like this, anyway? she thought. All they did was cloud the mind, confuse thought, distract.

Alison had been pinned to the wall, crucified upside down.

She was not naked, so that was something, thought Gordy, though not much. It was hardly a blessing, not when she took into consideration everything else. And the first thing that drew her attention was Alison's staring eyes.

Kneeling beside her to check the journalist's pulse, Gordy knocked into something she hadn't noticed, too drawn to the vision of terror in front of her. It was a large wooden bowl, and in it, blood from Alison's ruined eyes had collected, along with any blood that had managed to make its way down her body from her ankles. She also saw that two further bowls, both smaller than the first, had been placed under her wrists, which had also filled with her blood.

Gordy decided against moving the bowls, and adjusted how she was kneeling so that she wouldn't make a mess of the crime scene. She tried to avoid looking at Alison's eyes, but found herself constantly flicking back to stare at them, as though unable to accept what she was seeing was for real. Yet, it was, and she knew that this would haunt her for years to come, perhaps forever.

'They took her eyelids,' said Jameson, who had quietly come to stand beside her. 'Her eyelids, Gordy. Who does that? Who does any of this? And why? What the hell is wrong with people?'

Gordy couldn't say. She hadn't been able to find a pulse, so she stood back up.

'I'll tell you what's wrong,' Jameson continued, clearly not interested in Gordy providing an answer. 'People? They're a pack of bastards. All of them.'

'All?'

Jameson stayed quiet.

Gordy stepped closer to Alison, leaning in for a closer look to see exactly how she had been pinned to the wall.

'Christ ...'

Gordy wasn't one for that kind of language, especially after having fallen in love with a vicar, but right there and then, it was the only word that made sense. Yes, she'd said it as an expletive, but it was also a desperate prayer, a cry to whoever was out there listening, because she needed help to make sense of this.

'What is it?' Jameson asked.

'They pre-drilled holes. She's not nailed to the wall at all; she's screwed to it. One through both ankles, one each through her wrists.'

'What?'

Jameson stepped closer for a look.

'They brought a drill with them?'

'And the screws, probably even the Rawlplugs for the wall.'

Alison was in jeans and a plain, white T-shirt. Or it had been before everything that had been done to her.

'How the hell did they get her up there?' Jameson asked. 'She'd have struggled like mad, surely? You can't just hold someone up like that, can you?'

Gordy shook her head.

'And this is more than one person, isn't it? Someone held her up, made sure she was firmly in place and unable to move, while someone else ...'

'Secured her,' finished Jameson. 'What's with the bowls?'

Gordy couldn't give an answer, so didn't even try.

Around Alison's displayed body were symbols painted on the wall in what Gordy assumed was the journalist's blood. And there was a lot of it, all of it fresh, the lines of the symbols still dripping, joining them all up into some gory maze.

'Baphomet,' said Gordy, staring at a scarily accurate line drawing of a goat's head with huge horns.

'Pentagrams again,' added Jameson. 'They're really big into those, aren't they?'

There was even one on the ceiling. Blood from it had dripped down onto the neatly made double bed below, patterning it with a dot-to-dot of its mirror image above.

There was a gasp from the door.

Gordy and Jameson both turned to see Patti and Jack standing in the bedroom doorway.

'Don't come in here,' Gordy said, striding over to meet them and stop them from coming any closer. 'Anything outside?'

Patti and Jack weren't listening. They were staring over Gordy's shoulder, mouths open, aghast at what was before them.

Gordy repeated the question, and as she did so, managed to push herself out of the room and take Patti and Jack with her onto the landing.

'No, nothing,' said Patti. 'But then, Alison, she's in there, isn't she? So, we weren't going to find anything, were we?'

'Is there any sign of forced entry?'

'Sorry, we didn't—' Jack began, but Gordy stepped in.

'Right, I need you to check everywhere, understood? We need to know if the people who did this broke in.'

'They must've done,' said Patti.

'Why? Because the alternative is even more horrendous, that she knew whoever did this and let them in?'

'Yes.'

'Well, right now, we don't know which it is, and we need to know. I'm going to call Cowboy, get him and the SOC team over, and an ambulance. Did you get anywhere with tracking down Mr Rowe?'

'No,' said Jack. 'There are two running clubs in town. We spoke to members of both. No one knows anything about any Mr Rowe.'

'We're going to go along to both clubs, though, just to make sure,' added Patti, and Gordy saw Jack's lips go thin.

'Not a fan of running?' she asked.

'I tried it a while back,' Jack said. 'Even joined one of the clubs.'

'So, what's the problem, then? Why are you against going along, and as part of your job, I might add, so it's not like you have any choice, is it?'

Jack fell silent.

'Jack ...'

'There was ... an incident.'

'You mean you slept with someone and now it's awkward, is that it?' Gordy asked.

Jack's response was immediate.

'What? No! Of course I didn't!'

'Then what is it? What incident? How can something so bad happen at a running club?'

'I broke someone's ankle.'

Gordy glanced at Patti and saw her own mild shock reflected in her face.

'You ... what? How?'

'I was doing the park run,' Jack explained. 'It's on the path that goes around the field near the cricket pitch. It can be a bit of a scrum sometimes, when it's busy. I was trying to set a personal best, so I was really flying, wasn't I? Well, for me, I was, anyway. And, well, I went round this corner, and there was this bloke, and we kind of collided.'

'Hard enough for you to break his ankle.'

'Yes. Oh, and it was the club captain,' Jack added. 'I never went back. Just couldn't live it down.'

Gordy rested a firm hand on Jack's shoulder.

'Maybe they'll be pleased to see you,' she said. 'Water under the bridge and all that?'

'I put him out of action for over a year,' Jack said. 'So, I doubt that.'

'Well, I look forward to hearing all about it,' Gordy said. 'When do the clubs meet?'

'One's tonight, one's tomorrow,' said Patti, as a piercing

scream tore the house in two, chased by a cry of shock from Jameson.

Gordy snapped around and bounded back into the room, Patti and Jack behind her.

Jameson met her at the door, almost knocking into her as she arrived.

'She's alive, Gordy!' he said. 'Don't ask me how, but she is!'

## TWENTY-THREE

For the briefest moment, the shock of that scream, and of Jameson's revelation, caused Gordy to freeze. Alison was screwed into the wall. She had been tortured. She was alive. What the hell were they supposed to do next? What?

The next thing Gordy knew, she was kneeling beside Alison's head, cradling it as best she could, as Alison's scream broke itself on its own violence, shattering into cracked whimpers.

'Jack? The garage; the way this house is, my guess is that Alison has a toolbox of some kind in there, a power driver or something, or at the very least, a simple screwdriver. And bring a chair.'

'On it,' Jack said, and went thumping down the stairs and out the front door.

'Patti? Ambulance! Then call in the SOC team; we need this place ripped apart; there must be some trace here of who did this.'

'I'll grab the first aid kits from the vehicles as well,' said Patti, and was on the call as soon as she left the bedroom.

'Jameson?'

'All ears.'

'Her eyes, we need something to do something, I just don't know what.'

'Give me a minute ...'

Then Jameson was gone, and Gordy was left alone with Alison. She tried to think of something to say, some words of comfort, but such notions turned to dust in her mind, and were scattered to nothing by what had been done to the journalist. So, she busied herself by shifting the bowls of blood, careful to not spill any. The photos she had taken would be enough to show where the bowls had been before she'd moved them. And there would be no questioning as to why she had done so, she felt sure of that.

The detective in Gordy pushed her way to the front, as the caring side of her continued to stroke Alison's head.

'Who did this, Alison? Who? Was it the figure in the files you shared with me?'

Alison's answer was the cry of a cat trapped in a sack thrown into a river.

'We've got help on the way,' Gordy continued. 'Please, just stay with me, okay? I'm not going anywhere. I won't leave you.'

The cat in the sack was losing the will to live. Gordy couldn't allow that.

'I'm serious, Alison,' she said. 'Stay with me. Don't give up. Help us find who did this to you. Please ...'

Alison's body shuddered and Gordy saw fresh blood ooze from the wounds through which the screws holding Alison to the wall had been driven.

Jameson arrived carrying a bowl of water and some small towels.

'It's all I could think of to do,' he said, crouching beside Gordy, on the other side of Alison's head.

He took one of the towels, soaked it in the water.

'I know it's probably not hygienic, but it's better than nothing, right?' Then, to Alison; 'Alison? I'm going to rest something over your eyes, okay? It's just a damp towel, that's all. Try to not panic.'

To Gordy's surprise, as soon as Jameson laid the towel across the journalist's eyes, her body relaxed. Perhaps the darkness helped, she thought.

Patti and Jack arrived back at exactly the same time.

'Air ambulance is on its way,' she said, the two first aid kits in her hands. 'They'll drop down on the cricket pitch. Paramedics will stretcher her over once she's stabilised.'

Jack stepped forward. He was holding what looked like a small, plastic suitcase in one hand, a wooden chair in the other.

'Power driver, like you guessed,' he said. 'Fully charged, too. Chair's from the dining room. How do you want to do this?'

Gordy, with Alison's head still in her hands, took barely five seconds to decide.

'Patti, Jameson, and I will keep Alison steady and stable,' she said. 'You remove the screws, starting with the ones through her wrists. The three of us should be able to make sure that she doesn't suddenly drop. As soon as her wrists are free, we can take her weight, which will take the strain off her ankles. Use the chair so that you're right over where you need to place the drill. Once those are free, we can just carry her gently onto the bed. Everyone clear on that?'

Steely silence was the only response.

'Right then, let's get this done.'

Jack opened the plastic case and removed a power driver, quickly checking which screwdriver head to use, before fixing it into the chuck. He then crouched down by Alison's wrists ready to go.

Patti and Jameson stood on either side of Alison and held

her tight, bracing themselves and her against the wall, so that any movement as Jack removed the screws would be minimised.

'It's going to be okay,' Gordy whispered, her lips close to Alison's ear. 'But you're going to need to stay strong.'

Then, with a nod to Jack, she moved closer still, and took Alison's torso in her arms, pulling every ounce of strength she had into that moment.

Jack started on the first screw. Alison struggled, screamed, but the team held her tight, and the screw fell to the floor. The only sounds in the room were the whine of the drill, the screech of the screws complaining about being removed, and the awful cries and moans from Alison.

The second screw was out fast. Patti and Jameson held Alison so that she didn't fall, taking her weight with ease. Jack grabbed the chair he'd brought with him from the dining room, placed it against the wall, and moved on to the remaining screw at Alison's ankles. A few seconds later it fell to the ground.

'She's free,' Gordy said, and as though some unseen force was controlling their movements, they all worked together in quiet unison, gently bringing Alison down from the wall, then onto the bed.

Patti didn't wait for orders from Gordy and was straight on with the first aid kits, flushing out the wounds with saline solution, covering them with dressings. Gordy opened the other first aid kit, removed the wet towel from Alison's face, used more solution to wash her eyes as clean as she could, then covered each with a dressing.

A voice from the hallway downstairs bounded up to them.

'Paramedics! Where are you?'

'Here!' Gordy shouted back.

Footsteps raced upstairs and a woman and a man appeared in the door.

Gordy stood up as they approached, quickly ran through

everything that she could about how they'd found Alison, her injuries, that they'd just taken her down from the wall.

'I know someone somewhere is going to tell me that we should've left her there, that we risked injuring her further, but I stand by my decision; no way was I going to leave her hanging there.'

The paramedics stepped past Gordy and the others, and she watched them get to work, ushering the others out of the bedroom and onto the landing. The female paramedic dashed past and down the stairs, returning with a stretcher.

'We'll need all hands to get her to the air ambulance as quick as we can,' she said.

'Just direct us,' said Gordy.

With Alison stable and securely attached to the stretcher, the four police officers joined the two paramedics, and together they carried Alison to where the air ambulance was waiting. Once there, Gordy pulled her team away to let the paramedics get on with their job. Then Alison was away, and the low clouds swallowed the helicopter.

No one said a word as they all made their way back to Alison's house.

Outside the front door, Gordy brought them to a stop.

'Jack?'

'Boss?'

'You're Scene Guard. I know we didn't get the paramedics' names, but frankly, we had other things to worry about. Patti? Cordon off the house, then I want you and Jameson knocking on doors. This is a small place, as far as I can tell; someone must've seen or heard something.'

'And yourself?' Jameson asked.

'I'm going to have another look around the bedroom and be here for the SOC team. Patti, any idea when they'll arrive?'

Patti shook her head.

'Just as soon as they can. I told them what we were dealing with.'

And with that, Gordy sent them all off to get on with their tasks, then she made her way back upstairs.

## TWENTY-FOUR

With Alison now removed, the bedroom seemed all the more awful, as Gordy's focus was no longer on the victim, but on the evidence of what had taken place inside it.

Where Alison had been strung up, an imprint of her body remained. The hideous outline of where she had been hung was artistically presented to the world in red stains on a wallpaper of the most delicate wildflowers.

The bed was now all scrunched up from where Alison had been laid on it.

The three bowls were where she had left them, and the blood they contained still steamed a little.

Gordy moved in for a closer look at the symbols on the wall, hoping that something would click in her head, but nothing did. Alison was lucky to be alive, but her survival, she knew, was in the balance. The room was giving nothing up as to why she had been so cruelly attacked.

Leaving the room, Gordy quickly checked the last remaining bedroom, and found nothing untoward in it. The room they had found Alison in was the largest, and obviously her own, so she headed back for another look.

She saw the huge screws that had held Alison to the wall laying on the carpet, painted dark with blood and ripped scraps of flesh. She knelt beside them, and allowed her eyes to glide around the room in the hope that something would jump out. Nothing did. Which was when Gordy realised that perhaps that was exactly what she was noticing—the fact that nothing jumped out at her at all. The bowls though, they were calling to her. Why were they there? What was the point of collecting the blood?

Standing up, she walked back out onto the landing, trying to get her thoughts to make some sense. What was it Harry always said? Look for the thing that isn't there but should be, or the thing that should be, but isn't? That wasn't quite right, but it was about all her befuddled mind could manage right then. But it was enough to help her realise what it was that she was, or wasn't, noticing: there was no sign of a struggle.

Alison had been screwed to a wall, had her eyelids removed, yet the room looked undisturbed, so long as you ignored the evidence of what had taken place. When they had arrived, the bed had been neatly made, hadn't it? Covered in drips of blood from what had been painted on the ceiling in Alison's blood, but neatly made nonetheless. As far as Gordy was concerned, there was just no way what had happened to Alison in that room could have been done unless she had been unconscious, because surely the furniture, the bedclothes, would've shown signs of not just a struggle, but someone fighting for her life?

And there was another thing, she realised; Alison's wounds had been very obvious; the eyelids, the screws drilled through her ankles and wrists, but she'd not seen any evidence to suggest the woman had fought back. Where were the marks on her body, the signs of punches thrown, the bruising, anything at all to suggest she hadn't gone willingly?

Other questions were piling into her mind now, and Gordy left the bedroom and went along to what was Alison's office.

Sitting down at the desk, Gordy tried to imagine Alison at work. She wasn't about to try and boot up the computer resting on top of it; that would be something for the SOC team to be on with. But she decided a quick look through the drawers wouldn't do any harm.

The desk contained two small drawers and two large ones. The small ones were dedicated to stationery, though not much of it, a box of pencils, a box of erasers, a clean notepad, a stapler, and a tin of mints. The large drawers, however, held well-organised and clearly labelled files.

Gordy checked through the drawer on the left, and although she found plenty of interest—assuming she had any desire to sit down and look through numerous clippings from newspapers—she f ound nothing of importance. She moved on to the second drawer, flicked through more of the same, then slammed the drawer home.

Frustrated, she stood up, looked around the room, read what was on the two boards attached to the walls, stuffing her hands into her jacket pockets in frustration. Or she would've done if her right pocket hadn't been otherwise occupied. She pulled out Paul's notebook that Jameson had found in The Lamb and Fountain.

Flicking through its pages, then staring once again at page thirty-four, she heard the deep thrum of diesel engines outside, and knew that the SOC team had arrived.

She checked again everything that Paul had written or sketched out on the page, only this time noticing the numbers. She remembered assuming they were probably grid references or something, despite one or two of them being too long. And it was to one of those numbers she was now drawn; was it a mobile number? There were initials in front of it as well; DL. If it was a mobile number, then who on Earth was DL, and why were they so important that they would be on page thirty-four?

Gordy pulled out her own phone, was about to punch in the number, when something from one of the larger drawers burst back into her mind.

Stuffing her phone back into her pocket, along with Paul's notebook, she dropped back into the desk chair and opened the large drawer on the left. She flicked through the files, pulled out one dated twenty years ago. Inside were numerous newspaper cuttings. She'd not given them much time earlier as she'd flicked through, but something from them had hooked itself into her subconscious; but what?

A knock at the door caught her off guard, and Gordy swung around in the chair, the file falling from her hands to spill newspaper clippings all over the floor.

'Afternoon, Ma'am,' said Cowboy, his over-the-top western drawl front and centre. 'Hope I didn't disturb you or nothin'.'

Gordy dropped to the floor and quickly scooched up the spilled clippings.

'It's through there,' she said, directing Cowboy with a flick of her head to where they had found Alison. 'Third door along.'

'Need a hand?'

Gordy picked up the last few clippings, slipped them inside their folder.

'No,' she said, and stood up, which was when she remembered what she had seen.

Once again opening the file of clippings, she flicked through until she found the one she was looking for.

'There it is,' she said.

Cowboy came to stand beside her.

'There what is?' he asked.

Gordy lifted the clipping out of the clutches of the file that had held it for so many years.

The clipping contained a lengthy piece about a certain Mr Billy Parker. She skimmed through the text, caught references to the man's history, his crimes, how long he had been put away. But one thing jumped out at her above all, and that was the name beneath a photograph of the journalist who had penned the piece: Alison Read.

## TWENTY-FIVE

Come the evening, Gordy was shattered. The physical side of things was a given, because, like the rest of the team, she'd been on her feet all day, and the weariness in her legs was so bad that her feet were almost numb. Walking felt like she was dragging lumps of concrete along the ground, and every step was draining.

Emotionally, though, that was where the real exhaustion lay. There was just no amount of training, of preparation, of sessions with trained counsellors or whatever, that could prepare anyone for what they had found at Alison Read's house. Instead, you just had to face it head-on, and somehow try and maintain a distance from it all, otherwise that way madness waited.

The SOC team had got to work swiftly, the photographer coming in and this time managing to hold in the contents of his stomach. Then the others had taken over the house, marching in like a swarm of ants, going about their business in their PPE, collecting evidence, recording things, doing goodness-knew-what to make sure nothing was missed.

What had become apparent as the day had worn on, was that there had been no forced entry. Gordy had wondered about this from the state of the bedroom in which Alison had been found; it had shown no signs of a struggle, of her fighting back, fighting for her life. Unless Alison had accidentally left the house open, only to find her attackers waiting for her when she had returned from driving over to meet with Gordy, then they had entered freely.

That in itself was chilling, thought Gordy, as she pulled into an available parking space in front of the building where she lived. To enter freely implied that Alison had known her attackers, and well enough to allow them to enter. Gordy knew that there was always the possibility of her having been attacked at her front door, but again, there was no sign of anything like that having taken place. That they had somehow then gained access to her upstairs, and then done what they'd done, was puzzling. Why would Alison take them upstairs in the first place? And if she hadn't, how had they all ended up there?

Pulling herself out of her vehicle, Gordy made her way somewhat sluggishly up a short flight of concrete stairs to her flat. The front door groaned open, and she almost fell over the threshold. Heaving it shut behind her, Gordy's only thought then was that there was a very good chance her evening would comprise the sofa, some rubbish on the television, and a hefty glass of wine, perhaps even a takeaway. After all, Evercreech had a cracking little chippy, so why not?

With thoughts of a comfortable, cosy night ahead, Gordy pulled off her jacket and went to hang it up on one of the hooks in her small porch when she spotted an envelope lying on the doormat. Tempted as she was to ignore it, the inquisitive side of her was far too strong, and she opened it. Inside was a short note from John and Doreen, just to let her know that she had no need to bring anything, as food and drink would be provided, and that there was a good chance they would be joined by some others from the church as well, and that they hoped that was okay.

Stuffing the note back inside the envelope, Gordy yawned so loudly that the sound reminded her of the distant roar of the lions from Longleat Safari Park. She'd not yet visited the place, but it was only a few miles out of Frome, and she had, on a couple of occasions, driven past with her window down and heard the thunderous, echoing roar of hungry lions on the wind.

Was she too tired to go? Yes, of course I am! she thought. She was also very close to being late, seeing as it was already gone seven in the evening, and she was supposed to be there for seven-thirty.

All Gordy really wanted to do was shut the world out, rest, and recharge for the days to come, because she was going to need all the energy she could muster, of that she was sure.

With the envelope in her hand, she left the porch and shuffled down the hall to the kitchen, grabbing a bottle of wine on the way, before then taking herself into the lounge.

The wine was white, and just cool enough, thanks to the kitchen having no heating to speak of. She grabbed a glass from a small cupboard against the wall, removed the screw top, then sank into the sofa, where she filled her glass to the brim.

Gordy lifted the glass, realised she was about to spill the wine, and dropped her mouth to it to sip at the liquid as she raised it to her lips.

Leaning back into cushions so soft they threatened to swallow her, Gordy's eyes fell upon a collection of photographs she had on a small table beside the television. All sat within a hotchpotch of frames, most of which were bought from charity shops. The display was in many ways rather old-fashioned, but she didn't care; all that mattered, really, was the face of the person staring back at her from the opposite side of the room, the bright smile she wore, and those eyes so full of love.

'What?' said Gordy, as she took another sip, talking as she did now and again to Anna, the photographs working in so many ways to help her remember the woman who had captured her heart so easily, and looked after it so carefully. 'It's been a long day and I'm tired.'

Another sip.

'And I'll no' be going out tonight, either,' she added. 'I did well, I think you'll agree, to go to the church in the first place. Expecting me to start mixing with the congregation socially? That's a big ask. I'm not ready.'

The glass was soon empty, so Gordy refilled it, telling herself that with that one she would slow down.

'Looking at me like that isn't going to make any difference, you know,' she said, as the fresh glass was soon half empty. 'Anyway, I want fish and chips, don't I? Kind of got my mind set on having that now. And the idea of making polite chitchat around a dining table is not my idea of either a good evening, or the perfect way to relax.'

A knock at the door interrupted Gordy's one-sided discussion.

'I'll be back in a minute,' she said. 'This isn't finished, you hear?'

With glass in hand, she made her way down the hallway to the porch as another knock rattled through the flat.

Gordy opened the door.

'Doreen ...'

Doreen smiled so widely and warmly that Gordy felt the hard shell she had put on as soon as she had arrived home just crumble away. The woman gave her a huge hug, and it was all Gordy could do to not sag into it and cry a little.

'Thought I'd see if you wanted a lift?' Doreen said, stepping back out of the embrace she'd just given Gordy. 'I won't be drinking, anyway, so I can drop you back home afterwards as well.'

'You're only in the village though, aren't you?' said Gordy.

'You've surely had a hard day, though, yes? Thought I'd save you the effort of the walk. It's not far, I know, but there we are.'

'That's very kind of you.'

'Not at all! I can just wait here while you get yourself ready. John's on with the food anyway—he's the chef, you see—so there's really nothing for me to do except make sure our guest of honour arrives!'

Gordy couldn't help but be taken in by Doreen's wide-smiled kindness. Exhausted as she was, she invited the woman inside, showed her through to the lounge, and asked for ten minutes to freshen up.

In the end, it was just over fifteen minutes, but somehow Gordy had managed to jump in and out of the shower, and find some clothes that didn't look too un-ironed.

'Ready?' Doreen asked, when Gordy entered the lounge.

'Never more so,' Gordy replied.

Doreen led Gordy out of her own flat, then drove her to the edge of the village, parking up in front of a cottage with a lawn to the front and a small number of trees.

'Apples,' said Doreen, as they walked from her car to the front door. 'John likes a bit of cider, you see? So, he has a go at making his own.'

'What's it like?'

Doreen stopped, rested a hand on Gordy's arm, and said, 'Cleansing.'

Gordy screwed her face up a little.

'Cleansing? I've never heard of any drink I'd want to try described like that. Is it really that bad?'

'Not so much bad as terrifying,' said Doreen. 'One pint and you'll feel wonderful, trust me. His apple juice is just as good, but not so lethal.'

'By wonderful, do you mean drunk?'

Doreen's reply was but a smile.

Duly advised, Gordy followed Doreen through her front door and into the house.

'This way,' she said, guiding Gordy down the hallway to another door at the far end.

Gordy followed, then when Doreen opened the door, was nearly sent tumbling back down the hallway by the loud cheer from the other side.

Stepping into the room, Gordy found herself in the presence of over a dozen people, all of whom she recognised from her one visit to the church that Sunday. Clive was there, too, his arm around a woman who smiled at her and gave a little wave with her fingers.

'What's going on?' she asked, hesitating on the threshold.

John approached and handed her a half-pint glass filled with a bright, golden liquid.

'Just a little welcome party, that's all,' he said. 'Hope you don't mind?'

Gordy really didn't know what to say, lifted the glass John had given her to her mouth, sniffed the liquid, and immediately remembered Doreen's words about the cider her husband made.

A quick sip, and she lowered the glass.

'You really didn't have to,' she said. 'It was Anna who was supposed to be here anyway, not me.'

'And yet here you are anyway,' said Doreen. 'And we've all been so worried about you. I've not slept a wink for weeks!'

'Months, more like,' said John. 'Anyway, sorry for the shock. I'm sure you'll recover.'

Gordy, still somewhat taken aback, was tempted to turn tail

and run. But then she remembered Anna's photographs in her lounge and the awful look she would give her if she dared to return early.

She placed her glass on the side, and took off her coat.

'Only one way to find out,' she said, picking up her glass of cider and necking it.

## TWENTY-SIX

Gordy was at the hospital, sitting beside the bed of Alison Read. Alison's eyes were covered in bandages, as were her wrists. Her ankles were hidden beneath the bedsheets. Her skin, Gordy noticed, seemed not just pale, but grey, as though despite her still being alive, all life had left her, or perhaps her love of it had. There was no colour to it anymore, no one thing that would ever be able to take away what had happened, and somehow make everything seem, if not better, at the very least, okay.

Opposite her was a man with a beard coloured like a badger, his black beard cut through with stripes of grey bristles. He was small and wide, but not overweight, and he wore a waxed jacket as cracked as mud on a sun-scorched riverbed.

'Bloody glad her mum's not here to see this,' he said, his voice soft, but holding an undeniable strength within it.

The statement left Gordy unsure whether he meant that Alison's mum was simply elsewhere and couldn't get to the hospital, or had passed away. Not that such a detail was important.

'Mr Read,' she said, but the man shook his head firmly

enough to let her know she didn't need to say anything, and that indeed, there was nothing that she could say.

'Don't go wasting any of your words on me,' he said. 'I know this isn't your fault, so I won't have you saying sorry, or anything like that. Always warned her something like this would happen. Well, not exactly like this, but I said often enough that all that poking her nose in where it wasn't wanted would get it bitten off.'

The evening before had, quite to Gordy's delight, been a surprising amount of fun. The lift to and from the house by Doreen had been very much appreciated, especially when the evening came to a close. The cider had gone to her head a little, and when she'd walked outside, the fresh evening air had hit her hard. Having barely felt the effects of the drink in the house, outside, her legs suddenly felt a little unsteady. Cleansed she may have been, but pissed she was as well. Not much, but enough for her to think that the walk home would've undoubtedly taken considerably longer.

As well as the welcome and the cider, the evening had involved some lovely finger foods, lots of talking, and to her surprise, a jolly good sing-song. But instead of old folk tunes, or perhaps popular chart hits from the seventies and eighties that everyone knew, they had started off with various classics from primary school assembly. Gordy had been astonished to discover that she could still remember the words to classics like, 'All Things Bright And Beautiful,' 'Give Me Oil In My Lamp,' 'Kumbaya, My Lord,' and even 'The Ink Is Black, The Page Is White.' Duly warmed up, Gordy had then found herself belting out various hymns, most of which she knew because of Anna. Her voice had carried well, and by the end of the night, some of the other guests had done their best to try and persuade her to come along and join the church choir.

The evening done, and having been dropped back home by

Doreen, who had presented her with a couple of bottles of cider from John to keep in the fridge 'just in case,' Gordy had slept well and deep. Waking that morning with a craving for Crunchy Nut Corn Flakes, she'd found herself feeling considerably better than she had expected to, especially considering the amount of cider she'd drunk the night before. Perhaps it was cleansing, after all.

With none of her desired cereal in the house, and with enough time before she wanted to be in the office, she'd popped down to the Co-Op and grabbed a box, along with some fresh milk and something for dinner later on; just some fresh pasta, eggs, parmesan, and smoked streaky bacon. Spaghetti Carbonara was a favourite of hers, and was something she'd made for Anna often enough, so it would give her something to look for at the end of the day.

Back in her flat, she'd managed two bowls of the dangerously delicious cornflakes, and a large mug of tea. Despite the early hour, she'd tried the mobile number she'd found on page thirty-four of Paul's notebook. The call had gone straight to voicemail, so she'd left a message, made herself some sandwiches for lunch, then driven over to the office.

After a quick catch-up with Patti, who she had every faith in keeping tabs on the team, while also checking up on everything from Cowboy and the SOC team, Gordy had jumped straight back into her vehicle and gone to the hospital.

Alison's father had been at her bedside when Gordy had arrived, which had rather surprised her, not just because she hadn't been expecting to find anyone with her, but also because visiting hours were in the afternoon and evening, not the morning. As a police officer, such restrictions were easily waived, so she was intrigued as to how the man had managed to do the same. So far, he'd given no explanation.

'Been here long?' Gordy asked.

'Long enough,' the man answered.

Having introduced herself on arrival, she wondered at what point Alison's father would offer her his name beyond Mr Read. Perhaps he never would, she thought; he had no need to, really.

'Do you know if she's been awake at all?'

'There's too much in her system right now to have her anywhere near conscious,' Mr Read said. 'Probably for the best, I think, with what's been done to her.'

At this, he lifted his eyes to meet Gordy's, and she saw them narrow on her with the calculated coldness of a hawk readying itself to pounce on its prey.

'You mind if I ask you a few questions?' asked Gordy, holding the man's stare with sufficient ease to let him know she wasn't the kind of person he could intimidate or frighten, assuming, of course, that had been his aim. She suspected otherwise, however; the stare sent her way was only because the real culprit was yet to be found.

'Go ahead,' Mr Read said. 'It'll break the silence.'

'Do you know if Alison was expecting visitors yesterday?'

'Wouldn't have the faintest idea. I live over in Bruton, so it's not exactly far, but we don't see each other much. We talk most weeks on the phone, but time goes by without you realising, doesn't it? And Alison is a very private person. Never been married, either. Not that it matters, does it? Half the time, I think most of those who get married shouldn't have bothered in the first place.'

Gordy wondered if he was speaking from experience, but decided not to ask that question. And she knew where Bruton was, having driven through it a few times, usually when taking a thin lane out of Evercreech to vary her route to work. It was, quite clearly, a place occupied in the main by people with money, with high-end restaurants, private schools, and a very fancy art gallery.

'Her house is certainly a clean, well-ordered place,' she said.

'That's Alison; a place for everything, and everything in its place.'

'Why journalism?'

That question brought the thinnest of smiles to Mr Read's face, and it died as soon as it dared show itself.

'To annoy me, I think,' he said.

'How so?'

'As well as being a surgeon, I was a local member of Parliament for most of my life,' Mr Read explained, 'so I've little time for anyone who gets involved in that world. Had enough run-ins with the press to know half of what they say is made up, and the other half pure fantasy.'

A jaded view, for sure, thought Gordy, but she understood why some felt like that. And his confession of his career as a surgeon explained both how he lived in Bruton, and how he'd managed to get the hospital to waive its visiting hours.

'Did she ever talk about her work?'

'Incessantly. Frankly, it was all she talked about. No denying she's done well, either. Worked for some of the big papers, but the pressure got to her, so she moved back to Somerset a couple of years ago. How else do you think she afforded that house? Flogged a tiny flat in the city for a fortune. The place was no bigger than the outside privy my dad grew up with, as he was always so keen to point out, what with the luxury we had by being able to use a toilet you didn't have to use a map to find at the bottom of the garden, or take a hammer with you to break the ice.'

Mr Read was someone who liked to ramble a little, Gordy realised.

'When was the last time you spoke?'

'Monday evening.'

'And did she mention anything she was working on?'

'She did.'

Blood from a stone as well, it seemed.

'Can you remember anything about it?'

Mr Read leaned back in his chair, folded his arms across his chest.

'It was about Billy,' he said. 'That case, all those years ago, her reporting on it? That was her ticket into the big time. Next thing I know, she's telling me something's happened that's linked to him somehow. She didn't say much, but enough for me to warn her off.'

'How do you mean?'

'She didn't give me any specifics. All she said was that she'd heard about a body, a murder, and that its location, and who it was, made her think it was to do with Billy. I tried to warn her off, by which I mean I got a bit shouty, and she hung up. And now here I am, sitting beside her hospital bed. Being a parent, it never changes, you know? No matter how old you get, they're still your kids, and you'd still do anything for them. Anything.'

That last word was sent at Gordy with such laser-guided precision that she almost felt like it had burned a hole in her chest.

'Will she be okay?' she asked.

'Not for you to worry about,' Mr Read said. 'Your job is to find those responsible, isn't it?'

Gordy took out her phone, pulled up some screenshots from the Dropbox file Alison had left for her, then sat beside Mr Read and went through them slowly.

'Do you recognise who this is? Alison was following them, then they chased her. My gut tells me whoever this is, they had something to do with what happened to her.'

Mr Read stared at Gordy's phone.

'I never met Billy,' he said. 'All I knew about him was from what I read in the papers, what Alison told me, what she wrote. My guess is, that's him and that he's after a bit of payback.'

'Did Alison ever mention anything about Billy being involved in any kind of cult? Satanism, that kind of thing?'

Mr Read's expression was incredulous.

'Satanism? What? You're having a laugh.'

Gordy's face remained impassive.

'Of course she didn't. Satanism? He didn't need something like that to blame for how he lived. He was evil, plain and simple. The person I always felt sorry for was that mate of his, the one who helped the police apprehend him.'

Now that was an admission Gordy hadn't been expecting.

'You know about that?'

'Probably shouldn't, but like I said, Alison didn't half like to talk about her work.'

'Did Alison say anything else about him, about this friend?'

'I know he's the one who was murdered on Hatchet Hill.'

Gordy sighed, shook her head, felt a headache coming on. Whoever the source was that Alison had on the SOC team, she wanted to find them and wring their neck.

So, Alison knew more than she had been letting on. She also knew, or at least suspected, that Billy was involved. And, somehow, she'd managed to find him and follow him. Or that's what her dad thought, at least. And Gordy was inclined to agree. Billy was the most obvious suspect.

He was out on licence, had disappeared, then Paul is murdered, an old friend who, she guessed, Billy regarded as someone who had betrayed him. Then he turned his attention to Alison, maybe because she had found him, or perhaps he'd had had her in his sights anyway, because she'd reported on the case all those years ago.

But none of that explained the occult stuff surrounding both Paul's death and Alison's attempted murder. Because that's what it had clearly been; whoever had done it had expected her to die on that wall, not be rescued. Gordy had been given a full explanation by Cowboy as to exactly how that might have happened, had they not found her in time. Death would've been partly from blood loss, but also from the lungs being compressed by other organs, causing difficulty with breathing and eventual suffocation, and blood pooling in the brain causing blood vessels to rupture, the brain to haemorrhage, the heart to fail.

Gordy took one last look at Alison, rested a gentle hand on Mr Read's leg in some attempt at showing comfort, then rose to her feet.

'She's never had a problem sleeping, you know.'

The randomness of the statement had Gordy stop mid-step.

'Pardon?'

'Sleeping,' Mr Read said. 'Always slept well as a baby, right the way through her childhood, never had an issue with it. She's never complained about it, never mentioned it.'

'I'm sorry, I'm not sure I understand.'

'Flunitrazepam.'

Gordy said nothing, just waited for further explanation.

'It was found in her system. No one actually told me that, you understand? But it's amazing what you can find out when you visit your old workplace, isn't it?'

'And flunitrazepam is a sleeping tablet?'

'Better known as Rohypnol. Apparently, there was enough in her system to knock out an elephant. General view is she overdosed. Well, I know she didn't, because I know my daughter.'

'She was drugged, then?'

'How else do you think they pinned her to the wall?'

Gordy stared at Mr Read, her teeth clenched, wary now of the man and his hawk-like stare, the danger in it.

'Yes, I know what happened, what was done to my Alison,'

Mr Read continued, the words coming at Gordy through gritted teeth. 'And like I said, I'd do anything for her.'

'Mr Read, I think I need to make it clear that the police—'

Mr Read's reply erased Gordy's voice from the conversation.

'The police let Billy out, lost him, and now my daughter is probably going to lose her eyesight, and will spend the rest of her life haunted by what was done to her. Find him, that's all I'm saying. Find him. Old I may be, but I tell you, that makes me even more dangerous, doesn't it?'

'How?'

'I've lived my life, and I'm old,' Mr Read said. 'I've nothing to lose, and if you think what was done to Alison with a blade was horrifying, you can only imagine what the trained hands of a surgeon could do.'

For a moment, Gordy held Mr Read's gaze. He was hurting, and she understood that, and the heat of his rage had dried whatever tears he'd already cried. She knew that warning him further would be of little use. But this, it was an added complication. The last thing she needed was a vengeful parent spending his retirement roaming the streets to right a wrong. She'd have to keep an eye on him somehow.

'I'll be in touch,' she said, and at last broke free of Mr Read's stare, but as she left the ward, the old man sent a final few words to chase her out of the doors.

'I've nothing to lose, Detective, just you remember that ... nothing to lose at all ...'

# TWENTY-SEVEN

Gordy wasn't one for eating on the move. Dealing with a sandwich spilling ingredients all over her lap while driving wasn't setting a good example for other motorists.

As the main road back from Bath was scant when it came to places to pull over, she took a left down a narrow lane, just to see if there was something more interesting to look at than the rear ends of vehicles flying past.

The lane was lined by hedgerow, cutting off her view of the fields on either side, and around one corner she came face-to-face with two sheep happily munching on the verge. They stared at her as she came to a stop, then, with the air of teenagers sticking two fingers up at someone telling them to get a move on, they turned around and trotted nonchalantly up the lane.

Gordy followed, seeing that ahead there were no gates into fields to speak of. The sheep didn't seem to care; this lane was theirs and she was trespassing.

Eventually, the sheep came to a stop outside a gravel drive, beyond which Gordy could make out a large, detached house poking its windows through the branches of tall trees. They stared down at her like spying eyes.

Instead of dipping straight into the drive, the two sheep turned and stared at Gordy just long enough to give her the message that they didn't appreciate being hurried. Then, at last, they made their way up the drive, like it was theirs anyway. And perhaps it was, Gordy thought, because what better lawn mower could there be than two sheep?

After this brief encounter, the lane dipped and rose and twisted itself between field and woodland, before it ran itself out at a main road. Gordy turned right and was surprised to pass a castle, before then popping over an old bridge beneath which a wide river ran dark and slow. As she did so, she spied cars parked in a field to her right and, seeing the gate open, decided to go and investigate.

Driving into the field, she parked up, and saw someone sitting at a small table at another farm gate. It was a man clearly in his retirement years, and he was wearing a bobble hat and a thick jacket. On the table was a flask, a small Tupperware box, and a money tin.

'Hello,' Gordy said, coming to stand at the table. 'Just popped in as I could do with a quiet place to eat my lunch. That okay?'

'You a member?' the man asked.

'Do I need to be?'

'You do.'

Gordy looked through the gate. She could see a small gathering standing around a collection of bags. They were also all wearing bobble hats, and those god-awful robes outdoor swimmers wore.

'I just want to eat my sandwiches.'

'You don't want to swim?'

'Do I have to?'

'Well, I'm not going to force you to, but it's very good for you, you know.'

Gordy cast an eye up into the sky, the low cloud and cool temperature making her less than keen to even consider the idea of a dip.

'So I've heard,' she said. 'Where am I, by the way?'

'This is Farleigh Hungerford,' the man said. 'And this is the swimming club.'

'It's a field.'

'It is.'

'How is a field and a river bank a club?'

'Means we can keep it as it is,' the man explained. 'A nice, safe place for members to come and swim in the river. And it's the oldest river swimming club in the country, so that's something special, isn't it? Exclusive, I like to think. But, like I said, you need to be a member.'

Gordy watched the small group in the field beyond the gate remove their robes to reveal their swimsuits, and then make their way over to where she assumed was a place to throw themselves in.

Gordy was tempted to go and sit and eat her lunch in her car, but found herself asking how much a membership actually was.

'Twelve quid,' the man said. 'And I can take cash or card.'

'Twelve quid a month? To swim in a river?'

The man laughed.

'Goodness, no. That's for the year. Once you've joined, you're free to enjoy the river. It's not open all year, for obvious reasons.'

'And they are?'

'Well, to be honest, it can be bloody hideous down here in the winter. We can't have vehicles driving across the field and making a mess of it. The river is freezing. During the spring and summer, though? It's glorious.'

Gordy wasn't convinced, but something still held her on the spot.

'Twelve quid for the year?'

'That's right. Pay now, and then you're good to go.'

'Do I have to buy one of those robe things?'

'Only if you want to. You're right though, they are a bit of a uniform, aren't they? Worth it, though. Beats trying to change under a towel.'

Gordy's stomach rumbled. Then, before she knew what she was doing, she had her bank card out and had paid.

'You won't regret it.'

'You sure about that?'

The reply she received was a mischievous wink and a smile.

Pushing through the gate into the next field, Gordy heard yelps and laughs from the river, which was hidden from view by trees and thick bushes. She walked over to have a look, and saw the group she'd spotted earlier now floating around in the black waters.

'How is it?' she called out.

'Cold!' one of the group shouted back, a slim woman wearing a bobble hat. In fact, they were all wearing bobble hats, Gordy noticed; as much a part of the uniform as the robes. 'Lovely, though. You jumping in?'

Gordy shook her head, then added, 'I ... er ... forgot my swimming stuff.'

'I've some you can borrow, if you want? Seems a shame to come all this way and not get in, don't you think?'

Gordy was struck by the kindness of the reply, but as she desperately scrambled for a way to politely turn it down, her phone rang, giving her the excuse she needed to thank the woman for the offer and turn around to take the call.

'Detective Inspector Haig,' she said.

'Hello inspector,' came the reply. 'This is Dean Lucas. You left me a message to return your call?'

Dean Lucas? thought Gordy. She'd never heard the name in her life.

'Just having my lunch,' she said.

'You mentioned Paul Edwards,' Dean said. 'That's a name I've not heard in a while. Is everything okay?'

Gordy remembered then the number she'd found in Paul's notebook, and the initials DL.

'Would you be free at all to meet for a chat?' she asked.

'I'm free all afternoon, actually,' said Dean. 'And the rest of my life, if I'm honest. The joy of being seventy-one! Where are you? I live in Bradford-on-Avon, and I'm happy to drive. Are you at the station in Frome?'

'Right now I'm at Farleigh,' said Gordy. 'And I've really no idea where that is.'

'I'm a member of the swimming club,' replied Dean. 'You should join. A dip in the river is so good for you.'

Gordy laughed.

'I've just joined, actually. Not swimming though, just eating my lunch.'

'Well, if you wait there, I'll be down in twenty minutes. I could do with a dip anyway; good for the circulation, you know.'

'Perfect,' said Gordy. 'Just let me know when you arrive and I'll come meet you.'

Dean laughed.

'Oh, you'll know when I'm there,' he said, and hung up.

With the conversation over, and somewhat baffled by the cryptic way Dean had ended it, Gordy took a bite of a sandwich, called Patti to let her know that her plans had changed, and found herself half wishing that all police work could be as easy as the imminent meeting with Dean at the riverbank to arrange.

## TWENTY-EIGHT

Whatever Gordy had been expecting, Dean Lucas wasn't it. She'd had in her mind nothing more than an older man parking his saloon in the field, no doubt wearing warm clothes to ward off the cool of the day. Dean Lucas was not that at all, not by any stretch of the imagination.

The thunderous rattle of an old engine was the first sign she received that with Dean, things were a little bit different. Having made her way back to her own vehicle in time to meet him, and now leaning on its bonnet, she saw a large, bright red van turn into the entrance to the field. Nothing strange there, except for the chimney in the roof, huge chunky tyres, and an honest-to-God snorkel rising out of the bonnet and up the side of the windscreen.

Gordy didn't know for sure that this was Dean, but the timing was right, and the arrival was certainly memorable, as the van bounded across the field looking as though it wasn't going to stop in the field at all, but instead continue to the river and then drive through it to the other side.

The van came to a stop and Gordy, brushing herself free of crumbs from her sandwich, walked over.

The driver opened his door and fell out of the vehicle, so high was it on the enormous tyres, waving to Gordy on his way to meet the ground. Gordy thought that the vehicle looked extra high, like the suspension had been raised.

'Detective Inspector?'

'Haig,' said Gordy. 'Gordanian Haig. But please drop the inspector stuff and call me Gordy.'

She held out her hand and Dean shook it, which gave Gordy enough time to take in the full vista of the man standing in front of her.

The first thing that caught her attention was his hair; he didn't have any. He was bald, his scalp so shiny it looked polished. Not that his head was lacking in hair in other areas; a long, thick beard covered the bottom half of his face, and hung down past his Adam's Apple. Whereas Alison's father's beard had been almost striped with black and white bristles, Dean's was as white as snow. It was also groomed so perfectly that it looked as though it was a beard you could remove, a thing which would hook over Dean's ears when not needed, or perhaps when he went to bed.

He was, despite the temperatures, wearing tan cargo shorts and flip-flops. His torso was covered by a waterproof jacket, beneath which lay a thick, olive-green woollen jumper. Gordy suspected it was army surplus, but it would be no use for that life now, not with the numerous, brightly coloured darns it displayed holding it together.

'Fancy a cuppa?' Dean asked. Instead of waiting for an answer, he strode past Gordy and heaved open a side door of the van, before stepping up inside.

Gordy followed and discovered that the huge vehicle was also part tiny log cabin.

'Up you come,' Dean said. 'Make yourself comfortable and I'll get the kettle on.'

Gordy clambered up and perched herself on a comfortable seat tucked under a small table. Another seat sat opposite.

The rest of the van had all the things anyone could ever need to head off into the wilds, she thought. There was a small kitchen, plenty of cupboard space, nets hung from the roof and were filled with books and maps and the occasional bottle of wine. A bed lay across the van at the far end at about waist height, and she guessed that another door she spied led to a loo and shower. There was also a small wood-burning stove, which explained the chimney.

'Here you go,' Dean said, placing a mug of tea in front of Gordy. 'Sugar?'

Gordy shook her head.

'You'll have a biscuit though,' Dean added, and put an open tin of chocolate-covered discs in front of her. 'Homemade shortbread,' he said. 'Perfect after a swim, I can promise you that. And before as well. Hell, these bad boys are perfect any time of the day or night.'

Gordy took a biscuit, bit into it, then sipped her tea, and found herself briefly considering the idea of owning such a van herself.

'It's quite something, this,' she said, gesturing around them with a wave of a hand. 'Looks like you're set to head off into the wilds, even if there isn't a road.'

'Retirement was difficult,' said Dean. 'I couldn't find any purpose. My wife suggested getting a van, because then we could do a bit of travelling if we wanted to. Not sure she ever expected anything like this, though. Did it myself, you know? Most of it, anyway. Left the hard stuff, like the electrics and plumbing, to the experts. I'd probably get everything back to front and upside down and end up having to use the loo as the oven or something. But the design is mine, most of the cabinets, the floor, the bed.'

'Love the stove.'

'Me too,' Dean agreed. 'Gets very cosy in here very quickly. So, why the call? Something up with Paul?'

'How well do you know him?'

'Not well, really; we weren't friends or anything like that; he just asked me about some stuff he was looking into, that kind of thing.'

'What kind of thing?'

'I'm really into local history,' Dean explained. 'My day job was accountancy, which was about as interesting as the proverbial watching paint dry. All started because our house is rather old and I looked into its history. Next thing I knew, I was digging through all kinds of stuff in the local area, making a bit of a name for myself from it as well, doing talks around local groups, that kind of thing.'

'Is that how you met?'

'It was. Did a talk for a group into all that paranormal stuff. Not my thing, really; I'm not one for sitting in a dark room and waiting for a noise to terrify my overactive imagination. But I love the stories, that's where my interest lies. Also, most of the talks are in little back rooms or upstairs in pubs, so there's always a chance for a beer.'

'Surely you mean cider.'

'Can't stand the stuff.'

'You met Paul at the talk?'

'He contacted me afterwards, and we looked into a few things together.'

'Like what?'

Dean took a glug of tea from his own mug, then rested it on the table and stared at Gordy.

'Seems odd,' he said, 'that I've got a detective talking to me about stuff I researched for someone I've not seen in years, who, as far as I'm aware, probably works with you?'

'I can see how it would seem that way.'

'You're not telling me everything, are you?'

Gordy placed her mug on the table in front of Dean's.

'Paul's dead,' she said, and gave no time for that stark fact to sink into Dean's mind. 'His body was found on a bridleway leading off a lane called Hatchet Hill. I found your number in one of his notebooks, specifically on a page relating to Hatchet Hill, which is a location Paul has a bit of history with.'

'Billy, you mean?'

Gordy sat back.

'I was expecting more surprise at the news of Paul's death.'

'It's shocking, for sure,' said Dean, 'but like I said, I didn't really know him, and it's been a few years since we were in touch. What happened?'

'Can I ask what it was you were researching for him?'

'Of course, it's no secret. Ancient rituals, pagan stuff, and some darker stuff, too, like witchcraft and black magic. Somerset's soil is soaked through with the stuff in places, you know?'

'Please don't mention Glastonbury.'

Dean smiled.

'Fun place to visit, though, isn't it? I love it.'

'So do I, actually,' Gordy agreed. 'Not really sure why.'

She did, though, but wasn't about to start talking about having her cards read. That she kept very private indeed.

For a moment, neither of them spoke. Dean broke the silence.

'Paul never said too much about what had happened at Hatchet Hill. I know it involved an old friend of his, someone called Billy who'd been into stuff Paul had no time for, drugs I think? But that's all that he ever told me. I didn't pry.'

'I'm struggling to see the connection between any of that and you,' said Gordy.

'Paul never truly accepted that Billy got into all of that of his own volition. He just couldn't accept that a childhood friend he thought he knew could keep such a secret from him. He believed someone or something else had influenced him.'

'Like what?'

Dean stood up and opened an overhead cupboard, then sat down again, placing on the table a blue file.

'Something told me I'd need this,' he said. 'I mean, why else would a detective who works with Paul contact me? Seemed to be the only conclusion to draw.'

'And what's this?' asked Gordy, looking at the file.

'Show me yours, I'll show you mine,' said Dean. 'By which I mean, give me some idea as to why you're sitting here sharing tea and biscuits with an old bloke in a van. I can guess, but ...'

Gordy took Paul's notebook from her pocket, opened it to the page on Hatchet Hill, and turned it around so that Dean could see it properly.

'I see,' said Dean, then opened the blue file.

## TWENTY-NINE

By the time Dean and Gordy had gone through everything in the file, talked through all that Dean knew, the day had worn on and what was left of it was threadbare. So, with enough to be thinking about, she'd let Patti know she'd not be in until the following day. She also mentioned the concerns she had about Alison's father. Not that she really expected him to go out on some kind of manhunt, but it was worth her DS being aware. Once that was done, Gordy had then headed home to Evercreech.

The flat welcomed her as best it could, but the place was cold and even though she put the heating on, it just didn't feel warm, despite the quick increase in temperature. She needed company, it was that simple, and sitting alone with her thoughts wasn't going to do her any good at all. A call to Jameson solved that, the retired DCI jumping at the opportunity to meet at The Bell for a pie and a pint. And he'd been very specific about those requirements, too, as though anything else simply wouldn't do.

Arriving at the pub, with Dean's folder under her arm,

Gordy ordered a drink and then settled herself down at a small table in the corner. She wanted to be out of the way enough for her and Jameson to talk privately without being overheard and sure enough, when a few others mooched in to perch themselves down for food, they left her alone.

Opening the file, Gordy ran through what it contained. She'd already seen most of it during her chat with Dean, but she wanted to see if there was anything that she'd missed. She also didn't want to just sit there staring into space as she waited for Jameson to arrive. There was always the danger that doing so would have her spend too long thinking about Anna, which wasn't healthy. She thought about Anna often enough as it was, so when the opportunity arose to actively not do so, she jumped at it.

A shadow cast itself across the table.

Gordy glanced up, expecting to see Jameson. Instead, another face was smiling down at her with a warmth she could almost feel.

'Clive,' she said, seeing the man she'd first met outside the church Sunday morning.

Though not in his tweed suit this time, his beard was as dishevelled as it had been then, and she briefly compared it to the four other beards she had encountered that week, two of which belonged to members of her own team. That's a lot of beards, she thought, as she waited for Clive to speak, closing the file as she did so. Maybe too many.

'You on your own?' Clive asked, lifting a pint glass to his lips, and Gordy heard concern in his voice.

She shook her head.

'Waiting for someone, actually. Just thought I'd park myself here out of the way.'

'Well, that's no good, is it?' said Clive. 'Friendly place like

Evercreech and you sitting here all on your lonesome? Why don't I join you, just until your friend comes? It's no bother at all. To be honest, I'd like the company myself! Love a good chin wag.'

Gordy appreciated the offer. She was all set to talk things through with Jameson, and figured a distraction would be good, because it would stop her overthinking for a while.

'Thanks, Clive, that would be lovely.'

Clive pulled out the chair opposite Gordy and sat himself down, resting his pint on the table.

As he did so, Gordy stuffed what she'd removed from the folder back inside, and closed it. She didn't want any of what was in there to be seen by anyone other than those on her team.

'Great evening last night, wasn't it?' said Clive. 'So much fun! But that's what happens when old friends get together, isn't it? Can't beat it.'

Gordy smiled.

'It was excellent, thank you. You all made me feel so welcome. I really wasn't expecting it at all.'

'You've a good set of pipes on you, too; can't beat a good sing-song.'

'Took me by surprise, that, but it was a lot of fun. Amazed I was able to remember so many of the words, especially considering how much of John's cider I was drinking.' Gordy took a drink, then asked, 'You've known John and Doreen a long time, then?'

'Years and years. Can't really remember when we met. We had more hair and less around the waist, that's for sure. But you know what it's like when you just click with someone, when you have the same drives, the same beliefs, that kind of thing.'

'You just hit it off, then?'

Clive leaned forward.

'Sometimes, I think you're just meant to meet certain people, aren't you? Like the Universe, the gods, whatever, it all just conspires to put your kind of people in front of you.'

'You're probably right,' Gordy agreed, though she wasn't entirely sure that was the way things worked. But if that was what Clive believed, where was the harm?

Clive glanced at the folder sitting in front of Gordy.

'Bringing your work home with you?'

'Something like that, yes.'

'Bad habit. Suffered from it myself plenty enough. I'll warn you now, it's not healthy.'

'What is it you do?' Gordy asked. 'I'll be honest, I thought you were retired.'

Clive took another swig of his pint.

'Tree surgeon,' he said. 'And if I bring my work home with me, I end up filling the lounge with chainsaws, which isn't the best, is it? And you don't want to be messing with those when you're tired.'

'This is no reflection on you' said Gordy, 'but I would've expected someone doing tree surgery to be a bit younger. I'm impressed.'

'You don't need to be. I'm old and knackered and should know better. Need to ease off. Can't go dangling myself out of huge sycamores with chainsaws hanging off my belt for much longer. It's exhausting.'

'I can imagine. What does Eileen think?' Gordy asked, having met Clive's wife the night before at John and Doreen's.

'After all of the years we've been married, I think she's finally come round to realising she's not much of a fan of me doing something so dangerous. I'm not twenty anymore, am I? Should've retired, really, but I'm not very good at that. Need to keep busy. Bills to pay as well, and they won't do that themselves, will they?'

'Any ideas, then?'

'I own some woodland. All I really need to do is manage it well, coppice it, and I've a nice little earner with firewood. Even sell a bit of John's cider on the side, as well, but I probably shouldn't be telling you that, should I?'

Probably not, thought Gordy, but she wasn't about to arrest him for a few bottles of cider sold for cash.

'I do a bit of that already, and I've worked the woods for years, just need to really throw myself into it, but life throws things in the way sometimes, doesn't it?'

'Like what?'

Clive snorted the smallest of laughs.

'Our son was supposed to take over the business.'

'What happened?'

Clive gave an odd shrug, and Gordy wasn't really sure how to read it.

'You know how kids are. Grass is always greener.'

'Well, I'm sure you'll sort it out.'

Clive's shrug turned into a firm nod.

'We've got things in hand, now,' he said. 'I'm fairly sure everything will turn out just fine, and soon, too.'

'That's good to hear,' said Gordy, and she saw Jameson bundle through the main door of the pub.

He spotted her, waved, pointed at the bar, mimed drinking a pint, then walked over to put in his order.

'My friend's here,' she said.

Clive stood up.

'I won't keep you, then. Good to chat. Nice to have you in the village, Gordy.'

Clive had gone by the time Jameson arrived, his pint sunk and left on a table as he left.

'Who was that, then?' asked Jameson, sitting himself down, and placing a second pint in front of Gordy.

'That was Clive.'

'You're making friends, then? That's a good sign.'

'It's a friendly place is Evercreech. Ended up being invited round to someone's house last night. Food, a sing-song, and the best cider I've ever tasted.'

'That's quite the statement.'

'Homemade as well,' Gordy said. 'John and Doreen, they've some apple trees in their garden and they make it themselves. Never tasted anything like it. I've actually got some in my fridge; they sent me home with a couple of bottles.'

'Well, if it really is as good as you say, I need to try some. Quality control, you see.'

Gordy glanced at the fresh pint Jameson had brought her.

'I've not even finished my first.'

Jameson laughed.

'Best you get a wriggle on, then! So, what've we got?'

'You want to order food first, or get straight into it?'

'Already ordered; two chicken and mushroom pies, with chips and peas.'

'How did you know?'

'Read your mind.'

Gordy reopened the blue folder.

'What's that, then?'

Gordy gave a quick recap on her meeting with Dean Lucas, then took Jameson through the contents of the file, passing things over to him as she did so.

'More pentagrams.' Jameson sighed. 'Really? I know there's a lot more in here than just that, but ...'

'But what?'

Jameson finished his pint and as he did so, Gordy saw their food being brought over, so she quickly stowed the folder away down by her feet.

Once the steaming plates were set in front of them, Jameson spoke again.

'The local church I get,' he said. 'Sometimes I even go myself, you know? It's nice to meet with people, spend a bit of time contemplating life, that kind of thing, and bellowing out a good hymn can't half do you good. Plus, there's always those church coffee mornings, aren't there? And who doesn't like a great big slab of homemade cake and a cup of tea?'

'There's a but, though, isn't there?'

'There is ...'

Jameson jabbed a finger in the general direction of where Gordy had placed the folder.

'I don't see the attraction in any of that,' he said. 'There's enough darkness in the world, isn't there? So, why would anyone choose to go down that route, lined as it is with all kinds of unpleasantness?'

'It's not all like that,' said Gordy. 'A lot of it seems to be very much about being in tune with nature, that kind of thing. I can see the attraction in that, especially if organised religion isn't your thing. And people do like to believe in something, don't they?'

'That's not what we're talking about here, though, is it?' said Jameson. 'You've a file there rammed full of all kinds of stuff about ancient rituals, blessing the land with blood, that kind of thing. Hell, there's even something about human sacrifice, isn't there? And it's not just that, either, is it? You've got spells in there, some really weird stuff about raising the dead even, and that's just not normal, is it?'

'I never said that it was. It can't be, can it? Why do any of it? But it does all kind of link to what Dean gave me, doesn't it? The pentagram drawn in Paul's blood and his missing organs, the way Alison was strung up and those bowls left to collect her blood.'

Jameson shook his head despairingly, then stood up.

'I'll grab us another,' he said, and walked back to the bar.

When he returned, Gordy was staring off into the middle distance, trying to get her thoughts together on what she'd learned from Dean.

'Paul thought Billy was into something,' she said. 'Arguably, this looks like it was a bit of an obsession for a time, but as Dean said, it's been years. They were both into the paranormal stuff, weren't they? And everything in that file, in Paul's notebook, shows that Hatchet Hill has a history.'

'There's not a lane, a path, a field in the whole of Somerset—hell, the whole of England—that doesn't have a history.' Jameson sighed. 'This whole country is a patchwork of old battlefields and ancient burial sites, and is run through with all kinds of myths and legends.'

'But what if Paul was right?' Gordy said, picking up her knife and fork and breaking open the pie. A thin phantom of steam escaped and quickly disappeared, leaving behind the most delicious aroma. 'What if Billy was into something?'

'And by something, you mean witchcraft and black magic?'

'I've no idea what I mean,' said Gordy. 'All I do know is that Paul and Billy were old friends. They were into the paranormal. Billy, it turned out, had a secret life screwing up people's lives with drugs. Paul, broken by this discovery and feeling betrayed, was instrumental in getting Billy put away. Yet something niggled at him, probably the fact he couldn't quite accept that the Billy he thought he knew so well was the same Billy who'd been supplying drugs.'

'So, Paul put two and two together and didn't so much get five, as a whole world of crazy in which Billy has been taken over by the Devil, who then not only brutally murdered his old friend, but tried to murder a journalist?'

'That's not what I'm suggesting.'

'It's what I'm hearing, though.'

Gordy fell quiet, focused on her food. Jameson, for once, sounded agitated, and that wasn't like him at all.

'Everything okay?' she asked.

Jameson didn't answer right away, busy as he was making good headway with his own pie. Eventually, though, he rested his cutlery together on his plate and sat back, arms folded.

'Sorry.'

'For what?'

Jameson's answer was to pull out his wallet and flip it open in front of Gordy.

'It would've been her birthday,' he said, showing Gordy a picture of a woman with a bright smile and kind eyes. 'Grief's something you never get used to, is it? Why do you think I jumped at the chance to come here? Beats sitting at home on my tod, crying into a pile of old photograph albums, doesn't it?'

Gordy said nothing, as Jameson put his wallet away and started back on his pie.

'I still talk to Anna,' she said. 'I've this little display of photographs in the lounge. It's kind of like having her there with me.'

Jameson gave a knowing nod, and they both finished their meals in respectful silence.

When they were finished, Gordy yawned deeply, and reached down for the folder.

'So, we're back to thinking Billy did it, then, do you think?' she said.

'I think we're better to sleep on it,' Jameson advised. 'Get home, get to bed, see what tomorrow brings. Ask the team, chat it all through, see if you've missed something.'

'Like what?'

'Motive,' Jameson said.

'We have one, don't we? Revenge?'

When Jameson replied, his voice was quiet, and hard as a diamond.

'Whatever this is, it isn't that, not by a country mile.'

'Then what is it?'

Jameson held Gordy's eye for a moment.

'Evil,' he said, 'pure and simple.'

Gordy could only agree.

## THIRTY

The following day, Gordy woke up feeling a little shabby, but that was easily chased away by four slices of toast and marmalade, and a couple of strong coffees. She wasn't surprised though by her foggy head, not considering the pints with Jameson, and the amount of food she'd consumed; portion size at The Bell Inn was very much on the generous side of things, and certainly wasn't something she'd ever be complaining about.

Following a quick rummage through her fridge, and a rushed bowl of cereal, she'd left Evercreech for work. The journey to the office was uneventful, and she drove most of the way on autopilot, her mind trying to work out what on earth she was facing.

Paul's murder had been shocking for sure, but the attempted murder of Alison—she had no doubt that Alison had been meant to die on that wall—had been almost more disturbing. The way Paul had been killed had an almost frenzied air to it, as though someone had lost control. That didn't excuse it at all, but it did serve as an explanation, at least in part. The way his body had then been displayed ran counter to that, true, but to every murder, there was always something that either couldn't be explained or took an age to do so.

What had happened to Alison, however, was something very different indeed. It showed an appalling level of not just premeditation, but planning that strayed almost into the artistic. The way her body had been displayed, the pentagram on the ceiling, that she had been drugged to make sure she wouldn't struggle, and those bowls; all of it hinted at something considerably darker behind it.

The evening before it had been clear that Jameson held no truck at all with any of what Dean had presented, the links with Paul and Billy's history, and she understood that. But she wasn't going to ignore it, because it was just too damned in her face to do so. Whether it was all some elaborate distraction, a way to disguise the true reason behind what was happening, or central to what was being done, that didn't matter. What did matter, was that someone knew enough about it all to have done it in the first place. You didn't just go around putting pentagrams everywhere without good reason.

Arriving at the office, Gordy was surprised to find that Vivek was nowhere to be seen. Instead, Travis was manning the desk.

'Boss,' he said, as she walked over.

'No Vivek?'

'Death in the family,' Travis said. 'Had had to rush off in the night.'

'That's rough.'

'It is.'

As conversations went, it certainly wasn't memorable, but Gordy was too busy in her head to add to it, so left it there and strode up the stairs.

Walking into the main office, Patti was waiting for her.

'Travis smiling yet?' she asked.

'Should he be?'

'Apparently, he gets claustrophobic if he's behind a reception desk. And before you laugh, that's what he actually said.'

'He can't have done.'

'Said that he'd never worked behind a bar for the same reason.'

'Whereas I've never worked behind a bar because I just didn't want to.' Gordy noticed that Patti looked weary, and asked, 'How are you doing?'

'Not sleeping well, if I'm honest,' Patti answered, then seemed to look shocked that those words had fallen out of her mouth untethered. 'I'm fine, though,' she added. 'Absolutely fine.'

Gordy wasn't convinced.

'Case keeping you awake?'

'Among other things.'

'What other things?'

'Nothing really,' Patti said. Seeing the question in Gordy's eyes she backed it up with, 'Life's just a little tiring sometimes, isn't it?'

Gordy narrowed her eyes at the detective sergeant, and leaned against a desk.

'You do know you can talk to me if something's going on, don't you?'

'Nothing's going on, Boss,' Patti said, managing to force a smile. 'I'm fine, really.'

Gordy knew better than to push it, so moved on. 'Everyone in this morning?'

'They are. Made sure of that, seeing as you weren't able to get in yesterday. How did that go, by the way?'

'Well, I joined a river swimming club, and had tea and biscuits in a camper van that looked like it could survive the apocalypse. Then, I went to the pub for a pie.'

'River swimming? You mean Farleigh?'

'I didn't go in, before you ask.'

'Not been there in years,' said Patti. 'Let me know if you're heading down, and I'll join you.'

That was a kind offer, Gordy thought, but she had no intention whatsoever of ever heading down there. She'd initially liked the idea of going for a dip, but having watched a number of violently shivering swimmers head back to their vehicles, despite all of the warm kit they had been wearing post-swim, she'd been rather put off.

'I'll bear that in mind,' she said, then walked over to her office, pushed open the door, and allowed it to swing shut behind her as she slumped down at her desk.

Her phone rang.

'Just checking in.'

It was Firbank.

Checking in, or checking up, Gordy wondered, not entirely enamoured with the idea that the DSupt was keeping an eye on things. But then, that was her role, really, so it was fair enough.

'What have you heard?'

'I know about the journalist. How is she?'

'Stable.'

A pause.

'It's going to be very difficult to keep this quiet.'

'Understood.'

'I'll make sure it is, though. But I can't promise for how long.'

'Appreciated.'

Firbank hung up.

There was a knock at the door. Gordy looked up to see Patti on the other side and waved her in.

'Vivek's not here, so coffee isn't sorted yet. And frankly, the machine he has in the kitchen isn't one that any of us dare even go near; all those dials and levers, it's very complicated.'

'And my guess is, he's got it set just so, and we don't want to mess with that, do we?'

'His coffee is perfection.'

'Couldn't agree more. So, you have a suggestion?'

'I'm going to ask Helen to stop on the way. She'll grab coffee and doughnuts for all. Sound good?'

Gordy laughed.

'Coffee and doughnuts? What is this, New York?'

'Shall I take that as a yes it does sound good, or a no it doesn't?'

'Oh, it sounds good.' Gordy smiled.

Patti left the office, and through the open door, Gordy saw that most of the team had arrived and were already settling themselves in, switching on computers, chatting, throwing the occasional worried glance her way.

No, not worried, determined, that was it; they wanted this investigation done. They wanted answers. They wanted whoever murdered Paul caught and put in prison, and to have the key thrown away. They also probably wanted a lot more than that, but Gordy decided it was probably best to not go there. She couldn't blame them, though; the murder of one of their own was felt keenly. To say that it was personal would be a monstrous understatement.

With nothing in her own small office offering any good reason to stay there, bar shutting out the world on the other side of her door and hoping it would all just go away, Gordy headed out to join the team. As she walked out, the chatter died, and in the sudden, expectant silence, she couldn't think of anything to say.

She was relieved, then, when Helen and Jameson arrived at the same time, both of them armed with trays of coffee and a grease-spotted bag, the silence broken by the noise of the door swinging open, and the aroma of hot drinks and unhealthy snacks.

Gordy allowed the team a few minutes to get themselves sorted with what Jameson and Helen had brought, and made sure that Travis had been called up to join them. The addition of caffeine and sugar had an immediate effect, and the lift to the team's spirits was palpable.

With no direction at all from Gordy herself, everyone eventually migrated themselves across the office to where the rickety board was standing. They sat on chairs around it and waited for her to join them. When she did, Patti was already at the board, pen in hand.

'Ready when you are, Boss,' she said.

## THIRTY-ONE

Gordy was staring at Jack, not entirely sure she'd heard him correctly.

'You went along in disguise ...'

'Yes.'

'But, aren't you local?'

'Also, yes.'

'So, how is it that you were in disguise, then?'

'I went along dressed as a runner.'

'Of course,' said Gordy, because really, what else could she say? 'And was it effective?'

'Yes and no.'

Well, that was a confusing answer ...

'There's no real middle ground with the effectiveness of a disguise; it either works or it doesn't.'

'It worked right up to the moment it didn't.'

'Which was when?'

'Five minutes after I'd arrived.'

Gordy didn't know whether to hug Jack for being able to make her smile in the middle of a truly horrendous investigation, or kick him up the backside for making an arse of things and not getting to the point quickly enough.

Gordy waited for Jack to continue without being prompted, but when he didn't, she glanced at Patti and gave her just enough of a look for her to know she needed a little bit of help here.

'Get to the point, Jack,' Patti said.

Gordy felt that she could've probably said that herself, but it had perhaps sounded better coming from Patti.

'I still had my running gear, so I thought I'd go along and try to blend in,' Jack explained. 'The club met outside the rugby club and there was a good turnout, so I just sort of tagged along. I had to sign in, so I gave a false name. And, well, I sort of panicked at that point. I'd not really thought about it.'

'Sign in?' Gordy asked. 'Why?'

'Health and Safety.'

'In what way did you panic?' Patti asked.

'I just said the first name that came into my head.'

'And what was it?'

Jack shifted uncomfortably in his seat.

'Well, you see, right then, I was thinking about the darts, wasn't I? I don't know why, really, but my dad likes it, and he'd mentioned it to me when I was round there the other night, and my mind had kind of drifted, because I didn't really want to go running at all, so I was thinking about absolutely anything else to keep my mind off it.'

Gordy wasn't sure she was following, but decided it was best to let Jack finish.

'This woman approached me and asked who I was, and she was really smiley and I ... well, I just said it, didn't I?'

'Said what, Jack?' Gordy pressed.

'The name, the one I was thinking about. And they've all got nicknames, haven't they, darts players, I mean? Which I think is why she looked really confused.'

'The name, Jack,' said Patti. 'What was it?'

Jack gave an embarrassed shrug.

'Snakebite.'

Despite herself, Gordy laughed. And she wasn't alone in that either.

'You didn't!'

'Pete Wright, he's my dad's favourite. Wears all these brightly coloured clothes, does his hair really mad. His nickname is Snakebite. And it was out of my mouth before I could do anything about it.'

Gordy managed to curb her laughter just enough to speak.

'Do I need to ask what happened next?'

'The woman I was speaking to, she sort of just stared at me, and it took me a while to realise why, by which time, even my explanation that it was the nickname my parents had given me when I was a baby didn't really work.'

'When you were a baby? That's what you said? Honestly? That they named you Snakebite?'

'Then the captain of the club arrived, and it was the same one, you know? The one whose ankle I'd broken doing that park run? He recognised me immediately.'

'I'm hoping,' said Gordy, 'that all of the effort you went to was worth it.'

'I did the whole evening,' said Jack. 'Couldn't really back out at that point, even if I'd wanted to, mainly because the club captain stuck by me like glue. Ended up doing hill sprints. Have you ever sprinted up a hill? It's impossible. You can't. It makes you dizzy and sick. Why would anyone do that for fun?'

'You tell me, Snakebite,' said Travis, and a ripple of laughter went around the room again.

Gordy waited for the laughter to die down.

'Well, firstly, Jack,' she said, 'I can only applaud you on your dedication to your duty. I'm genuinely impressed.'

'Thank you.'

'Secondly, you're not a secret agent, you're not working undercover, so in future, don't. Is that understood?'

It was a gentle slap on the wrist, but a slap of the wrist nonetheless, and Gordy was pleased to see that Jack looked sheepish enough to understand.

'Yes, Boss.'

'So, what did you find out?'

'A couple of things, actually. No one knows anyone by the name of Rowe.'

'Figured as much, but why did this Mr Rowe say he was a member of the running club? What's that about?'

'My guess,' said Patti, 'is that it was all part of the cover story, a way to convince Paul to head out at that time of night.'

'It's very specific though, isn't it?'

'And it's not a great cover story either,' said Jack. 'Everyone I spoke to at the running club said they'd never go running that way on their own in the middle of the night. It's different as a group, but solo? Asking for trouble.'

'Why?' asked Travis. 'It's not like every tree and bush is a secret hiding place for a murderer, is it? No one's out there with a bag of knives just hiding in the branches on the off chance someone runs past. I know it's a dark thing to say, but there are easier ways to go about killing someone.'

'It's more the safety aspect of running solo,' Jack explained. 'If you're doing long-distance stuff, and you're on your own, you make sure someone knows where you're going and when you'll be back. Running at night adds to the danger, the darkness making it considerably easier to trip over stuff. Obviously, you'd be wearing a torch and have a fully charged mobile phone with you, but it's still a higher-risk activity.'

'I see what you mean,' said Gordy. 'Have an accident in the middle of nowhere in the middle of the night, and it's going to be a little more problematic finding you.'

'But it was the old railway line,' said Travis. 'That's dead easy to find and access, isn't it?'

Gordy looked to Jack, waiting for a response.

'The point I'm making,' Jack said, 'is that the members of the running club don't go trying to smash a personal best on their own in the middle of the night on a lonely path in the countryside. Not only does Mr Rowe not exist, his story doesn't hold together either.'

Gordy wasn't in the least bit surprised.

'Anything more on the van and the axe?' she asked, turning her attention to Helen and Travis. 'Anything useful there?'

'We've looked over the footage from the security camera at Mr Mason's property a few times now, and it doesn't provide us with much,' said Helen. 'The driver's face is hidden from view the whole time he's on the property.'

'And what about from where the van was taken?'

'Zilch,' said Travis. 'No security cameras, nothing picked up anywhere. It's actually frighteningly easy to nick a vehicle, isn't it?'

'Why take it, though?' asked Pete. 'Surely it can't have been to just make off with an axe; that makes no sense at all.'

What does in this case? Gordy thought.

'And where is it?' she asked. 'Do we have any reports of it being seen?'

'On that, yes, we do,' said Helen. 'Which is something. Only came in this morning, actually.'

'How and where?'

'The numberplate was picked up on a mobile speed camera, over near Shepton Mallet. The van itself was taken from a road in Radstock.'

None of this was helping, thought Gordy, doing her best not to show her frustration.

'Can you be any more specific than near Shepton Mallet?'

'It was seen on the main road, which heads off towards Wells, and it took a right to head into Dinder.'

'And what is in Dinder?'

'Sod all,' said Travis. 'Pretty much just a farm or two, a bit of woodland out the back, a village hall, a church.'

'That's not the bit we've heard today, though,' said Helen. 'Well, we have. It's just that information was recorded last night, you see, but didn't get to us until this morning.'

'There's more, then?'

'Someone called in about a van, matching the description of the one that was stolen, parked up on their property, which just so happens to be very near Dinder.'

'Nice to know something's actually going our way for once,' Gordy said.

'I've already said we'll go and check it out once we're done here.'

'Some actual positive news at last.'

'Gave his name as Gatcombe.'

That name rang a bell, and Gordy said, 'Clive Gatcombe?'

'Yeah, that's him. He mentioned you when he called, said to tell you he'd found a van on his land and wondered if you could remove it. You know him, then?'

Gordy couldn't help but smile.

'Did you get his number? I'll give him a call.'

'I did,' said Helen, 'but you do know that's not how policing works, right, Boss? You're not at the beck and call of Joe Public, even if you do know them personally.'

'I get that, but sometimes I think what we're lacking more than anything in the police is that personal touch. I'll call him when we're done. What about the axe?'

'Now that is a bit weird,' said Travis.

'How so?'

'It had been sharpened.'

'Elaborate.'

'It's razor-sharp,' Travis explained. 'And according to Mr Mason, the person it was stolen from, he'd not sharpened it for months as he'd not seen the need; apparently, it was plenty sharp enough to chop wood.'

'It was also sharpened differently to how he'd have done it,' Helen added. 'Mr Mason used an angle grinder, which would sharpen, but leave a rough edge. Now, though, the axe blade is like a razor.'

Gordy sighed, felt her shoulders sag under the weight of it all.

'Considering what it was used for, my guess is that the killer wanted to make quick, easy work of what they had planned with Paul. Anything else?'

The team remained quiet, so Gordy moved on.

'You'll be pleased to know that Alison Read is stable. She's in a bad way, and will be for a long time, considering what was done to her. But at least she's alive.'

'Why was she targeted?' asked Jack.

'I think it's because Alison reported on Billy, the trial, everything,' said Gordy. 'She also sent me photos and video footage of her following someone in Shepton Mallet; that's what she wanted to see me about when she turned up here, if you remember? After seeing what she'd sent, we headed over, and we found what we found. I also was informed when I visited her that flunitrazepam was found in her system. You'll all know it by its more common name of Rohypnol. I've had no confirmation yet, though, of how it got into her system, or how her attackers managed to get enough into her to make her easy to handle and do what they did.'

'Do you think it was Billy, then, this person she followed?' asked Pete.

'Whoever it was, they were wearing a dark jacket, and their face was hidden by a ski mask balaclava thing. Impossible to tell.'

'Why not make sure she was dead, though?' Jack asked. 'Why leave her like that?'

'Maybe it was to make her death more painful,' Jameson suggested. 'Which is an awful thing to suggest, I know, but we have to consider it.'

'And what about those bowls?' asked Patti. 'The link to what happened to Paul is obvious, what with the pentagram stuff in the room, and her connection to what happened to Billy, but those bowls? They were just so weird.'

'I've been thinking about those a lot myself,' Gordy admitted. 'I'm still none the wiser.'

'They were there to collect Alison's blood. That, at least, is obvious,' said Jameson. 'Maybe it's all part of some ritual? Or made to look like it is, anyway; all part of the theatre the killer likes to do.'

'The killer has to be Billy, right?' said Pete. 'There's no one else to pin this on at all.'

'And he's not been seen since he disappeared on licence,' said Jack.

'Do we have any up-to-date photographs?' Gordy asked. 'There would be some from his leaving prison to go on licence, surely.'

'There are, but I reckon it would be easy for us to miss him, even if he walked past us on the street.'

'How so?'

'Huge beard,' said Jack, miming one on his face. 'Bigger than Travis's. He's probably shaved it off.'

Gordy rolled her eyes.

'What is it with blokes and beards now? They're all over the place. Years ago, no one had a beard, and now everyone seems to be wearing one. Anyway, what does that matter? If he's shaved it off, he'll look like he did before, won't he?'

'And he's put on a lot of weight while in prison,' Jack added. 'I checked against the photos from when he started his sentence, and you just can't believe it's the same person. Beard or not, he's not recognisable.'

Gordy wanted to scream. Not least because Billy's photographs should've been something they'd discussed much earlier in the week. She suspected it would've made no difference to where they were now, but even so, it was a misstep on her part. Paul was dead, Alison had been left to die, and here they were trying to pull together threads so thin that—

Something stopped Gordy's thoughts in her tracks.

'The bowls,' she said. 'They were there to collect blood, right? That's what we think, isn't it?'

'No other conclusion to be drawn that I can think of,' said Jameson. 'Why do you ask?'

Gordy held up a finger, asking everyone to give her a moment.

'Why, though, that's why,' she answered, knowing that what she'd said didn't make much sense to those listening, despite it being crystal clear in her own head. 'Why collect the blood at all?'

'Like I said, it's all part of the theatre of what was done, isn't it?' said Jameson. 'Makes us think it's a ritual. Probably to have us thinking one thing, when it's actually something else. Mislead us.'

Gordy shook her head.

'I'm not so sure, because why put those bowls there to collect it if you weren't going to do something with it?'

'They did, though,' said Patti. 'They painted that pentagram on the ceiling, didn't they?'

'Then why leave the bowls to keep catching the blood? What's the point?'

'What are you thinking?' Patti asked.

'I'm thinking,' said Gordy, 'that whoever did this expected to come back. They strung Alison up, and didn't think that anyone would find out, that they would be able to pop back later, when she'd finally died, and collect the blood.'

'That's genuinely horrifying,' said Helen.

'It's not just horrifying,' said Gordy, 'it's bloody terrifying, and do you know why?'

Everyone on the team was quiet, waiting for Gordy to answer her own question.

'Because if they meant to come back, then we got in the way of that, haven't we? By saving Alison's life, cleaning up the crime scene, we've ruined whatever it was that they had planned.'

'So what?' said Travis. 'Isn't that a good thing? Alison's alive, isn't she?'

Gordy saw realisation dawn in Jameson's eyes, and he nodded solemnly.

'You think they'll go after someone else now, don't you?' he said.

'I do,' said Gordy. 'And what's worrying me now isn't so much why, but who ...'

## THIRTY-TWO

Gordy's words sat in their midst, daring anyone to challenge them. No one did. Even Gordy herself shied away from them, the stark reality of what she'd said potent with terror.

'What now, then?' Pete asked. 'We've got a suspect, but he seems to have disappeared months ago, and any photos we've got aren't any good. Paul's dead. That journalist is never going to be the same again. We don't really know why any of this is happening, whether it's revenge, some weird cult stuff, perhaps both. And now you're suggesting that there's more to come. How the hell do we stop it, stop them, whoever they are, because we're not even sure it's Billy, are we?'

Pete's summation was bang on, Gordy thought.

'I want the evidence we have looked over again. We might have missed something. No idea what, but you never know; stuff slips through, it always does. I want both crime scenes examined again. Someone needs to go have a wander around Hatchet Hill, and someone else needs to visit Alison's place. I also want Paul's wife and daughter looked in on. I know Uniform are still keeping watch, so this is a courtesy call, really, but again, something might float to the surface mid-conversation over the usual tea and biscuits. Patti, can you sort that out, please? I'll give Clive a ring and go check out this van; we'll need to have it picked up by the SOC team as well; they'll need to look at it in situ, then take it back to theirs and give it a good going over.'

'Remember, I'm a part of the team,' Jameson said. 'So, you've an extra pair of hands.'

Gordy gave that a couple of moments, then said, 'I think your experienced eye would be good over at Alison's,' she said. 'We've got a spare set of keys for the front door, so get yourself over there as soon as we're done and see if anything jumps out. You okay with that?'

'Of course.'

'Let me know if you find anything, and that goes for the rest of you, too; stay in touch, not just with me, but with each other.'

Gordy clapped her hands together, and despite everyone's heightened level of alert, they jumped.

'Any questions?'

Silence.

'Good, then let's get cracking, shall we? And as we do, make sure you all remember what I said earlier in the week: A, B, C: assume nothing ...'

'Believe no one,' said Pete.

'And check everything,' said Helen, and with that, they disbanded.

Grabbing the location of the abandoned van from Helen, and Clive's contact number so that she could give him a call and arrange to meet him there, Gordy made her way across the main office to head on out to Dinder. As Jameson headed off, she remembered something and called him back, quickly dashing back to her office to return with a bottle in her hand.

'Here,' she said, and handed it to him.

'And what's this? The colour is disturbing; rather too much like a generous sample for the doctor ...'

Gordy ignored that and said, 'The cider, remember? You said how you absolutely needed to taste it because of some kind of quality control thing; so, now you can.'

Jameson laughed, tried to return the bottle, but Gordy wasn't having any of that.

'You'll love it, I promise. And I've a feeling there's plenty of it back at John and Doreen's, so if you like it, I'll see if I can get you some more.'

Jameson thanked her, then pushed his way out of the office. Gordy was about to call Cowboy when Patti jogged over.

'I'll come with you to check on this van,' she said.

'No need,' replied Gordy. 'I know Clive, and it's just an abandoned vehicle, right? It's not like I'm walking into the valley of the shadow of death, is it?'

That got a glazed-over look from Patti.

'Psalm twenty-three?'

'And you know it off by heart?'

'Just that bit.'

'Bleak.'

'It is that.'

'Well, I'm still coming with you.'

Gordy gave Patti a quizzical look.

'You do know I'm the boss, don't you? In fact, you're even getting the hang of calling me that, instead of that god-awful ma'am.'

'I can call Cowboy on the way,' said Patti, clearly ignoring what Gordy had just said.

'I was just about to call him right when you interrupted me.'

'And now you don't need to. Come on.'

Gordy was given no chance to answer as Patti pushed through the doors and headed for the stairs.

The journey to Dinder was uneventful, the main road from Frome built for speed but offering only slow vehicles spaced out just far enough to promise the opportunity to overtake, and then welch on that same promise. Gordy didn't mind, though, as she'd never been one for overtaking, always thinking it was better to arrive with a calm mind and a moderate heart rate, than stressed and with your pulse threatening to crack your chest.

Patti called Cowboy, who said he'd be at the location in ninety minutes at the latest, and by the time that conversation was over, they'd driven through Cranmore, the tiny village of Dean, and were approaching the market town of Shepton Mallet. Three sets of traffic lights slowed their progress, again supporting Gordy's belief that rushing was futile, and then they were turning off the main road and driving into Dinder.

Patti called out directions, and soon they were circling around the perimeter of a large woodland.

'So, how do you know this Clive, then?' Patti asked as just ahead she spotted a lane. 'Down there, I think.'

'Churchwarden, or something like that, I think,' said Gordy. 'I decided to go along to a service at the weekend. Been putting it off since I arrived. I'm not a churchgoer, really, but it's nice to sit and think in a place like that sometimes, I think. Mainly though, I went because it would've been Anna's church, and I need to put that ghost to bed.'

'That's quite a brave thing to do,' said Patti. 'But then again, I think you're brave just living in Evercreech in the first place.'

Gordy laughed.

'It's not that bad!'

'No, that's not what I meant! Evercreech is lovely! No, what I'm saying is, that living in the place you were supposed to share with your partner; that takes real courage.'

'Well, we'll see how it goes, shall we?' said Gordy, not really wanting to get into the reasons she'd decided to not only go ahead with the job down in Frome, but also the move.

There were the practical reasons, obviously, like how the job was already sorted, as were the arrangements for where she was going to live, and she'd not had the energy to change anything, not then. Moving away from the Dales had been essential, because otherwise she'd have been bumping into memories of Anna every day; a fresh start, though hard, made sense. But the trouble was, that last reason didn't quite sit all that well with the other reason, did it, the one which rose above all the others as the true explanation for her move not just to Somerset, but Evercreech? And that was, quite simply, because by moving as she had done, she'd allowed herself to pretend she was leaving everything behind, whereas, in fact, all she did, was go ahead with the move anyway, and had included Anna in every part of it.

As painful as it was, and as desperate as she was to escape, she still wanted to hold on. There would be no moving on, not yet. God, not yet ...

'Gordy?'

Patti's voice broke Gordy out of her thoughts.

'Yes?'

'You missed the lane, the one I said you needed to take? It's back there, and it heads into the woodlands, I think. Probably why the van was dumped there; nice and out of the way, probably didn't think anyone would find it so soon.'

Gordy apologised and swung the vehicle around as soon as she could.

Approaching the lane, she turned off the main road, and forced from her mind all thoughts of Anna, and all the good and bad reasons for her move south. She had a job to do, so that was what she was going to focus on.

The lane ferreted its way forward, scurrying almost into the woods.

'There it is,' Patti said, pointing.

Ahead, Gordy spotted a small white van. A man was standing beside it, staring at them as they approached, a carrier bag in his hand.

'And that's Clive,' said Gordy. 'Fun fact, he's got a hell of a singing voice on him.'

She pulled the car up onto the side of the lane, thinking to leave clear access for the SOC van when Cowboy and his team arrived.

Climbing out of the car, she walked over to meet Clive, and remembered something he'd told her at the pub before Jameson had arrived.

'Are these those woods you were telling me about, then?' she asked.

Clive said, 'I feel right at home when I'm among the trees. There's something special about places like this, isn't there?'

Gordy had to agree, taken in by the mottled sunlight in the trees, and the faint whistle of the wind as it led their branches in an eerie dance.

'Here,' Clive said, and gave Gordy the bag he was carrying. 'A little gift from John and Doreen.'

Gordy opened the bag and spotted something wrapped in greaseproof paper, and a small, clear bottle filled with a golden liquid. She remembered their conversation in the pub, and Clive's mention of him shifting the occasional bottle of John's cider while selling logs.

'You're sure you're not trying to flog me this?'

Clive smiled, shook his head.

'I'd not be so foolish,' he said. 'And that's apple juice, not cider. Can't have you or me drinking on the job, can we? And some apple cake, too, if I'm not mistaken. I've some myself.

Doreen and John thought you might welcome a snack.' He checked his watch. 'And it's gone mid-morning now, hasn't it? Sounds like a good idea to me.' He removed duplicates of the parcel and bottle from his pocket. 'Join me?'

Gordy took the bag.

Clive opened his bottle and handed it to Patti.

'Best apple juice on the planet,' he said. 'You have to try it.'

With a sheepish glance at Gordy, Patti took the bottle and had a sip, before handing it back.

'No, you have it,' said Clive. 'I've more, anyway.'

'You sure?'

'Of course!'

As Patti drank the apple juice, Clive opened the parcel and offered her some of the cake, which she took eagerly, spilling crumbs as she took a bite.

'Come on, Gordy,' Clive said, looking at her and winking. 'How can you resist?'

Gordy laughed, then opened her own bottle and parcel, and joined in. The apple juice was sublime, just like the cider she remembered from the evening at John and Doreen's. It wasn't as earthy as the cider, probably because it hadn't spent months getting all alcoholic. Instead, the taste of apples was so bright, so vibrant, and so sweet, that the bottle was half drained before she even had a nibble of the cake. But when she did, that, too, was a thing of wonder.

'Delicious,' she said.

'Can't say as I would ever disagree with you,' said Clive.

Walking over to the van, with Patti to one side and Clive on the other, and with the cake stowed away, so as not to drop crumbs all over the crime scene, something started to scratch at the back of Gordy's mind, but right then she had no idea what. The woods were peaceful, the day surprisingly bright, and there was even the chance that the discovery of this van could be just the break they were looking for. Always a glass half full, she thought, because that was just a better way to live. And on that thought, she finished the rest of the apple juice, enjoying the buzz from the sugar, and popped the bottle into her jacket pocket.

'When did you find it?' she asked.

'Just this morning,' Clive answered. 'Came over to fill a trailer, and there it was, just sitting there. Figured it was best to call you and see what you'd suggest I do with it, what with you being in the police and all. Made sense, I think. Nice to meet another member of your team, as well.'

At that, he gave a nod to Patti.

'What it is to have a detective inspector on speed dial,' Patti said, a cheeky smile curling the edges of her words.

Gordy took a walk around the van. It was smaller than the kind of van a builder might use, she thought, and from the badge, she could see that it was a Volkswagen.

'Keys are in it,' said Patti, leaning in to stare through the driver's side window.

Gordy pulled on some disposable gloves, gave the passenger door handle a heave, and pulled the door free of the car, the hinges barely making a sound.

The inside of the vehicle looked clean, normal, and gave nothing away immediately to suggest why it had been taken, and why it had been dumped. It had been used by Paul's killer though, and the person or persons who had attacked Alison, so there had to be some clue, didn't there? Surely ...

Heading around to the rear of the van, Gordy opened the door, and it swung out to reveal, well, nothing at all. She leaned in for a closer look, and found that the back of the van was empty. She could see no reason as to why it had been stolen in the first place, never mind what connection it had to what had been happening that week.

Pulling herself back out of the van, Gordy stood up to find a startled Patti staring back at her from the other side of the open van door.

'Patti?'

Patti didn't answer. She was leaning against the side of the van, her face pale.

'Sorry, Boss,' she said, 'but I don't feel right ...'

She shook her head, as though trying to dislodge something, then dropped out of sight.

Gordy dashed around and found the detective sergeant on her knees.

'Patti? What the hell's wrong?'

Patti didn't answer.

Gordy dropped down beside her, then called for Clive, who came to stand beside her.

'Something the matter?'

'Yes, but I've no idea what,' Gordy said. 'Patti? Can you tell me what's wrong? How did you feel when you got up this morning? Were you okay? Or has this come on suddenly now?'

'I ... I don't know,' Patti replied. 'I was fine this morning. It was just then, when you were looking in the van. My head, it started to swim, and I felt really dizzy. I'm sorry ...'

Gordy helped Patti turn around so that she could sit on the ground and lean her back against the side of the van.

'Just take a moment,' Gordy said, standing up and giving Patti some space. 'Let your head clear.'

'I feel terrible, Boss, like I'm going to pass out. What's going on? What is this?'

Gordy hadn't the faintest idea. She pulled out her phone, went to make a call to the office, when her own vision blurred.

'Patti ...'

Before Gordy knew what was going on, the world around her was swimming and swirling. She struggled, fought against it, but a queasiness started to take over and soon she was feeling groggy. Then her legs gave way, and she was on the ground next to Patti.

If Gordy hadn't known better, she'd have said she was drunk. But she knew damned well that she wasn't, it was impossible. It was apple juice she'd drunk, and she knew the difference well enough, so what was this? What was happening to her and Patti? It didn't make sense.

'Clive? Clive! I think you're going to need to call an ambulance. Please ...'

As she waited for Clive to come to her, to make the call, unconsciousness finally got the better of her. As she drifted off into nothingness, the thing that had been scratching at the back of her mind resurfaced; if Clive had driven to the woodlands himself, then where in the hell was his vehicle?

## THIRTY-THREE

Jameson arrived at the house of Alison Read with no urge to go back into the crime scene. But this was something he'd done numerous times before, and he appreciated the reason that Gordy had sent him over. He'd expected this to be Patti's job at least, but he could see how it was best to keep her with the rest of the team and send him out here.

The house was still cordoned off with crime scene tape. It flapped in the faint breeze as though deeply unhappy at where it had ended up, perhaps having expected to be used for grander designs, more newsworthy crimes. Though what was more newsworthy than the attempted murder of a journalist, Jameson wondered, and was happy that the story hadn't yet broke, because that really would bugger things up; a swarm of chattering, questioning, pestering keyboard egotists was not what any of them needed right then, especially not Alison.

Ducking under the tape, Jameson walked over to the front door and went inside. The house was cold and still and he was struck by the sensation that the very walls of the place knew something truly terrible had happened inside them.

He'd noticed similar so many times before, how a building would retain an awful silence after terrible events had taken place inside it, the memory of it seeping into the very brickwork. Didn't matter if that building was the grandest mansion in the country, or a tiny one-bed apartment at the top of a high-rise, the sensation was the same, and it made him shudder.

Chastising himself for letting his imagination get carried away with itself, Jameson headed straight upstairs. Best to get the worst part over and done with first, he thought, and went across the landing to the room in which they'd found Alison.

The door was closed, and having slipped on some disposable gloves and covers for his shoes, he opened it slowly, reverently, his mind playing back for him what they had discovered on the other side.

When the room was in full view, a series of flashbacks piled in, and Jameson was again seeing Alison on the wall, the blood, the markings on the ceiling. He could smell it, too, the sweet, metallic reek of blood, and something else, too, behind it, sweeter perhaps, but what, he had no idea. He wasn't sure he'd noticed it the other day, wasn't surprised either, considering what they'd had to deal with. The discovery of it all had been enough to be going on with, but when Alison had revealed to them all with that raw scream that she was still very much alive, everything else had been pushed to the side.

Stepping into the room, a wave of rich, pungent aromas assailed Jameson's mouth and nose and he ducked back out immediately, leaning against the wall to gather himself.

Come on, he muttered to himself, you've seen worse, been to worse, so pull yourself together ...

A quick dab of vapour rub under his nose, and Jameson forced himself to go back inside. With jaw clenched, he swept his eyes left and right, forcing his other senses to be fully awake, no matter how overwhelming it all seemed.

The blood on the walls, the ceiling, the bed, had turned black, some of it flaking, all of it reeking to high heaven. Though that description didn't quite fit, he thought, because the only place such a stink belonged was in the bowels of hell.

With a closer look at the bed, and under it, he saw nothing that he hadn't spotted before, and moved over to where Alison had been hung.

The shape of her upside-down body had been preserved. The outline of her body had been captured by the blood it had released, sketching a rough, almost childlike image of her on the wallpaper. Sweat stains filled the spaces between the black lines of blood, showing where her body had rested against the wall.

Jameson had no problem imagining the pain Alison had been in, the fear she must have experienced, and it only drove him on to try and find something, anything, that would bring them closer to those responsible.

He saw that the bowls they'd found beneath her head and wrists had been taken by the SOC team and was pleased to not have to see them again. That detail had been almost too much, because, as Gordy had later pointed out, it had shown that the ones who had done this to her had perhaps intended to return and collect the blood.

Leaving the room, Jameson decided to have a sweep around the house, and made a point of going through each and every room slowly, methodically. He opened drawers and cupboards, with no idea what it was he was really looking for. He checked under cushions, behind curtains, under rugs, but nothing came to light. Alison's office was interesting, but after twenty minutes of looking through files, reading what was pinned to the walls, he found nothing that he could link in any way to what had happened.

Downstairs, the story was very much the same. This was a neat house, cared for by its owner, and he doubted very much that she would ever live here again. If he could sense the trauma of the place, he dreaded to think how even just stepping through the front door would make Alison feel. No, she wouldn't be moving back here, no chance of that.

In the lounge, Jameson checked the sofa, the armchair, flicked through books on shelves, even lifted ornaments to see if anything was hiding underneath. The room had the faint back note of burned wood, thanks to the fancy-looking wood-burning stove in the wall, and he was able to easily imagine Alison enjoying snuggling up in front of it after a long day.

Moving on into the kitchen, he attacked his search with a frustration borne of wishing something would just leap out at him and smack him in the face. He was starting to feel helpless, that whoever was responsible had got away with it and would never be caught. It was a despair that came with the job, and he knew how to push through it, forcing such destructive thoughts back into the box in which they belonged, locking that box shut, and throwing away the metaphorical key.

Turning from the kitchen to go and check out what was left of the house, which was really only the garage and the garden, Jameson realised he'd not looked in the fridge. There was no point, really, because finding anything in there that would have any relevance at all to what had happened in the bedroom above was a stretch, to say the least. But still, he preferred to be thorough, so he stepped back inside and opened the door.

Cool air pushed out, and a bright light welcomed Jameson to a fridge stocked well with far too many vegetables for his liking. He saw not one single pie, just carrots and salad and tomatoes and cauliflower. Now, if there was ever a vegetable he had simply never understood, it was that. Nothing made it taste good. Not even cheese.

Beyond the vegetables, there were other things, too, like soya milk and some kind of yoghurt drink that seemed a little too proud of how good it was for gut health. In the door, he saw a bag of coffee beans sealed with an elastic band, more soya milk, more yoghurt, a bottle of juice, and a solitary, and very small, bar of dark chocolate. Because of course it was dark, he thought; Alison was obviously someone for whom even the thought of milk chocolate would probably break her out in a rash.

Heaving the fridge door shut, and with a scant look through the freezer below, Jameson finally gave up and headed outside, walking past the neat pile of logs for the stove, and on towards the garage. He opened it, stepped inside, and started to look through the neatly stored items against the wall when something he'd seen scratched at the inside of his skull, like a hook in the back of an eyeball.

He winced, shook his head, wasn't quite sure what the something was that had decided to make itself known. So, he stood there for a moment, gave it time to reveal itself again. And then, there it was, and before he knew what he was doing, he was racing back inside the house, crashing into the kitchen, and ripping open the fridge door. There, in front of him, he saw the bottle of juice, pulled it off of the shelf it was sitting on, shook the golden liquid inside to make it swirl. He popped the lid, sniffed it, and that smell … That was what he'd noticed upstairs, wasn't it? But why? That wasn't all though, not by a long shot. He'd seen exactly the same bottle before, earlier that day; it was the twin of the one he'd been given by Gordy.

## THIRTY-FOUR

When Gordy came to, she saw speckled sunlight above, and it stabbed at her eyes, daring her to keep them open. So, she closed them again, the pain of the brightness too much too quickly.

Opening them again, this time much more slowly, she became aware that what she was seeing was the tops of trees far above, and beyond them, a grey sky being slowly bissected by golden rays.

The last thing she remembered was ... was what, exactly? She wasn't sure, because what her mind was trying to show her really didn't make any sense at all.

She and Patti had left the office to meet with Clive at the van he'd found in some woodland near Dinder. Yes, that was it. They'd arrived, found the van, with Clive waiting for them. They'd had a chat, Clive had given her the very kind gift from John and Doreen of apple juice and apple cake, both of which had been utterly delicious. Then what?

Gordy closed her eyes, shook her head, tried to rub it, and discovered then that she couldn't move her arms. What was wrong with them? Had they gone to sleep? They felt numb, like she'd been lying on them for some time, but why would she be doing that? She was at work, for goodness' sake!

'Patti? Patti!'

No answer.

Gordy struggled again, tried to turn her head to see if she could work out where she was, what had happened.

Patti had fallen ill suddenly, hadn't she? That was it. She remembered that very clearly, how she'd seen her slump to the ground, sick as a dog, checked on her, then for some reason, started to feel rough herself.

She called for Patti again, heard no reply, tried to move, couldn't.

Had they both caught something at the same time? That didn't make sense, did it? What kind of illness takes two people down within minutes of each other?

A shadow fell across Gordy and she looked up to see faces staring down at her. She couldn't make them out, the light stabbing through the tree canopy above rendering them faceless.

'She's awake, then.'

'Looks that way.'

'Best give her some more, then, like the other one; it'll have her asleep in seconds.'

'You sure?'

'We've plenty. Don't want them struggling, do we?'

'Kind of her to bring a friend, though, wasn't it?'

'Oh, for sure; made up for her rescuing that journalist before we could go and get what we needed.'

'We going to bleed the other one out properly this time, just to make sure?'

'I think it's for the best, don't you?'

Whatever they were talking about, Gordy had no idea, and she was about to ask for an explanation, for some help to get her free from whatever held her, when hands grabbed her head, her jaw was yanked open, fingers pinched her nose, and a sweet liquid was poured into her mouth. She spluttered, coughed, couldn't breathe, then a hand was clamped over her mouth and she had no choice but to swallow if she wanted to ever breathe again.

'There we go.'

'Went down a treat, didn't it?'

'Always does; why do you think I make so much of it?'

All Gordy heard was laughter, as the world around her closed in, and she faded once more into a thick, black nothingness, her last thought was the realisation that she recognised the voices.

JAMESON WAS on the phone to Cowboy.

'Yes, apple juice,' he said. 'There's a bottle of it in the fridge, and I'm damned sure I could smell it upstairs in the bedroom where we found Alison as well. Was there anything in what the SOC team found about it?'

'I've not had the chemical analysis back yet,' Cowboy said. 'I can check, but I'm not sure how long—'

'What about from the hospital? Must be something from there, right? We know Alison was drugged, that's how they managed to do what they did without her putting up a fight. They must have some idea as to how it was administered.'

'That would make sense. Stomach contents, that kind of thing, but really only if she vomited.'

'My guess is that she did,' said Jameson. 'If there was enough inside her to knock her out, then you add that to the shock and trauma of waking up upside down, what that would do to the body, then it probably wanted to get rid of whatever was inside her, and quickly.'

'I'll call them now. This the number to get you on?'

'It is,' said Jameson. 'I need to call Gordy immediately, let her know what I've found.'

'I'll be in touch.'

Jameson hung up, then pulled up Gordy's number.

'Come on ... come on ...'

No answer.

He waited for it to go through to voicemail, hung up, then tried again.

Still nothing.

'Where the bloody hell are you, Gordy? Answer the damned phone!'

His phone rang, and he answered it without even looking at the incoming number.

'Gordy?'

'Cowboy.'

'What've you got?'

'You were right,' Cowboy said. 'Alison vomited in the air ambulance on the way to the hospital. Analysis showed she had ingested very little that day, clearly the kind of person who views a coffee and a cigarette as breakfast.'

'Apple juice?'

'Yes.'

'Bingo ...'

'Not a version of that game I'd want to play, though, if you don't mind me saying so,' said Cowboy. 'Winning doesn't seem like much fun, does it?'

With Cowboy's confirmation of what Jameson had suspected, he marched out of the house, quickly locking the front door behind him, then made his way over to his car. He tried Gordy twice more, then called the office.

Travis answered.

'Anything from Gordy?'

'Nothing,' Travis said.

'Is Patti there? I need to speak with her right now.'

'She's with Gordy.'

Jameson froze mid-step.

'She's what?'

'They both went to check up on that van,' Travis explained. 'The one found in the woods over by Dinder, remember?'

'Yes, I remember,' Jameson replied. 'You able to send me the location and the details of the person who reported it?'

'No problem. Is something up?'

'Yes,' said Jameson. 'Very much so. And I know I'm not your senior officer here, and I've no right to tell you want to do ...'

'But you're going to, aren't you?'

'Yes,' said Jameson. 'So, listen up, because right now, the lives of Patti and Gordy absolutely depend on what we do next.'

## THIRTY-FIVE

'She's still unconscious, then?'

'Looks that way.'

'You gave her too much!'

'It's not an exact science, is it? We just have to wait, that's all; it's not like another hour or two's going to make any difference, is it? The power we're drawing on, it won't matter in the end, and we'll have him back. And that's only just the beginning!'

'And to think we believed that God was all-powerful!'

'We were fools.'

'No longer though, eh? No longer …'

Gordy had stirred a few minutes ago, woken to the same horror of being unable to move, and with no knowledge of where she was, where Patti was, or what had happened to them. But the memory of her last waking, and not only that but of what had happened before at the van, had been strong enough to make her keep her consciousness a secret. She needed to know things, and sometimes, just listening was enough. Now, though, she knew so much that even if she could've moved, she wouldn't have been able to. This fresh knowledge seemed so wrong, so terrifying, that it held her fast, and she didn't know what to do with it.

There were four voices dancing around her, sometimes close, sometimes far off, and she recognised them all. Such knowledge didn't make her situation any better. Far from it. If anything it only made it all the more terrifying.

John and Doreen were there, and Clive and Eileen. Why they were there, though, and why they'd done what they had done, she simply couldn't fathom. What were four seemingly kind, elderly churchgoers doing being mixed up in something so utterly horrifying? It made no sense in the slightest. Why had they killed Paul? Why had they drugged and tried to kill Alison? And what the hell did they want with her and Patti? None of it was adding up.

If anything, this new information was only serving to make things seem even more complicated and difficult to understand. But she needed to understand it, and she needed to be free of whatever held her tight, so for now, she would remain as lifeless as she could, and hope something came to light.

Having not heard any of the four voices for a while, Gordy eventually decided to open her eyes the tiniest of cracks. And what she saw took her breath away. Patti was with her, not too far away, in fact, but she wasn't lying on the ground. Instead, she was strung upside down from a tree, her eyes closed, her arms hanging down, like the fresh kill of a hunter who had spent the day stalking it.

Risking movement now, Gordy opened her eyes further, and managed to turn her head just far enough to allow her to see that she was lying beside a raised platform of rough branches, beneath which logs had been piled. She also saw that lying on top of the platform was something covered in a sheet. And that something had to her mind the very recognisable shape of a body; had they killed someone else? And if so, who? What had she missed?

Gordy could see little else, but understood now that her wrists and ankles were tied. She tried to move both, but escape wasn't possible, not if she wanted to do more than hop away from the four pensioners who had, for a reason as yet undisclosed, kidnapped her and Patti.

For now, Gordy knew she had no choice but to use all her energy to remain calm, to think through everything she and the team had uncovered, and to be ready for any opportunity to escape, or at the very least, delay whatever was planned for her and Patti. Because whatever it was, she had no doubt that it wasn't good.

HAVING DIRECTED Travis to get straight to where Gordy and Patti had gone to check out the van, and to take Helen with him, Jameson had raced over to Evercreech, not to Gordy's flat, or to The Bell, but to the vicarage. He'd also instructed Pete and Jack to get over to him as soon as they could, and to be fully ready for him to call them with a change of location.

The address had been easy to find thanks to a quick check of the vicar's details on the church's website, and he skidded to a halt on the gravel drive. That the church had been able to find a replacement vicar for Anna was a good sign, he thought; it meant that whatever was going on with certain members of the congregation, there was a good chance that he had nothing to do with it and no knowledge of it either. All Jameson wanted was information.

Jogging over to the front door of the vicarage, Jameson hammered the heel of his fist against the wood, waited, and hammered again. He was just about to have another go, when the door opened, and he greeted the man who had opened it in a somewhat more threatening fashion than he would have wished for.

'Can I help you?' the man asked, more than a little hesitantly.

'Are you Reverend Alan Parker?'

'I am, but between you and me, I've never liked that title? Reverend; it sounds so damned pompous, doesn't it?'

'I need your help.'

'Well, that's literally my job description,' said Alan. 'Helping people. I'm sure some would disagree, and give me some flim-flam about how it's all about bringing people to the Lord, filling the pews, that kind of thing, but that's not really me, I'm afraid.'

'I'm here about some of your parishioners.'

'You are? Why? Has something happened? Do you need to come inside? I've a fresh pot of tea on.'

Jameson shook his head.

'No time,' he said. 'Do you know of someone called Clive Gatcombe?'

'Of course. He's a churchwarden. Welcomes people to the church, that kind of thing. Lovely chap.'

'Do you have his address?'

That question drew a frown from the vicar.

'I'm a police officer,' said Jameson. 'Retired, anyway. I'm a colleague of Gordanian Haig? She was here on Sunday, I believe?'

'Gordy? The poor woman whose partner died? Yes, I know her, and you're right, she was here on Sunday. What happened, it was terrible. I'm only here in the interim, really, sort of like an emergency vicar, if you will! This kind of thing doesn't usually happen, a replacement found so quickly, I mean, but it was felt that under the circumstances special measures needed to be put in place.'

'I think something's happened to Gordy,' Jameson said, realising now that Alan was someone very much blessed with the ability to just talk and talk; another part of the job description, no doubt.

'And you think Clive's involved? What on Earth is going on?'

Jameson had no idea how to explain, mainly because he wasn't sure himself, and he didn't want to give too much away and risk terrifying the vicar into going mum.

'Gordy arranged to meet with Clive at a woodland over by Dinder, something about a van he'd found there.'

'Perhaps that's where they are, then?'

Jameson wasn't so sure; if Clive and whoever else he was working with were planning on doing harm to Gordy and Patti, he couldn't see them advertising it so clearly to the police by arranging the meeting, then staying there; that was just stupid. But what if there was somewhere else?

'I've already sent officers there,' said Jameson. 'And I've other officers on their way to join me here. Do you know of anywhere else?' Another thought occurred to him. 'Is there an orchard nearby, perhaps?'

'Orchard?'

'Clive makes his own cider.'

'No, he doesn't; that's John. He has a few apple trees in his garden and honestly, it really is very, very good. I had some myself last week. He made it last year, so it's had plenty of time to just sit and mature, and you know, I never really liked cider much at all, but this? It's quite something!'

Getting a word in edgeways wasn't easy with someone like Alan, but Jameson pushed on.

'Does John have an orchard, then?'

'No, just a few apple trees at home, like I said. Clive could be at his woodland though.'

'I don't think so,' said Jameson. 'Gordy headed over to the one by Dinder earlier and—'

'No, he doesn't own that one, just manages it, doesn't he? I mean his actual woodland, the one out the back of Evercreech. It's about a mile away, that's all. Has a lovely little river running through it. I've been out there a few times myself, to help me think, especially when I'm writing a sermon. Nature's very inspiring, isn't it?'

A car whipped into the driveway behind Jameson's vehicle and he turned to see Pete at the wheel, Jack sat beside him.

He looked back at Alan.

'Tell me where it is,' he said. 'Now!'

## THIRTY-SIX

Rough hands grabbed Gordy and she felt herself being dragged across the ground.

'We need the blood first.'

'Get on with it then!'

'I'm not doing it.'

'It's simple; all you have to do is get the knife and cut her throat; she won't struggle, and even if she does, it won't make any difference.'

'What about the sound? Won't she scream?'

'With her throat cut? No chance of that, just a gurgle as it drains out of her. Get the bowl.'

'Why aren't we doing it like we did before, to that journalist?'

'No time.'

'But the ritual ...'

'I don't care about the ritual! I want the blood and I want my son, because that's what this is all about, isn't it? So, cut the bitch's throat and let's have it done! Now!'

Gordy knew she had to do something, but what? She was

tied up, groggy, had no doubt at all that violence was coming her way, and soon. But what about the team? How long had she and Patti been gone? Would they have started to grow concerned at the lack of contact? And if so, is there any way at all that they could be on their way to wherever they were now?

'I know you're awake ...'

The voice was close enough for Gordy to feel hot breath on her skin. She opened her eyes and found Clive staring down at her.

'Hello, there.' He smiled, though the warmth she'd seen in it before was gone. 'How are you doing?'

'Clive ...'

The backhanded slap came out of nowhere, as Clive raked the side of her face with his rough, hard knuckles. She saw bright lights flash in front of her eyes, and pain exploded in her head.

'Didn't ask you to speak none, did I, little miss Detective Inspector?'

Gordy shook her head to dislodge the pain and help her think straight.

'You ... you can't do this.'

'I can, and I'm going to,' said Clive. 'Done it before, haven't I? That friend of Billy's, it was easily. I actually enjoyed it, carving him up, hacking at him like a tree that's come down in a storm. Which, I suppose, he had, really, hadn't he? He just didn't know it.'

The pain in Gordy's head eased.

'What's Billy got to do with this?' she asked.

'He's got everything to do with this,' said Clive. 'Everything!'

A figure came to stand behind Clive and, through bleary eyes, Gordy saw that it was John.

'I've told you what you need to do,' Clive growled.

'I know, it's just that I'm not sure I can.'

For a moment, Clive just stared at Gordy, then he said, 'Excuse me for a moment, Officer,' and stood up.

The next thing Gordy knew John landed on the ground beside her with a yelp.

'What the hell did you do that for?' John said, rubbing his chin.

Clive's meaty hands grabbed John and dragged him to his feet. The man's strength was ferocious, born of so many years working the trees, and Gordy knew then that fighting him wasn't going to work; she'd need to do something else, but what?

Clive was yelling at John, shaking him as he did so.

'They took our Billy away for years, and now here you are, dithering? You remember how important he is, don't you? He's the one we were promised all those years ago. There's plans for him already written in the stars, aren't there? You want to get in the way of that?'

'What if it doesn't work?'

Gordy heard the sharp sound of flesh meeting flesh.

'We've everything we need. You know the power we work with, what it can do, or have you lost your faith, is that it?'

'No, of course I haven't!'

'Then prove it! Show me, and show your true master, just how strong your faith is!'

Gordy, still baffled by the insanity of what she was hearing, knew she had to do something. If there was going to be any chance of anything being done, then she was going to have to do it herself. Patti's life, and her own, clearly depended on it.

With John and Clive still fully engaged in their argument, which had now moved away a little as they continued to argue, Gordy looked around. Her hands were tied in front of her, and that meant she could, if she pushed hard enough, and forced her body to work through the pain of having been left to seize up on the ground, stand. What she would do then, she'd work out at that point, but right now, any distraction would be something.

Rolling onto her side, then onto her knees, Gordy grimaced and pushed. Pain lit her like fire, but she was on her feet.

She saw John and Clive still arguing, neither of them aware that she'd moved. But now what?

As she looked around, her eyes came to rest on Patti just long enough to see that she was stirring. Whatever drug they had been forced to take was wearing off. Her eyes came to rest on the wooden platform she had been laid beside and there was no doubt in her mind now that beneath the sheet was a body.

Around the body were laid a number of bowls, two of which were empty. One, she saw, contained a large, decomposing organ, and though it was already rotting, even her scant memory of what she had studied at school told her that it was a heart. Another contained something considerably smaller, but no less horrendous, and she guessed it to be the pineal gland, and whatever else had been cut away with it to make sure it could be removed. There were three other bowls, one of which contained black liquid, which, like the contents of the other bowls, she guessed to belong to Paul, and it to be his blood.

The two empty bowls must have originally been for what they had wanted to collect from Alison, and that they were now planning to take from Patti. What then, was her own role in this? she wondered. Or was she just here as a spectator? No, that wasn't it, surely. Then what?

A shout brought her up sharp and she knew she had been spotted. Then, as Clive and John came at her, she did the only thing that she could, and threw herself headfirst onto the wooden platform.

. . .

WHEN JAMESON CAME SPEEDING around the corner of the small track at the edge of the woodlands Alan had directed him to, the last thing he had expected to see was two women lifting a large picnic basket out of the back of a beige saloon. And judging by the look on their faces as he sped towards them, slamming on the brakes just in time to stop from crashing into the back of the car as they jumped out of his way, they hadn't expected to see him, either.

Giving no thought as to what it was that they were doing, Jameson jumped out of his car and pelted over to them, as Pete and Jack came to a juddering stop behind him, sending a cloud of dust and grit into the trees.

The women dropped the picnic basket and started to scream into the woods, doing their best to make a break for the trees themselves, but as Jameson made after them, he was quickly overtaken by Pete and Jack, who tackled them both to the ground.

The women both kept screaming and yelling, but were soon both sat on the ground, their wrists in handcuffs.

Jameson stood over them both.

'Hello,' he said. 'Now, my guess is that although you weren't expecting to see me or my two friends here, you've a bloody good idea as to why it is that we've shown up, am I right?'

The women glanced at each other, then stopped screaming.

'That's better. Now, how's about you tell me where they are? And by they, I mean Detective Inspector Gordanian Haig, and Detective Sergeant Patti Matondo.'

The women both shook their heads. One of them decided it would be a good idea to spit in Jameson's face.

The phlegm caught Jameson on his right cheek. He stood up, wiped it away, then crouched back down.

'Here's the thing,' he said, his voice calm, quiet, and so thick with menace that he nearly scared himself. 'Either you, or people you know, have done terrible things these past few days, to a journalist, to a friend of ours, and now I think you're planning to do more of the same to two more people we know very well indeed. Now, you're probably thinking that you can keep quiet, that by doing so you're serving some greater power, perhaps, because judging by all the black magic bollocks I've seen this week, that's what you're into, isn't it? Devil worship or something? Not that I really care. But you should. And do you know why?'

The women stared back impassively.

Jameson reached down and grabbed a handful of dirt.

'Because whatever power it is you believe in, and whatever reason you can give for what you've done, if you don't tell me right now where my friends are ...'

He lifted the dirt and slowly, ever so slowly, crushed it in his hands and allowed the grains and lumps to fall to the ground.

If he was honest, Jameson had no idea what he was doing at all, because really, what did letting dirt fall through his fingers mean? He was just hoping that there, in that moment, and knowing what was going on in the woods behind them, the two women would be disturbed enough, and scared enough, to give him just enough information to find Gordy.

'Follow the path,' one of the women said. 'But you're too late! You're already too late!'

Which was when a scream ripped through the trees, and birds scattered with callous cries.

GORDY WAS ON THE GROUND. She was lying on top of a body which, judging by its pudginess, and the beard she could now see on the rotting face of its owner, belonged to the missing Billy. The stink of it was eye-watering. The bowls had all scattered, sending Paul's heart, pineal gland, and blood across the woodland floor.

'What have you done? What the bloody hell have you done?'

It was then that Patti opened her mouth, and her lungs let rip, her scream loud enough to shatter glass.

Gordy felt herself be lifted up with ease as Clive heaved her off of his son's revolting corpse, then threw her to one side like a piece of rubbish, before turning his attention to Billy.

'My son! What have you done to my son?'

'So, you're his parents, you and Eileen?'

Clive wasn't listening. He was sobbing, trying to drag his son's reeking husk back to the wooden platform.

'I thought you disowned him. You didn't even visit him in prison!'

Clive had Billy's body halfway up on the platform now and was trying to move his legs, but the dead don't always want to play, and no matter what he did, Billy just kept slipping back off the platform and onto the ground.

'We had to disown him! It was the only way. Otherwise, people would've found out, they would've known!'

'Known? Known what?'

This was making less and less sense, thought Gordy, but she didn't care, because the more she was able to keep Clive talking, then perhaps the more chance there was of someone finding them. There was clutching at straws, and then there was this, Gordy knew that, but what else did she have to cling onto? And just where the hell had John got to?

'He's the chosen head of our order,' Clive said. 'And no, we're not Satanists, before you ask, and neither do we follow the teachings of that limelight-loving Crowley. We follow mine, you hear? My teachings! My ways! The true way to bring about a new awakening!'

Gordy felt her soul crack. Clive, it was clear, was a religious nutjob, yet another twisted fool who'd somehow managed to persuade others that he had some kind of answer they probably hadn't even realised they'd been looking for. She remembered what Clive had said in the pub, something about how the Universe and the gods conspired to put your kind of people in front of you.

'You're a cult, then,' she said, disappointment lacing her words like arsenic. 'How pathetic.'

Her words clearly hit a nerve as Clive began to shake with rage or a mad belief, or both.

'A cult? We're so much more than that, Gordy. I have been called, I have gathered my followers, and now my son will take his rightful place at—'

'You're pensioners!' Gordy laughed. 'About the only thing any of you could gather is enough energy to make yourself a mug of hot milk and honey before bedtime!'

Clive's shaking grew more violent.

'Pensioners? We are ageless! We have been chosen! And Billy will—'

'How did you actually meet, then?' Gordy asked, refusing to let Clive start preaching. 'If you've known each other for years, something must've drawn you together? What was it, some evening class on paganism? A coffee morning for people who will believe any nonsense you tell them?'

'Sex is how we met,' said Clive. 'We are all celebrators of the freedom of having an open relationship with your beloved.'

Once again, Gordy's laugh spat from her, only now it threatened to consume her whole, so ridiculous was what she was hearing.

'You were into wife swapping? Seriously? That's how this all began? You all chucked your keys into a bowl for a fumble with the neighbours, and next thing you know, you're dancing naked under a full moon and convinced you're Lucifer's envoy? God in Heaven, if only you could hear yourself.'

'God does not belong in Heaven!' Clive shouted back. 'That kingdom will be thrown down and a new one made!'

'But you go to church,' said Gordy. 'That's literally where I met you!'

Clive managed to calm down for a moment, though was still struggling with Billy.

'Hiding in plain sight, you see? No one would suspect, would they?'

'Didn't move far away, though, did you?'

'We did, but we came back, years later. John and Doreen first, then me and Eileen. We left it long enough for no one to remember who we were, made sure we didn't visit the places we used to, kept ourselves to ourselves, until such time as Billy was free and we could finish what we started.'

'Which is what, exactly?'

Clive turned all of his attention to Gordy, Billy now back on the platform. He dropped himself down beside her. She saw a wildness in his eyes.

'He is the master's vessel,' he said, a wildness in his eyes that was terrifying. 'Asmodeus will fill him with his greatness!'

'Sounds painful. And seeing as Billy's dead, my guess is that it's not going to be as easy as you expected it to be.'

'Billy, he didn't understand. We tried to explain, but he wanted nothing to do with it. Got mixed up in things we didn't agree with. And then he was in prison, out of reach. We had to disappear, to work out what to do next. When he was released on license, we found him, but he wanted nothing to do with us. So, we had no choice ...'

That sounded ominous, thought Gordy, and she realised why.

'You kidnapped him, didn't you? That's why he disappeared.'

'We did all we could to persuade him, but he wouldn't listen, and things went too far ... we went too far ... and ...'

'Wait ... you killed Billy? You killed your own son?'

'He wouldn't listen! We had to make him understand!'

'By torturing him? Is that really what you're telling me?'

Clive took a breath to calm down.

'We ... educated him,' he said. 'But he would not listen, would not learn. But he will now, I assure you.'

'Once again,' said Gordy, 'I feel I need to point out the fact that Billy is dead.'

Clive got in Gordy's face.

'It doesn't matter, though, does it? We have what we need. We have the heart and the soul of the one who betrayed him. We will have the blood to bless and drink.' His eyes burned even more wildly then. 'And we have you!'

And this was where I'll find out, isn't it? thought Gordy, not sure at all she wanted to know.

'Me? Why? What for?'

'You've been a part of this since you arrived in Evercreech,' said Clive, calm once again, his emotions swinging violently left and right. 'In fact, you've already gone through three parts of the ritual without even realising it. All that remains now is the sacrifice, the prayers, and the feast!'

Those words took Gordy back to Paul's notebook.

'Procession, purification, hymns,' she said. 'But when have I done any of those? And why? What's the purpose of any of it?'

'Doreen drove you to our house, did she not? That was the procession. The purification? Do you not remember what she said about John's cider?'

'Cleansing ...'

'Exactly! Because it was blessed by me beneath the full moon and—'

A cough cut into the moment.

'Going to have to interrupt you there, I'm afraid,' the voice said.

Clive snapped his head around. Standing behind him, Gordy saw Jameson.

'You're nicked, mate,' he said, and with a strength Gordy had no idea Jameson possessed, he dragged the man off her, flipped him onto his chest, and cuffed his arms behind his back.

Clive spat and roared and yelled, but Jameson simply ignored him as he knelt down beside Gordy, helping her to sit up.

'Patti,' Gordy said. 'You need to cut her down.'

'Jack's on that already,' said Jameson, as he got to work on untying her. 'You okay?'

'No.'

'No, you don't look it.'

'What about … There were others. I saw one, and I think there's two more, two women. Eileen and Doreen.'

'Oh, we have them,' said Jameson. 'Caught them carrying a huge picnic basket. Looks like quite a feast was planned.'

'And the other man? John?'

'Ran right into my arms.'

For a moment, neither of them spoke.

Jameson broke the silence.

'Between you and me, I was hoping my first case with you as a consultant was going to be a little less …'

'Batshit crazy?'

'Something like that.'

Free at last, Gordy stood up, rubbing her wrists as blood started to flow and her skin tingled.

Patti was being checked over by Jack, Clive's shouting had

turned to a mumbling, and Billy's body was staring, lifeless, into the trees above.

'Anything you need?' Jameson asked.

'A bath,' said Gordy.

Then with Jameson helping her, she grabbed Clive out of the dirt of the woodland floor, and marched him away from the body of his dead son. On the way, she called Cowboy, and quite to her own surprise, the sound of the man's truly terrible John Wayne impression was just the medicine she needed. And despite everything that had happened, she laughed.

## THIRTY-SEVEN

Gordy was standing in the kitchen of her flat in Evercreech. Her hands, indeed her arms, were covered in flour, as was much of what she was wearing. Standing on her left was Jameson, and to her right, Vivek. On the work surface in front of each of them was a large lump of soft, white dough.

'You're doing brilliantly,' Vivek said.

Gordy glanced at Jameson to see that he was wearing even more flour than she was.

'Remind me again why we're making bread?' he asked.

'Because,' said Gordy, 'I'm trying to take back a bit of control.'

'By learning to make your own bread?'

'Doesn't make much sense right now, I know, but it will, I'm sure.'

Vivek then instructed Gordy and Jameson to start kneading their dough.

'Remember,' he said, 'don't be shy with it. Stretch it and fold it and punch it. Show the dough who's boss. Really go for it!'

Vivek, having returned to work from visiting his ill relative, had been very easy for Gordy to persuade to teach her a bit of baking. It wasn't that she'd never baked in her life before, just that it had been decades, perhaps not even since school.

'My arms hurt,' Jameson complained. 'How long do we have to do this?'

'For about ten minutes, I would think,' Vivek replied. 'The dough should spring back at you when you poke it.'

'I'd probably do the same if you poked me,' said Jameson.

Gordy held back her laugh.

After the truly awful events that had transpired over the last week, the team was still reeling. She'd thought over everything so many times, the horror of it, the oddness, and in the end realised that perhaps trying to understand everything wasn't really all that helpful. Paul was dead, Alison was recovering, Patti had bounced back from their abduction with surprising ease, and she herself had pretty much just brushed that bit off as nothing more than a bad day at the office.

A funeral was now being planned for Paul, though when that would take place, no one was sure. His wife and daughter, Gill and Kelly, were being provided with a huge amount of support, not just from the police, but from social services and the local community, with friends circling the wagons to keep them safe.

Aspects of the case were still unclear, but that was no surprise. That a truly tiny group of seemingly innocent, harmless people could believe in something so fervently that murder would be so easily carried out wasn't just shocking, it was impossible to comprehend. As was the way so much of it had been planned, from the stealing of the van, to ensure their own vehicles would not be linked to what they were doing, to the story of the lost delivery driver, designed to not only get their hands on an axe they couldn't be connected to, but also sow enough seeds of confusion to throw everyone off their scent.

Clive had access to more than enough axes himself, but he knew, from his wood deliveries, that one was easy to get his hands on, and that it would draw eyes a way than to him buying even more from his usual supplier. He also clearly had a flair for the dramatic, a need for the story to involve a fair amount of theatre. And as to what it was that he and his swinging wife and friends actually believed, no one could really tie it down. Books had been found in drawers at John and Eileen's house, all of them filled with ramblings that made no sense to anyone, but to John, to the others, they somehow held their thrall.

'Right, it's time to roll out the dough,' Vivek instructed, and handed Gordy and Jameson each a rolling pin.

'I thought we were making bread,' said Jameson.

'This is a sweet dough,' said Vivek. 'And you'll be adding fruit, sugar, and lard to it.'

Gordy saw Jameson's eyes widen.

'What, we're making our own lardy cake?'

'You are.'

Gordy saw Jameson's enthusiasm for rolling out the dough increase dramatically, as he attacked his with gusto.

A few minutes later, and with the dough rolled out, the lard and sugar and fruit applied, and the dough folded again, a process that was repeated three times, both loaves were plopped in a tin each, covered, and left to rise.

'Time for tea, then, is it?' Jameson asked.

With a wash of their hands, a fresh pot was made, and the three of them strolled through to Gordy's lounge.

Sunlight was rushing in through the windows to spill across the floor, and she saw how a golden puddle of it was now drenching her photos of Anna.

Vivek walked over and picked up one of the photographs.

'This is a woman with a kind smile,' he said. 'It shines, doesn't it?'

'She shone,' said Gordy, 'brighter than the sun.'

Vivek placed the photograph back down, lifted another.

'Grief, it can be both heavy and light all at once, can't it? One moment, we're weighed down by our loss, and the next we're lifted by the memories of the love.'

'I'll admit, it's been heavy more than light most of the time,' said Gordy. 'But I'm trying to change that now, a little, anyway.'

Jameson sat himself down on the sofa.

'And how's that going for you?' he asked.

Gordy gave herself a moment to think of an answer, but in the end, just started talking and hoped something would make sense.

'Moving here was the best and the worst decision I could've made,' she said. 'I'm here without the one person I was moving here for in the first place. But I think staying where I was, well, that would've been worse; too many ghosts. Here, well, it's new, isn't it? Though Anna was supposed to be here, she never was, not with me, anyway. But there's also the fact that she actually is, because I've brought her with me, haven't I?'

'That's hard to deal with,' said Vivek.

'It is, but I think I've allowed it to be harder than it needs to be, if you know what I mean?'

Neither Vivek nor Jameson responded, so Gordy kept talking.

'I've allowed it to weigh me down so much that all I've been doing is struggling to just get through every day, and I know that's not what Anna would want. What happened, it wasn't her fault, it wasn't anyone's fault, and me trying to blame the world, to just give up, what use is that?'

'Not much,' Jameson agreed. 'But don't put yourself under too much pressure. It's been, and it is, rough. I know. I'm talking from experience.'

'The only way this works, the only way I can make any

sense of it, is to somehow use it to grow, to change, to become something more than I was before. That's what Anna would want, I'm sure of that now. I'm a better person for having Anna in my life. I learned so much about life, about humanity, about love, about me, and I'm not going to just throw that away. I can't.'

Jameson raised his mug of tea to Gordy.

'You know, I'm starting to wonder if I can hear the echo of Anna's voice in your words. I never knew her, but my guess is, she's damned well proud of you, Gordy.'

Gordy smiled at those words, as Vivek checked his watch, drained his mug.

'Time to get those lardy cakes in the oven,' he said.

Later that day, when Gordy was alone, and it was just her, the coo of a pigeon sitting on one of her window boxes, and a slice of warm lardy cake in her hand, she looked over at the pictures of Anna, and saw so many smiles shining back. She remembered each one, and more besides, and for the first time in a long time, instead of tears, the only thing that came to her was her own smile shining back.

---

## STOP!

SCAN THE QR code below to grab your copy of *Death Springs*, the thrilling third book in the Detective Inspector Haig series.

You can also sign up for my VIP Club to get exclusive short stories and a regular newsletter.

# ABOUT DAVID J. GATWARD

David had his first book published when he was 18 and still can't believe this is what he does for a living. Author of the long-running DCI Harry Grimm series, David was nominated for the Amazon Kindle Storyteller Award in 2023. He lives in Somerset with his two boys.

Visit www.davidjgatward.com to find out more about the author and his highly-acclaimed series of crime fiction.

facebook.com/davidjgatwardauthor

Printed in Great Britain
by Amazon